drowning
is
inevitable

SHALANDA STANLEY

drowning

is

inevitable

Alfred A. Knopf

NEW YORK

THIS IS A BORZOI BOOK PUBLISHED BY ALFRED A. KNOPF

All rights reserved. Published in the United States by Alfred A. Knopf, an imprint of Random House Children's Books, a division of Penguin Random House LLC, New York.

Knopf, Borzoi Books, and the colophon are registered trademarks of Penguin Random House LLC.

Visit us on the Web! randomhouseteens.com

Educators and librarians, for a variety of teaching tools, visit us at RHTeachersLibrarians.com

Library of Congress Cataloging-in-Publication Data
Stanley, Shalanda.
Drowning is inevitable / Shalanda Stanley.
pages   cm.
Summary: After seventeen-year-old Olivia and her friend Jamie accidentally kill Jamie's abusive father, two other friends, Max and Maggie, join them in running away from St. Francisville, Louisiana, to hide out in New Orleans while they try to figure out what to do next.
ISBN 978-0-553-50828-4 (trade) — ISBN 978-0-553-50829-1 (lib. bdg.) — ISBN 978-0-553-50830-7 (ebook)
[1. Runaways—Fiction. 2. Best friends—Fiction. 3. Friendship—Fiction. 4. Homicide—Fiction. 5. Mothers and daughters—Fiction. 6. Fathers and sons—Fiction. 7. New Orleans (La.)—Fiction.] I. Title.
PZ7.1.S735Dro 2015
[Fic]—dc23
2014042580

Printed in the United States of America
September 2015
10 9 8 7 6 5 4 3 2 1

First Edition

In memory of my brother Shandon,
who taught me to be brave
and that it's okay to be loud

Chapter 1

I think you've heard what happened. Most people have. We made national news. You don't know the truth, though. The newspapers didn't tell the whole story. They said horrible things about Jamie that I won't repeat. They said I made bad choices. But there are times in life when you tell your best friend you'll do anything for him, and you mean it. My dad says that's only true of high school best friends, and as I grow older, I'll realize there are things you shouldn't do—even for a friend. I don't know about that, but I want you to hear the truth from me.

Forgive me for telling the parts you already know, but it's important to say everything. I should warn you, some of it might be hard for you to hear because of what happened on Fidelity Street. It'll be easier for me to tell you if we pretend we don't know each other, like this is a confession to a small-town priest.

St. Francisville, Louisiana, where I was on unofficial suicide watch, is hidden between green bluffs and the Mississippi River. I wasn't particularly sad about anything, but I was almost eighteen, and being that my mom killed herself on her eighteenth birthday, people were worried that suicide was genetic. To their credit, my life had paralleled my mom's up until I didn't get pregnant at seventeen.

My bedroom wasn't my own, but my mom's. It had stayed exactly the way she left it, down to my crib still standing in the corner. I sometimes thought about taking down her pictures and posters and putting up my own, or at least cleaning her clothes out of the closet, but it was easier to keep looking at her things. Now that I was her age and closer to her size, I even wore her clothes.

I hadn't always been allowed in her room. It was off-limits to me when I was younger, a shrine left untouched. I was eleven before I was brave enough to sneak inside, looking for answers to the questions I was too scared to ask. It was always in the middle of the night. I'd steal secrets from the folds of her things—her favorite CDs, books with highlighted passages that I'd read over and over by flashlight, too young to understand them but still searching between the words for clues to her. She was the ghost I was always looking for.

It was different now. I had open access, which in some ways was worse.

Standing in front of her closet looking at the proof that

Seattle's fashion trends had once made their way south, Jamie said, "You'd probably have more friends if you stopped wearing your mom's nineties grunge clothes."

It was true that I didn't have a lot of friends. Not because I didn't want more friends, but because everyone's parents remembered *her.* Apparently people were worried that suicide was contagious, too. My mom was St. Francisville's only suicide. No one in town had died unnaturally since her, unless you counted the boating accidents, which nobody did. I guess death by boat couldn't be unnatural, seeing that the Mississippi River pressed against the town and the False River was just a ferry ride away. Drowning was inevitable.

"What good would changing my wardrobe do?" I said. "Nobody can tell us apart anyway."

"You don't help," he said. "Now come on and pick out something to wear tonight." He yanked a flannel shirt off its hanger and threw it at me, but he missed and knocked a picture off my mom's dresser. It was one of her and my dad. Pictures of the two of them were scattered around the room. In almost all of them, he was looking at her instead of the camera, his love for her burning in his eyes. My mother was beautiful, and not in the all-mothers-are-beautiful way, but in the look-at-her, what-is-she-doing-in-this-town way.

"Fine, but it's too hot for flannel."

Jamie looked back in the closet and smirked. "Good luck."

I shoved him out of my way and snagged a dress off a hanger. "I'll be quick."

I went into the bathroom to change. There were pictures of my mom and her friends stuck around the edges of the mirror. She was always smiling. She was a liar. Happy people didn't kill themselves. My dad said she had "a way" about her, said she had a way of believing in you so you felt like you were special. She could convince you to do anything with her eyes. She was beautiful, with poor impulse control—a combination that did nothing but keep her in trouble.

My mom walked into the Mississippi River at night wearing only her nightgown. I was three days old. She didn't leave a note. Sometimes I followed her trail from the back door to the river, imagining which trees she might have touched, wondering if she paused before stepping into the water.

On coming out of the bathroom, I found Jamie flipping through her CDs. "We've got to get you some new music."

Jamie was my favorite person in town and friend number one. He'd always lived next door, but we didn't officially meet until the first day of kindergarten, when he had been sporting an unfortunate shorn look. His mom had shaved his head to combat his obsessive hair twirling, a thing he did when he was nervous or sleepy. This had caused a huge problem at nap time, so I had scooted my mat close to him.

"You can twirl my hair," I'd said.

He'd returned the favor by giving me his bag of chips at snack time, because my grandmother had forgotten to send me to school with a snack. We'd been taking care of each other ever since.

From that first day of school onward, we spent every afternoon playing together. What started as a friendship born of proximity became something deeper. Jamie never treated me like the daughter of the town's most infamous dead girl. He only saw *me*. He even let me keep his secrets.

When I was little, I used to pretend I was Jamie's sister, because I thought his family was perfect and I wanted to be a part of it. My grandmother's kitchen window looked right into their dining room, and I would watch them eating dinner, talking and laughing. His parents would look at him like he was the most important person in the world, and Jamie would look like he agreed. I'd watch them like they were a TV show.

But that was BDBD, as Jamie would say. Before his dad became a drunk.

"We're gonna buy you some new music," Jamie said. "Today. We fix this today." He pulled a CD out of the stack. It was the Smashing Pumpkins. "Here, put this in your box. This proves your mom had terrible taste."

I looked everywhere for answers to the question of who she was. Some people collected rocks or stamps. I collected clues about my mother. I put everything in a box, a collection of evidence. Every clue was a piece of the mosaic I was making, hoping one day it'd reveal a clear picture of her.

Exhibit A: a newspaper clipping detailing a hunger strike she had organized when the Tackett boys didn't have money to pay for their school's hot lunches and the cafeteria lady had served them peanut butter sandwiches. She got all the other kids to agree not to eat until the Tackett kids could eat the regular lunch. It worked. Exhibit A showed she was kindhearted and passionate.

Exhibit B: a picture of her taken at Thompson Creek, which had been stuck to her dresser mirror. She once went cliff diving there when the water was too low, and someone had taken a picture of her right before she'd jumped. On the back she'd written, *The rush was like nothing else.* Exhibit B showed she was impulsive and reckless.

I took the CD from Jamie. "I'll be sure to add this piece of information."

Jamie nodded, his face serious.

There was a knock on the door. My grandmother stuck her head in the room. "Lillian, that other boy is here. He's on the porch. I told him you didn't want to see him, but he won't listen."

"That other boy" was Max Barrow, my on-again/off-again boyfriend since sophomore year. My grandmother couldn't remember names. Jamie was "that boy" and Max was "that other boy." By the way, my name isn't Lillian. Lillian was my mom's name. My grandmother started calling me by it when I was in the sixth grade.

At first it was a tiny slipup that she quickly corrected: "Lillian, will you bring me the— I mean, Olivia, will you bring me the paper?"

Soon she was slipping up more and more. Then one night she caught me sneaking out of my mom's room, back when I hadn't been allowed in, and the "Lillian" had escaped from her mouth in one loud breath.

Her eyes were distant with sleep. "What are you doing up? You couldn't sleep?"

I was scared stiff, unable to find any words. I braced myself for what I thought would be a verbal lashing. Instead, she reached for my hand and led me to the bed.

"Lillian, you need your rest."

My grandmother had pulled back sheets and covers that had not been touched in eleven years and tucked me in snugly. She hummed a lullaby and rubbed her hand across my hair, and my eyes burned when she dropped a kiss on my forehead. Just like that, I became *her*.

I didn't sleep that night. I thought about getting up and sneaking back to my bed, just pretending it hadn't happened. It was only a two-bedroom house, so I slept on a twin bed in the corner of my grandmother's room. I didn't budge, though, just stayed wide-awake in my mom's bed, under her dust-covered quilt, doing my penance. After that night, my grandmother stopped seeing me altogether: this was the consequence of my curiosity.

Jamie hated it.

"Her name's Olivia," he said now.

He corrected her every time. It didn't make any difference. My grandmother would look at him with slightly unfocused eyes that never saw the things in front of her clearly, and go back to calling me Lillian.

My grandmother was old, but my dad said losing Lillian had aged her even more. She didn't have my mom until she was in her forties. She hadn't been trying for a baby.

My grandfather didn't want kids. He was a traveling sales-man who'd come through town and swept her off her feet. They got married, and he stayed for a few years, but he was a "wanderer," according to my grandmother. He wan-dered into town and then wandered out of it. "He left me on a Tuesday," she'd said. She found out she was pregnant a couple of weeks later.

"I don't like it when that other boy comes over, Lillian," she said now. "He's no good for you. Boys like that can make a girl change her plans."

That was funny, since the reason for my most recent breakup with Max was that I didn't have any plans.

My grandmother came into the room and picked up the shirt Jamie had thrown at me, then put it back on the hanger and hung it in the closet. On her way out of the room, she bent to pick up the picture on the floor. She put it back in the exact spot Lillian had left it in.

Jamie stared at the shut door for a time and then said, "You need to go talk to that other boy."

"I don't want to."

"Sure you do," he said. "Go tell him you love him and you're ready to have his babies."

"But I don't and I'm not."

"You do love him."

"I'm not ready to love him."

"That's the first true thing you've said all day. Go ahead, go talk to him. I know you've already forgiven him."

"How do you know?"

"Because you're always forgiving him for the wrong things."

"Fine, I'll go talk to him."

"Do you mind if I hang here?" he asked.

"No, of course not."

These days, Jamie avoided going home at all costs. *Everyone* avoided going to Jamie's house. There were many reasons for this, the main one being that his dad was unpredictable. Jamie picked up the magazine on the nightstand and plopped down on the bed. It was a *Rolling Stone* from 1995.

"Cool, Soul Asylum is planning another tour."

It was a June edition. I'd read it cover to cover. I'd read everything in the room cover to cover.

Max was sitting on the swing, his head in his hands. His clothes had that slept-in look. At the creak of the screen door, he lifted his face to mine. Max was beautiful, in the same hard and brown way as a lot of boys in St. Francisville. He was the size of a man, but when you looked in his eyes, a boy looked back at you. When he was near me, he made it hard to breathe. And not in that he's-so-dreamy-and-perfect way, but because he was the physical reminder of the last bad choice I'd made. He was the kind of boy you could make a lot of mistakes with. He was also magnificent and fearless. He loved me too much.

The first time Max told me he loved me was during junior year. We were standing in the school parking lot between the buses and teacher parking. That was also the year he told me he knew I was the girl he'd marry someday.

"I love you," he'd said, the sun making him squint and his words making my heart rate double.

"You can't," I'd said.

I'd turned and walked away, his "Why not?" a whisper behind me.

Then he'd yelled out, "Yes, I can love you! I *do* love you."

"Why?"

The look on his face said he hadn't expected to be questioned. At first I thought he wouldn't answer.

"You see the real me," he'd finally said. "My dad, my friends—they see me how they want to see me. But you see me for *me*."

Max loved me for the same reasons I loved Jamie.

Now he was looking at me, and there was fire in his eyes. Sometimes he looked at me like my dad looked at my mom in those pictures. I didn't know how to tell him his love burned me up.

"Hey," he said. "I've been looking for you."

"I've been here." I took the seat next to him on the swing.

"Is Jamie here?" he asked.

I nodded. Max had always accepted my friendship with Jamie and was never threatened by it. Everyone knew we were a package deal.

The air between Max and me was thick. I kept replaying the last things we'd said to each other. Judging by the look on his face, he was doing the same thing. He reached for my hand and flipped it over. He traced the scars there, something he did every time he held my hand. He reached for the other one and did the same thing, like the lines were a code he was trying to break.

"I shouldn't have been driving that night," he said, his soft touch an apology.

"No, you shouldn't have been."

He grimaced.

A few months ago, we were coming home from a party when a deer ran across the road. Max had been too drunk to drive, but I couldn't convince him not to. Max swerved, but we still hit it. The impact sent us off the road and into a ditch. The truck flipped over. Sometimes I still heard the sound of metal crunching in my sleep, my subconscious replaying that night. We'd landed upside down. Max was no help. I had to kick the window out to get us free, and I cut my hands on the glass climbing through. Everyone said I shouldn't have been strong enough to break the glass. I tore up my hands pretty bad, and Max couldn't forgive himself.

After the accident Max started thinking I was a liar.

"I forgive you," I'd say.

"I don't believe you. How can you?" he'd ask. "I almost killed you."

"But you didn't. It was an accident. That deer came out of nowhere. You would've hit it even if you were sober."

"Don't make excuses for me," he'd argue.

No matter what I said, he wouldn't believe me. Since

then, it was like he was on a mission, loving me more to atone for his sins.

He rubbed my scars now and shook his head. "I love you," he said. "And I'm sorry."

He was wild, throwing around words like *love*. He pushed most people away, but not me. With me, he was dying to be saved. I wanted to tell him that love never saved anybody. It didn't save my mom.

"That's done," I said. "You don't have to be sorry about that anymore."

He had other things to be sorry about. "I'm sorry about what I said the other day."

I pulled my hand from his. We both knew that wasn't true.

"I'm sorry for *how* I said it," he said.

That I believed.

"I didn't know asking you to come to Baton Rouge at the end of the summer would be a deal breaker."

"I can't see myself there."

"Even though that's where Jamie will be?" he asked.

Both Jamie and Max were going to LSU in the fall. The thought made me hollow. It was only about thirty miles away, but you couldn't measure the distance from St. Francisville in miles.

"I can't see myself anywhere."

"Look, I get it," he said.

But he didn't. Max had always had a place, in the past, in the present. Max had a future, even if it was one he didn't want. His dad was a prominent attorney in town who expected his son to follow in his footsteps. Max would be pre-law of course, and his dad had already added the *and Son* to the sign outside his office.

There wasn't a lot of new ground broken in St. Francisville. Most people just did what their parents did, which was why almost everyone who knew me half expected me to follow my mom into the water. No one asked me, "What do you want to be when you grow up?" To be honest, it was a question I didn't want to hear. In two months I'd be eighteen, and a day after that I'd outlive her. I had no idea what I wanted to do with the rest of my life, because there had never seemed a point in planning past eighteen. I figured if I pulled through, then I'd make some decisions. This frustrated Max to great extremes and had been the catalyst for our last fight.

"Olivia, you have to pick something. You have to do *something*!" he'd yelled.

"I am doing something!" I'd yelled back.

"You're playing dress-up in a dead girl's clothes. That doesn't qualify as a life plan."

My eyes had watered and my nose had stung at his words, like he'd struck me. "Should I keep doing whatever it is we're doing?" I'd asked. "Having sex in your truck on turnrows and getting day-drunk for no reason. Is that a better life plan?"

It was his turn to look like he'd been kicked in the gut. "I haven't had a drop of anything since that night, and you know it."

I did know it, but I couldn't keep myself from rubbing

13

salt in his wound. I'd wanted to hurt him back. "I know. I'm sorry."

"I try every day to do the right thing," he'd said. "My dad says I have to be honest, own up to my mistakes. And that's what I'm trying to do, but you make everything so hard."

"How do I make things hard?"

"Because you're not honest back. You're always pushing me away. You won't let your guard down. You won't let yourself be with me, really *be* with me."

"What does that have to do with me forgiving you for almost killing me?"

We'd been standing in my grandmother's front yard, not far from where we were now, and he'd picked up a rock and thrown it. It had hit one of my grandmother's flowerpots and shattered it, soil and petals flying everywhere.

"I'm sorry," he'd said. He'd started cleaning up his mess, gathering the pieces of clay pot and cussing. His nickname on the football team was the Tasmanian Devil. He wrecked everything in sight, and I had the scars to prove it.

"I don't want to do this anymore," I'd said.

He'd dropped the pieces of flowerpot. "You're gonna break up with me again?"

"Yes."

"How long this time, do you think? So I can plan out my week."

"God, Max!" I'd screamed. "You're impossible! You always want more. You push and push. You're never happy with the way things are."

Our yelling had brought my grandmother outside, and she stood there staring Max down.

"I'm sorry about your flowerpot, Ms. Josephine. I'll clean it up."

"No, that's fine. Just leave."

"All right, I'm leaving," he'd said, his face looking dejected. "Olivia, you don't have to come with me to Baton Rouge. Just pick a direction and go," he'd added much more quietly. He hadn't meant that, though. He'd wanted me to follow him.

That brought us to our current problem. "Whatever I do has to be mine, Max."

"I get it," he said again.

This is what Max said anytime he didn't understand something. We were in stare-down mode when the front door opened.

Jamie stepped onto the porch and said, "Your grandmother started cleaning around me. I took that as my cue."

He nodded in Max's direction. "Hey, man," he said. "I hear you've been a dick lately."

"I'm trying to apologize," Max said.

"Good luck with that." Jamie looked at me. "Are we still meeting at Bird Man's later?"

"Yeah, I'll see you there."

I watched Jamie walk away. The closer he got to his house, the more his shoulders slumped: Jamie's attempt to make himself smaller.

There were a few moments of awkward silence, and then

my grandmother appeared in the front window, giving Max her death glare.

"I think that's my cue, too," he said. "Will I see you later tonight?"

"Maybe," I said.

"Maybe," he sighed. He stood and walked down the porch steps. With his back to me, he said, "You know you love me." He got in his truck, a gift from his dad to replace the one he'd totaled, and drove away, the dust kicking up from his tires.

It was true. It was my gut instinct to love him. He was broken, but he was mine. I was scared, though. I'd seen the consequences of love in my dad's eyes.

My dad was a shadow in my life, standing in the corners, only coming close when absolutely necessary or in his most lonesome moments. He watched me warily, as if I was a clue to her, as if the time I'd spent inside her body had given me a secret and one day I'd tell him what it was. I was scared to love or be loved in that way.

It was on this street—Fidelity Street—that he'd promised her he'd love her forever. They were sixteen and standing under the gigantic live oak tree across from my grandmother's house. I once asked him to show me exactly where he stood and exactly where she stood.

"Tell me word for word what you told her," I'd said.

"I told her that even though we were only sixteen, I knew I'd love her for the rest of my life."

"What did she say?"

"She said she'd love me for the rest of hers."

He didn't know his love would outlive hers by a life-time. Then I'd asked him why he'd never moved on. He'd paused, then grunted and said, "Lillian was enough."

He didn't live with us. He wasn't comfortable in my grandmother's house. Then again, nobody had expected him to move in after my mom died. He lived in a one-room apartment above the garage where he worked. I once asked him why he didn't want me to live with him. He said there wasn't enough room. I didn't think that was it. One time he admitted, "Sometimes it hurts to look at you."

I stood up from the swing and walked to the tree where they'd declared their love. The big branches swept to the ground, and all it took was a little balance to get to the sweet spot. I could see this tree from my mom's bedroom window. When I was little, I imagined the branches were arms, always open, a constant invitation. Over the years I had occasionally woken up in this tree, having sleepwalked there.

I climbed up the huge branch that was rolled out like a red carpet. I sat in the seat, its handholds worn smooth from years of my touch, and looked down the street into everyone's yards. If I strained my eyes, I could see all the way downtown. There were small towns, and then there was St. Francisville.

It stretched three miles along Highway 61 and was home to less than two thousand people. People could say what they wanted to about small towns and small minds, but the people here knew how to do things without being taught. No one remembered learning how to swim, or how to tell a harmless snake from the ones that killed you. Knowledge was passed down through the generations. The babies were born wise.

I looked down along the bluffs to the river. People were boarding the ferry to New Roads, the town we shared the Mississippi with. There were rumors that we might be linked by a new bridge, but for now it was up to the ferry to get us back and forth. I wanted to learn how to steer the ferry. It couldn't be that hard, just going back and forth all day long.

Fidelity Street dead-ended at my grandmother's house, which was pale pink with the required front porch. There was a pathway that led around the side of the house to a trellis wrapped in flowers. The trellis opened into a garden that was wild and whimsical, leaning heavily on the whimsy. Nothing in it resembled a straight line or hinted at a plan. In one corner was a swing from which, if you swung way out on it, you could get a peek at the river below. One of my earliest memories was of being in this yard with my grandmother, back when she called me Olivia. She used to push me on the swing.

"This was your mother's favorite thing to do when she was your age," she'd said. "She once made a promise, right out loud to the house, that this would always be her favorite place in the entire world, and that she'd never leave."

That made sense, because in pictures from my mom's childhood, the house and yard looked like something out of a storybook. The kind of house your fairy godmother or the tooth fairy might live in, or the kind of house a five-year-old might pledge her undying love to. Not so much anymore. The paint was peeling, and some of the windows were cracked; nothing broken ever got fixed. The only thing my grandmother tended to was the garden. The house itself looked abandoned.

I saw Jamie in his backyard. He was sitting on the patio and writing in his journal, one of those speckled notebooks. He'd filled up dozens of them, and they took up whole shelves in his bedroom. He only wrote in them in his backyard, where he was now, pretending not to notice me watching him from my tree. His brow was furrowed and he was writing furiously, like the words were screaming from his hand. Sometimes when he couldn't say things out loud, he took them out on his journal. I heard the sound of his parents' fighting coming from inside their house.

Jamie's dad had a split personality. If you went over there in the morning, Mr. Benton could be kind and loving, even funny, but in the afternoon he was sad and mean and terrible. His mood slowly slipped down as the day wore on, his whiskey consumption the deciding factor.

The only person I hated in the entire world was Tom Benton. I forgave him for his meanness; it was his niceness that was truly unforgivable. It gave you a glimpse of the man he could have been all the time, if he could've stayed sober. He beat his wife—though she was quick to point out it was only when he was drunk.

"He's never laid a hand on Jamie," she'd say in her husband's defense.

This was true. He had never laid a hand on Jamie. In

fact, Jamie couldn't remember his dad even touching him since he was ten. That was the year Mr. Benton lost his job and found the bottle. Even though he found work again, the jobs never lasted long, and he never stopped drinking. Sometimes I caught Jamie watching his dad expectantly, like he was waiting for him to turn back into the man he was before.

He stopped touching Jamie. He stopped looking at him. I once begged Jamie's mom to leave and take Jamie with her. I begged her to make it quick, because I was worried Jamie was being completely erased. She didn't even think about it.

"I made a *vow*," she said. "I made a vow for good times and bad."

She'd made this vow in their backyard. We took promises made on Fidelity Street very seriously. Once Jamie tried to promise me he'd always be my best friend. I made us walk two streets over before he made any declarations, just in case he wanted out later.

"Lillian! Come down out of that tree and help me bring in the laundry." My grandmother was in the side yard, fighting the wind as she tried to fold sheets.

Jamie lifted his head from his journal and looked at me. His parents' shouting was getting louder; then there was silence, followed by his mom's screaming and the crash of a slammed door. Even at this distance, I flinched. Jamie didn't, though. He just held my eyes. Sometimes his eyes were the saddest thing you'd see for two parishes.

I still pretended I was his sister. I didn't want his parents as my family anymore, though—just him. He and I made our own family: the invisible children of Fidelity Street.

"Lillian!" my grandmother yelled again.

"I'm coming!"

From a distance my grandmother looked like a grandmother was supposed to look. She was small and round and soft in all the right places. She smelled like peppermint and old-lady perfume. Her face was lined like a map, which made you think she had the answers to all life's questions, but the map offered no direction. I loved her completely, and she loved me back, even though it wasn't my face she saw. I couldn't explain it, but I could still feel the love from when I was just me. She was my protector, even if she couldn't remember who she was protecting.

"Lillian, I love you," she said.

With the billowing sheets between us, I replied, "I love you, too."

Chapter 2

Maggie, friend number two, worked at Bird Man Coffee and Books. It was a cross between an art studio, a restaurant, and a dive bar, complete with local musicians and sculptures, and decorated with books, endless books. Oh yeah, it also sold coffee.

Maggie was behind the counter, wiping it down with fast, angry strokes. I was petite, but Maggie only came up to my shoulder. What she lacked in size, she made up for in volume. She was a singer, songwriter, artist, and fighter—a bewilderment of beings. No one matched the sheer velocity with which she approached life. Once, in the first grade, she gut-punched Brad Henderson, a boy three times her size, when he said I was the only person in the class who didn't have a mother. Everyone needed a Maggie.

"Hey, how's it going?" I asked.

"If I have to serve one more cup of coffee today, I'm

going to lose my mind. And your sometime boyfriend came by looking for you," she said.

"He found me."

"I told him to leave you alone. He never listens. He doesn't listen to anyone." She exhaled loudly. "I'm sorry. I'm just in a bad mood. I'm ready to get out of here." She stopped wiping and leveled a hard look at me. "I *have* to get out of here."

Maggie was moving to New York in the fall. She had a scholarship to the School of Visual Arts in Manhattan and planned to major in fine arts. She didn't listen to or read anything dating to after 1976 because "nothing current is original." She had no filter and would say anything that came into her head, and her eyes were so big that when she looked at you, she always saw more than you wanted her to.

"I'm off soon," she said. "Are you and Jamie coming to Magnolia's?"

Magnolia's was an actual juke joint that sat behind the coffeehouse. Jamie and I spent most every free night of the summer there—at least the nights Maggie was singing.

"Yeah. He's meeting me here."

"Good. My dad is coming." She rolled her eyes. "He's bringing the new girlfriend."

Maggie was one of only three kids in my graduating class to come from a broken home. Her parents' divorce was big news at West Feliciana Elementary. In St. Francisville, Louisiana, marriage was forever.

Maggie's mother was a folk singer who spent most of her time in New Orleans working on a drug habit and hoping to be discovered. Maggie joked that the only thing her mom ever gave her was her voice. Her dad, meanwhile, gave her everything else. He was a local artist who taught Maggie about art, books, music, and, according to Maggie, how not to love a woman.

"It's gonna be a good show," said Maggie. She beamed. Maggie was a born performer.

The door opened and Jamie walked in. You couldn't tell from his face that anything bad had happened earlier. Jamie was good at that. He snuck up behind Maggie.

"Maggie, my love," he whispered in her ear. He reached for her hand and spun her out and then brought her back in to his chest, swaying with her even though there was no music. It didn't matter. When Jamie and Maggie were in a room together, there was always dancing. He dipped her. "When are you going to quit this job so you can spend more time with me?" he asked.

"When you give me the money it takes to afford my life."

"If I had it, darlin', it'd be yours." He let her go and sank down on the couch. "How long before you get off?" he asked.

"I'm headed to Magnolia's now to help set up. Will y'all be over in a little bit?"

"You know it," he said. "Can you get me a cup of coffee before you go?"

She threw her dish towel at him. "Get your own coffee."

No one carded at Magnolia's. This accounted for the rowdy state of many of the teenagers in the room. Jamie and I picked a spot in the corner, not too far from the stage. Maggie started belting out a song, so loud and beautiful.

Jamie leaned in toward me. "I'm going to get a water. Do you want one?"

I nodded. As soon as Jamie walked away, Lyle Williams snaked up next to me. Lyle had graduated a year ahead of us and been solidifying his reputation as the town asshole ever since.

"Ticktock, Olivia. Your birthday's coming soon," he said. "You don't have much time left." He stepped closer to me, invading my space, his hot breath on my face. "Why don't you make the most of it?" His hand slid out to grab my waist and pull me even closer to him.

"Screw you." I shoved his chest.

"What? You broke up with Max again. You're fair game."

I looked over my shoulder to see Jamie coming back to me, having abandoned his quest for water. Jamie was usually pretty easygoing, but he became a different person when someone was messing with me. I knew if I didn't do something to defuse the situation, Jamie was going to get into a fight. He'd gotten into more than a few of them because of me.

After the last fight, when I was cleaning his cut lip in my mom's bathroom, I'd told him, "You have to stop taking up for me. They're not gonna stop, and you're gonna keep getting hurt."

He'd looked down at the floor, watching the patterns his blood made as it dripped onto the tile, and mumbled, "Better me than you."

Not wanting a repeat of that performance, I jerked free of Lyle's hold.

"Shut up," I said.

I turned and walked outside, but stopped short at the sight of Max sitting on the front bumper of his truck. Since Max had stopped drinking, he didn't come into Magnolia's.

Lyle followed me outside. "Hey, don't walk away," he said. He reached out and snagged the back of my shirt.

I turned around as Jamie stepped between us.

"Leave her alone," he said.

Lyle let go of me. "If it isn't Olivia's lapdog. Run along. We were just having a little chat."

"No." Jamie put his hands on Lyle's chest and gave him a push. "I said leave her alone."

Lyle's hands fisted at his sides. Even though Jamie knew what was coming next, he didn't look scared. He held his ground and, with a little chin lift, gave Lyle a look that said, "Come on, man, hit me."

Just when I thought there was no avoiding a fight, Max stood. Lyle jerked his head up in response. Max didn't have to say anything; Lyle tucked his tail between his legs and walked away. For people like Jamie and me, it took busted lips. Max only had to stand. This was because when Max *did* fight, he didn't lose. I turned my anger on him.

"We had it under control," I said.

"You looked like you had it under control," said Max,

and then, trying to change the subject, "Maggie sounds great tonight."

"As she does every night," Jamie added.

Max nodded. "You might want to be careful about going back in there. Lyle is stupid and doesn't learn from his mistakes."

"You're right," Jamie said.

Max walked to us and reached for my hand. "Let's get out of here." He leaned down to my ear. "You and me, let's go somewhere."

"Why would you think I'd go anywhere with you?"

"Olivia," he sighed.

"Max."

"Why do you fight me on everything?" he asked. "Just come for a ride with me."

I looked at Jamie.

"I'm fine to stay here with Maggie," he said.

"See? Jamie says it's fine. Let's go." He tugged on my hand. "I've missed you. Please?"

"Where do you want to go?"

With a mischievous glint in his eyes, he said, "Let's go to Thompson Creek."

"Wait," Jamie said. "You don't need to go out there at night."

"Sure she does. Everyone knows that's the best time to go cliff diving."

Max knew I wouldn't be able to resist that invitation.

"It hasn't rained in over a month," Jamie said. "The water's too low."

"I know a place that's safe to jump. It's supposed to be over twenty feet deep. Come on, Olivia. Live a little."

The rush was like nothing else.

I could tell Jamie knew what I was thinking, because he let out a loud sigh and threw his hands up. I didn't always do the right thing; sometimes I channeled self-destruction. It was a feeling that started in my toes and quickly headed north. I knew what people would say if word got out that Lillian's daughter had gone cliff diving, but there were times when I felt dared to meet their expectations. What they didn't realize was that I didn't do these things because I was suicidal. I just wanted to feel closer to her. We had limited options when it came to mother-daughter bonding.

"My mind's made up," Max said. "I'm jumping off a cliff. You can come with me or not." He turned and walked to his truck.

"Wait for me," I said.

Jamie looked pissed.

"You heard him," I said. "His mind's made up. I can't let him go alone."

"Sure you can. He doesn't have to be your problem."

"But he is," I said. Max was always my problem.

"Am I supposed to pretend I don't know why you're really going?"

"Yes." I couldn't keep the excitement from my voice. I always got excited when I was about to do something I knew she'd done. I got this irrational feeling, like I was close to finding her.

"Dammit, Olivia. Try not to die."

I ran to catch up with Max. He pulled open the passenger door and then leaned in to try to kiss me.

"No, Romeo. I'll jump off a cliff with you, nothing more."

He smirked and got in the truck.

I caught Jamie's eyes as Max cranked the truck. They pleaded with me, but I stayed put. No matter how many times Jamie stepped in, there was no saving me from Max or myself. Jamie knew that on nights like this, he had two options: he could be the witness, or he could go home. He turned and walked back inside.

The creek was only a few miles away, so it wasn't long before we were standing at the edge of what passed in St. Francisville as a cliff. I was starting to rethink my decision to jump, but I couldn't bear to let anyone see me back down, especially Max. I did try to stall, though.

"You can't even see the water from here," I said.

The night air whispered around us, dead black.

"It's there. I promise."

"Are you sure this is a good idea?" I asked.

"Kids jump all the time. It's safe."

He kicked off his shoes, and I did the same. I placed my hands in his and he twisted us closer to the edge, looked down into my eyes, and breathed, "Trust me."

Never—but I closed my eyes and nodded slowly. I thought I could hear voices in the background and imagined that one of them was Maggie's.

"Are you ready?" he asked.

"Yes," I said, but my heart was beating so loudly in protest that I was sure he'd hear it.

His thumbs rubbed my palms. He lifted them to his face and planted kisses there. It took my breath away.

"I'll never put you in danger again. I promise. You can do this. The water is deep enough."

I nodded.

"One, two . . . deep breath . . . three."

We stepped off the edge of the world and plunged into the night. The wind rushed by us. I heard screaming before I realized the sound was coming from me.

The water was as black as the night. There was a flash of light as a car headlight swept over the water below, and I closed my eyes when my feet stabbed through the surface. There was no sickening snap of bones, but the water grabbed me fiercely, ripping my hand from Max's. I turned around, then up, then down, disoriented.

But I didn't panic; in fact, the opposite happened. I felt my muscles relax as I slowed, no longer a speeding bullet. My heart stopped hammering and picked out a slow beat while the water moved around me, warmer than I expected. I opened my eyes, but saw nothing. I stayed like that for some time, quiet and peaceful, in the silence of the murky water.

I stayed under for what felt like minutes. My chest started to burn. My lungs protested. I should've swum toward the surface, but I remained perfectly still. I felt closer to her when I was underwater. I wanted to try death on for size, to see how she might have felt.

Then my reflexes took over. My arms pushed the water

out of my way, my legs kicking frantically as panic set in. There was no light and no hint I was going in the right direction. I faltered, then committed and pushed through the water faster and faster in the same direction.

There was never sweeter air. I heard my name being called, and the voice was panicked.

"Olivia!"

The water splashed around me and on me, but I continued to suck in air. Max reached me and yanked me toward him. Then he half dragged me to the shore.

"I can swim."

"Are you sure?"

We stumbled up the bank and collapsed onto our backs on the grass. I closed my eyes and concentrated on breathing in and out. Max lay next to me.

"What the hell, Olivia?!" he yelled at the sky.

"I'm sorry," I said.

I opened my eyes to the sound of twigs crunching and saw Maggie and Jamie walking toward us. I take back what I said before. On nights like these, Jamie had three choices: he could be the witness, go home, or get backup. Maggie leaned over Max's wet form and drew her hand back. I flinched at the sound of the slap she gave him, hard against his face.

She leaned in closer and yelled, "The last thing she needs is everyone in town knowing she jumps off cliffs for fun! If you tell anyone about this, I promise you, you'll regret it."

I could tell he believed her.

Then she turned to me. "I know you think there's a black hole waiting for you, but you can go around it."

Max looked truly remorseful. He locked eyes with me and said, "I'm sorry. I wanted to jump off a cliff, and I didn't want to do it with anyone but you."

It was one of the nicest things he'd ever said to me. He hefted himself off the bank and walked away from us, dripping, never looking back. Jamie helped me up and I avoided his eyes, not because I'd done anything that terrible but because I knew I'd aged him.

Maggie looked at me hard, her lips twitching like she was getting ready to say more. Instead of ranting, she turned and led the way back to her car. We stayed a couple of paces behind her.

Jamie whispered, "Don't be mad at her. She doesn't like being scared." Then, his voice louder this time, "Maggie's the kind of girl you'd go the whole world to find."

It was like he was reminding us both. I wasn't mad; I agreed.

Riding back to Fidelity Street, my clothes wet and clinging, I thought about the moment underwater when it had stopped being my decision whether I stayed there, when my reflexes had screamed, *"Swim!"*

Maybe there was something inside you that wanted to stay alive and would scream to be heard, no matter what you'd been through. I wondered whether it had been like that for my mom, whether she'd changed her mind as the black current of the Mississippi River pulled at her. Flipping my hands over to study my scars, I wondered if she had fought.

❧

Late in the night, my cell phone rang, Jamie's familiar ringtone filling the air. I answered it.

"Bob Costas," he said.

"Carly Simon," I countered.

"Selena Gomez."

"G-Greg . . . I mean, wait—"

"No, you lose this round. And George Harrison."

"That's what I was trying to say."

"I know. Drew Barrymore," he said.

"Bob Barker," I countered.

"Ooh, double whammy."

It was a game we played anytime one of us couldn't sleep, filling up the night air between us with names. You had to name a celebrity using the first letter of the last name the other person said.

"Bette Davis," he said.

"Good one. David Letterman."

"You find a way to bring David Letterman into every game."

"What's wrong with David Letterman? He's sexy."

Jamie laughed.

"What?" I said. "He's smart, and smart's sexy."

"Good to know," he said.

There were a few moments of silence. "Did you find any answers at the bottom of Thompson Creek?" Jamie asked.

"No, just more questions."

"Your mom wasn't there?"

"No."

"You'll find her," he said. "Was it a rush?"

"Like nothing else."

More silence.

"Good night, Olivia."

"Good night."

Chapter 3

Summer in St. Francisville was hot, the kind of hot that could kill old people and babies. The weatherman routinely told us we should stay inside until dark. You'd think this would prevent the town from planning outdoor activities, but St. Francisville loved festivals. I secretly loved them, too. The music and spirit were special, despite the heat.

It was the second day of my favorite festival, the Day the War Stopped. When I was little, I didn't understand the significance; I just liked watching the parade and seeing everyone dress up in clothes from the 1860s. The festival was a reenactment of the funeral of a Union captain, one John E. Hart. You might think it strange that a Union captain got a festival every year in Louisiana, but Hart was a Mason, and he died on his ship when it was docked along the bluff on Bayou Sara. At the time, dead bodies were chucked over the side, not without ceremony, and the fighting continued.

However, according to Masonic rites, Captain Hart needed to be buried on land. The Union soldiers sent word to the Masons in St. Francisville, and after some negotiating, they agreed to bury him. The Masons met the soldiers at the dock with a coffin, white flag and all, and marched Captain Hart through town to Grace Episcopal Church, where a preacher was waiting. The town put down the war for four hours to bury a brother. The beauty of this didn't escape me, and neither did the irony: Captain Hart had died by his own hand.

The procession began at the banks of the bayou and then continued into town. When I was little, I'd fall in at the end of the line. No one ever stopped me as I broke through the crowd, stepping into the street to take my place. I'd work my way closer to the coffin, and I couldn't help but look up at it. Once everyone was in the graveyard, I'd take a left instead of a right and go sit at my mom's grave. Sometimes I'd close my eyes and imagine the tribute was to her.

Most years, Jamie walked with me. It was never a plan we made, just this unspoken thing between us. We'd sit with Lillian as the rest of the town rewatched Captain Hart's funeral. As we got older, we stopped walking in the procession altogether and came straight to the cemetery.

I tried not to linger on the fact that the people of this town, who looked at me with nervous eyes, gathered once a year to re-create the funeral of a suicide victim. I knew it wasn't the death they were honoring, but the bonds of brotherhood. I also knew I wasn't being fair, but I felt scorned. My dad tried to help me understand. He said it wasn't malice, it was regret. The people of the town—the good and the bad alike—were made of one fabric. If there was a tear, we all felt it. When my mom died, my dad said the whole town felt it, and everyone gathered around my grandmother, trying to hold her up. Lillian was everyone's daughter.

This year, Jamie and I planned to meet Maggie at the art tents before going to the grave. We met under my tree and started walking, but Jamie stopped suddenly in front of his house.

"What time did you tell Maggie we'd be there?" he asked.

"No certain time. Why?"

"I just remembered I have something for you."

He walked toward his house. I saw his dad's truck in the carport and slowed my steps. Jamie noticed.

"Don't worry. He's working the night shift now. He's sleeping."

"Okay." I planted a smile on my face and pretended that walking into his house didn't make my stomach hurt.

I used to be as comfortable in Jamie's house as I was at my grandmother's. We played hide-and-seek all over the house, and every Tuesday night was game night. We played board games, all four of us gathered around the kitchen table while Mr. Benton read aloud the rules of whatever game we were playing. He was a stickler for the rules, but if you won, he'd make you feel like a million bucks, like you were the smartest kid that ever lived, because you'd beaten him at Candy Land. It made me sad to be in Jamie's house with those memories. I was pretty sure it made Jamie sad, too, but he didn't talk about BDBD days.

Mrs. Benton was sitting at the table sipping coffee as we snaked around the kitchen and down the hall toward Jamie's bedroom. She acted like she didn't notice us, not even a blink. I held my breath as we passed his parents' room. The door was open a crack, and I caught a glimpse of Mr. Benton on the bed.

The first time he'd hurt Jamie's mom had been after one of our games. For a while, after he lost his job, we pretended not to notice that Mr. Benton was sad and drunk. We all ignored his mean comments. But one night we couldn't. Mrs. Benton told him he'd had enough to drink and tried to take the bottle away from him. He pushed her, and she fell into the table, the glass in her hand shattering on the floor all around her. He didn't help her up, just walked away from her. That was our last game night.

Jamie picked up his journal from his bed and added it to the collection on his shelf. I stood and ran my fingers over the spines.

"What do you put in all of these?"

He shrugged. "Just stories, ideas."

He went to his dresser and slid it over a bit. It made a loud scraping noise against the hardwood, and Jamie stopped instantly, his head snapping in the direction of his door. I stopped breathing and started praying, something I never did unless I was in Jamie's house. *Please, please, please don't let that have woken him up.* I didn't look at the door, only Jamie's face. It seemed an age before he blinked. No noise came from his dad's room. Relief washed over his face, and he dropped to his knees and pulled up a loose floorboard.

I met him on the floor. He slid a few planks toward me and revealed a hole. There were two journals stacked inside it.

"Those are more personal," he said. He reached his hand in and pulled out an envelope. He handed it to me.

I knew instantly what was in it. "She left another one? When did you get this?"

"Last night. I went by the graveyard on my way home. It was in the flowerpot. I was going to bring it over right away, but your lights were out. So I put it somewhere safe."

My mom's childhood best friend, Beth Hunter, wrote her letters, and she always put them in the concrete flowerpot at her graveside. I had never met Beth, but my mom's bedroom wall was speckled with pictures of her. Beth was smiling in all of them, her face usually tight up against my mom's. It'd been over a year since the last letter. I quickly tore open the envelope.

When I was younger, I didn't read them. Not out of some sense of moral high ground, but because I couldn't read cursive. I kept all of them where Lillian had saved things that were important to her: in a shoebox under her bed. The box held ribbons from pep rallies, movie ticket stubs, her lift ticket from her one and only ski trip, a matchbook from a café in New Orleans, my dad's class ring.

Beth and my mom had made all these plans, this life list that was still tacked to the corkboard hanging in my mom's bedroom. I assumed Beth had her own copy, because according to her letters she was working her way through it. There were 126 things on this list. I knew because I'd counted each one again and again, memorizing the things my mom wanted to do but never did, this life she didn't live. Each new letter detailed something on their list. So far, I'd crossed off twenty-eight things. Beth snuck into town and left a letter each time she checked something off, telling my mom what she'd missed. I didn't know how she managed to do it undetected, because this town missed nothing.

I quickly read the new letter.

"Which one?" Jamie asked.

"Number thirty-six, move to New Orleans." Beth didn't go in order. So far my favorites were: live in Denver and work at a ski lodge, spit gum off the Golden Gate Bridge, and wait tables in Hawaii. Some things were easily done, like be kind to a stranger, and some were huge and seemed as though they could never be crossed off, like number eighteen: love everyone all the time. I knew that before I went to bed tonight, I'd put this letter with the others and cross number thirty-six off my mom's list. I was going to find Beth someday, but like a lot of things I was going to do, so far nothing had come of it.

Jamie put the planks back in place, and even though he was as careful as possible moving his dresser to its original position, it still made a noise. He froze again, and I hated that he had to be so quiet in his own house.

The bed squeaked as Mr. Benton got up. Jamie looked from the door to the window, like he thought it might be a good idea to jump out of it instead of trying to get out the door. With Mr. Benton you never knew who you were going to get, the monster or the man.

Jamie quickly herded me toward the door. "Let's go."

We skirted past them in the kitchen, Mr. Benton wrapping himself around Jamie's mom, all soft touches and words, kissing apologies across her cheek.

"I'm sorry. I love you. I love you," I heard him say, his hand running over the fading finger marks on her face. She didn't say anything, but her eyes said she was tired of being loved that way.

"I'm sorry," Jamie muttered once we were outside.

"It's okay."

We didn't talk about it on the way downtown. We never talked about it.

We were walking behind the bank building when we saw Max across the parking lot. I hadn't seen him since we went cliff diving, and there was this weird morning-after feeling. He was leaning against the side of his truck.

"When are you and him gonna figure things out?" Jamie asked.

I didn't get to answer him, because we suddenly came face to face with my dad.

He nodded. "Jamie."

Jamie nodded back. "Mr. Hudson."

"Do you mind if I talk to Olivia for a minute?"

"No, no, sir." Jamie looked at me and said, "I'll go find Maggie. We'll meet you later."

"Bye," I said.

"It's hot out here," my dad said. "Walk with me to my truck. I've got some water in my cooler."

I was about to tell him I wasn't thirsty, but he gave me a look that said not to argue. Once he got to his truck, he started pacing.

"I heard you went cliff diving at Thompson Creek."

My eyes shot over to Max, who looked back at me questioningly.

My dad followed my stare. "He didn't have to say anything. In this town, even the trees talk." He rubbed the back of his head, something he did when he was really upset.

"It wasn't a big deal. A lot of people do it," I said.

"It might not be a big deal for a lot of people, but we both know it is for you. How can you be so immature?" His eyes burned into mine.

"I'm not immature, I'm seventeen. My actions are age appropriate."

For a second I didn't think he had anything to say to that, but then he lashed out. "If you want people to stop comparing you to Lillian, then stop acting like her."

"I don't know how to be different," I admitted. A hard lump formed in my throat, because the truth hurt.

His head dropped. Most dads wanted the world for their children; mine just wanted me to live through my mistakes.

Time passed. I'm not sure how long it was, but I sensed when he wanted to be released of his parental burdens and obliged. "I'm going to her grave, if you want to come with me."

He looked younger at just the mention of her. For a second I glimpsed the boy my mom had loved, and that made me sad. I also knew that it would do the trick, and what his answer would be.

"No, you go ahead." He stepped backward, putting distance between himself and me. "I'll go with you next time." He said that every time.

Once he'd turned the corner, I looked back over at Max to see him still watching me. He motioned for me to join him, but I had a dead girl to visit. I shook my head and walked in the direction of the graveyard.

Whenever I went to the graveyard, I tried not to look at the tombstone itself. There was something jarring about seeing her name in stone, her birth and death dates the same, just separated by eighteen years. Instead, I leaned against it. The cemetery was beautiful. The oak trees were older than the town itself. I wondered at the things they must have seen.

I saw Jamie and Maggie down the street, making their way toward me. They were talking, and Maggie said something that made Jamie laugh. Once they got to me, they plopped down on either side. I rested my head on Jamie's shoulder, a habit. We turned our attention to the funeral procession as they carried the empty coffin toward us and into the graveyard. We didn't say anything as the ceremony began, the gun salute to Captain Hart our soundtrack, the cold of the stone pressing through my shirt.

Chapter 4

My grandmother's house was built a hundred years ago, and it had a skeleton key that locked all the doors from the outside. Recently she'd started using it to lock me in my room at night. The closer it got to my eighteenth birthday, the stranger she got. She knew something bad had happened to Lillian on her eighteenth birthday, and it was as if she was trying to save her the second time around, as if locking her—or me—in would keep us away from the river. It became a nightly ritual, and I'd hear her leaving her room and padding down the hall to my mom's room.

One night, as usual, I heard the knob click.

Through the door she said, "Good night, Lillian."

Later that night I heard her cry out in her sleep, and then heard her bedside lamp crash onto the floor.

"Olivia!"

She only remembered who I was in her nightmares. I

ached to go to her, to comfort her, but my door was locked. Instead, I pressed my forehead against the door, palms against the wood, like I expected some magical power to allow me to slip through it. I stayed that way until she quieted down.

The next morning I woke to an empty house. My door was unlocked. I looked out the kitchen window to see my grandmother working in the garden. She was weeding and watering, and her lips were moving. I knew she was singing.

I heard the sound of the screen door bouncing off the jamb, and Jamie walked into the kitchen. He took his usual seat at the table and stared out the window, saying nothing. It had gotten pretty loud again at his house the night before, and the sounds had carried across the yard. Jamie was beginning to lose his talent for keeping things from registering on his face. Today he looked tired.

"Hey," I said.

He didn't look at me, just kept his head down, picking at some invisible thing on the table. Jamie was retreating. I felt him backing away even as he sat there in the room with me. Nobody was quiet like Jamie Benton.

I tried to change the mood by being extra cheery. "What are we doing today?"

No response.

"Do you want to go to Bird Man's? Maggie gets off at noon. I'm sure we could find something to do, go see a movie."

He looked at me and nodded. "You'll have to drive," he said. "My mom took my car to work today."

"What's wrong with her car?"

"Don't ask."

I had a feeling it had something to do with Mr. Benton going for another DWI to add to his collection.

Maggie was just getting off work by the time we made it to Bird Man's. Jamie and I did a quick loop around the coffeehouse to check out her new collection. Her paintings were angry this time. No one knew for sure what had inspired that emotion, but I had a pretty good idea.

"What's wrong?" Maggie asked Jamie as soon as they made eye contact.

"Same ol', same ol'," he said. "I don't want to talk about it. What's going on with you?" He motioned at the paintings behind us.

"I don't want to talk about it."

"Since we're not talking, let's go see a movie," I said.

We were quiet while we waited in line. But I had to ask, "Are you going to see your mom before you leave?"

Maggie looked up and answered me with a shrug. "I've been thinking about it, but I'm not sure. I don't even know how to get ahold of her. Her cell was disconnected the last time I tried calling. But that was forever ago."

"Your dad hasn't heard from her?"

"She checks in every so often. He fills her in on what's going on in my life. But she never asks to talk to me. She probably doesn't want to see me."

"I bet she would. We should go down together. A road trip could be fun."

She looked at me hard. "And play Where's Waldo with

my mom in New Orleans? Believe me, anywhere she's staying is nowhere we want to be." She flicked her cigarette to the ground. Maggie didn't smoke, not really, but she tried every now and then. I didn't mention her mom again.

After the movie we rode around town before dropping Maggie at home, and then Jamie and I headed back to Fidelity Street. He sat quietly beside me. The sun was setting, but I'd be back in plenty of time before lockdown.

"Do you want to come home with me?" I asked.

His look said *yes.* I smelled supper while were still in the carport. My grandmother might be short on sanity, but she made up for it with her cooking.

Sitting around my grandmother's kitchen table that night, watching her dote on "that boy," my life seemed almost perfect.

"More peas, baby?" she asked him.

"Yes, please, Ms. Josephine," he answered.

It was perfect as long as I ignored a few blaring untruths. Like the fact that in my grandmother's house, I pretended to be my mother, and my grandmother pretended she wasn't crazy, and Jamie, sitting across the table from us, pretended everything in his life was normal.

Later that night, after my grandmother had locked me in, I went to the window and saw Jamie sitting in the seat of my tree. He was looking in my direction, but he didn't see me. I climbed out the window and walked over to the tree. Jamie stared straight ahead, giving no sign he was aware of my presence.

"Jamie," I said.

No response. Sounds of breaking glass and his dad's yelling came flying out of his house. I turned to look at it and saw that the back door was open, like Jamie had walked out and not bothered to shut the door.

"Are you okay?" I asked. "What are you doing? Come down and talk to me."

Nothing. I turned to look at his house again and saw his dad standing in the doorway.

Jamie didn't see him, because he was still staring straight ahead. Mr. Benton leveled his gaze at me. Then he stepped back inside the house and slammed the door.

His look was a promise of something terrible, but instead of scaring me, it made me feel brave.

"Don't worry about him," I said. "Everything's okay. You can come down now."

Still no response.

"If you come down, I won't let anything bad happen to you. I promise."

A promise made on Fidelity Street.

"I'll take care of you."

Jamie tilted his head down and looked at me, then slowly climbed out of the tree. I took his hand and led him back to my window. We climbed into my mom's room. Jamie sat on the end of the bed, his head down.

"I had to get out of there," he said. "I needed a quieter place."

"I understand," I said. "Come to me next time." I pulled a sleeping bag from under the bed. "You can sleep here when you need a quieter place."

He nodded. I unrolled the sleeping bag and handed him a pillow.

"Do you think you'll be able to sleep?" I asked.

"Maybe, since you're here," he said. His voice sounded old.

I turned off the lamp, and he lay down on the floor. I got in the bed and scooted over to the edge.

"I'll let you twirl my hair," I said.

He laughed quietly. "I'm good."

Silence followed.

"Marlon Brando," I said.

"Brad Pitt," he whispered.

"Paul Simon."

"Sammy Davis, Jr."

"David Letterman."

"Good night, Olivia."

"Good night."

When I woke in the morning, he was gone.

The next night, after my grandmother locked the door, I turned to see Jamie at the window, waiting to be let in. He didn't say anything, just pulled out the sleeping bag and lay down. The next night it happened again, and then again. It went on like that for a solid week. Things at his house were going downhill fast. Each day when I woke up, Jamie was gone and the door was unlocked, making me wonder if it was really happening at all.

"Do you think you can come to my house for supper tonight?" Jamie asked.

We were sitting in the middle of my mom's bed. We'd been rereading Beth's letters and guessing which number she'd do next.

"Why?" I asked. "Can't you just eat here, like usual?"

"That's the problem. I'm usually over here, and my mom's feelings are hurt. She wants me home more."

"But she knows why you stay away," I said.

Jamie nodded. "My dad's going in early for the night shift. He'll be gone by five-thirty. It'll just be the three of us, if you want to come."

"I'll come," I said.

"You sure?"

"Of course. It'll be fun."

"I wouldn't go that far," Jamie said.

Just in case, I waited until six before getting ready to go to Jamie's. My grandmother was sitting on the back porch, looking out at the river.

"I'm going over to Jamie's to eat supper."

"All right, baby," she said. "Tell that boy's mother I say hello."

"I will." I leaned down to kiss her cheek. "Be back later."

Jamie and his mom were in the kitchen when I came in the back door. No one knocked on Fidelity Street.

"You're just in time," Jamie said. He and his mom were elbow-deep in some concoction and there was flour everywhere, on the counters, cabinets, Jamie's forehead.

"In time for what?" I asked.

"To help cook."

"Wait a second. You invited me to eat. Nobody said anything about cooking."

"It was implied."

"I don't think it was."

"Shut up and get over here," he said.

"What are we making?"

"My mother's chicken and dumplings," Mrs. Benton said.

"Nice," I said. I'd had them before. They were amazing, and apparently very messy to make.

"Olivia, will you light the stove?" Mrs. Benton asked.

"Sure."

"Thanks, sweetie. We're almost through kneading. Grab that skillet and put it on the fire." She nodded toward the counter. It was one of those seasoned cast-iron skillets. It took both hands to lift it.

Mrs. Benton rolled out the dough and began cutting it into smaller pieces.

"Olivia, turn some music on." Jamie gestured with his head to an old radio sitting on the counter.

"What station?" I asked.

"What it's on is fine," he said.

It was a classic rock station, and the music filled the room.

"Turn it up," Jamie said.

"When you were little, we used to dance around this kitchen all the time," Mrs. Benton said.

"I remember," Jamie said.

I did, too.

"It's been a long time. Let's fix that." He wiped his hands on his jeans and pulled his mom to the middle of the room, twirling and spinning her like he'd done to Maggie so many times. He moved her around the kitchen and she laughed loudly, the kind of laugh where your head falls back.

"Come dance with us," Jamie said to me.

"No, I'm good here. I'll just watch."

"Nope, no watching," he said. He reached for me and pulled me into the fold.

Once I was sandwiched between him and his mom, we swayed and laughed to the Steve Miller Band singing about getting their lovin' on the run. This was a good day. We bumped into the kitchen table and knocked over a chair, but that didn't slow us down.

The music was loud, and we were laughing so hard that we never heard Mr. Benton's truck pull into the carport. We didn't see him until he was standing in the middle of the kitchen, his face a mixture of anger and disbelief. He reached and turned the music off. The room plunged into silence, and I couldn't breathe. We stumbled apart as if we'd been caught doing something wrong.

"What the hell's going on here?" he asked. The monster was back.

No one answered.

He threw his hands up. "What in the *hell* is going on here?" He reminded me of a pissed-off bear, like the ones you see on nature shows, standing tall on their back legs, waving their arms in the air, showing all their teeth.

Mrs. Benton scrambled around the kitchen, swiping at the counters with her hands. "I'm sorry. We were getting supper ready. We made a mess. We were just dancing, being silly. What are you doing home?" she asked, breathless.

"They had too many guys working tonight. They cut me loose." He looked around the room again, taking in the disarray. "Is this what y'all do when I'm not here?"

"Is that why they sent you home?" Jamie asked. "Or was it because they smelled the alcohol on your breath?"

My eyes went round. To my knowledge, Jamie had never poked the bear before.

"What did you say to me?" Mr. Benton asked.

"Did they smell the alcohol? Were you cut loose for the night, or were you fired?"

"You don't get to talk to me that way." Mr. Benton's voice shook, and he pointed his finger at Jamie. It was shaking, too.

"He didn't mean it," Mrs. Benton said. She came around the table to stand between Jamie and his dad. She put her hands on Mr. Benton's chest. "He didn't mean it," she repeated.

"I think he did," Mr. Benton said.

"Yeah, I think I did," Jamie agreed.

"Jamie," I whispered.

Jamie turned to me, and his eyes softened. I think he'd forgotten I was there.

"I think you should go home," he said.

I thought so, too, but Mr. Benton was between me and the door.

"Now, why would she do that?" Mr. Benton asked. "It looked to me like the party was just getting started."

I heard the slur in his voice now.

He knocked Mrs. Benton's hands off his chest and turned the music back on. "Y'all wanted to dance, so dance."

"I don't feel like dancing anymore," Mrs. Benton whispered.

He ignored her and turned the music up. She attempted to step away from him, but he grabbed her. "I don't remember asking you what you wanted to do." He shoved her toward the center of the room, and she stumbled. Jamie caught her.

"You wanted to dance in the kitchen with your boy. So carry on."

He turned to look at me. "You can finish cooking supper. I'm starving."

Jamie and his mom held hands but stayed still.

"That's not dancing," Mr. Benton bellowed. He went to the shelf and pulled down a bottle. "Come on now. You have to move to dance." He took a glass off the shelf and poured himself a drink. "Don't make me tell you again."

They swayed awkwardly, and my hands started sweating.

"The food's not going to cook itself," Mr. Benton said to me.

I faced the stove and turned the heat off under the empty skillet. My fingers shook. I picked up the dough cutter and finished cutting the strips Mrs. Benton had been working on.

"I'm sorry," Mrs. Benton said as she tripped on Jamie's feet. Her voice trembled.

Mr. Benton sat at the table and watched them. "Isn't that sweet?" he asked.

It took me a second to realize he was talking to me.

"Don't you think? Isn't that just the sweetest thing you've ever seen?"

The way he said *sweet* made my stomach hurt. He was looking at me expectantly, so I nodded.

He knocked his drink back and slammed the glass on the table. "It's my turn." He stood and pulled Mrs. Benton from Jamie. "When's the last time we danced? Hmm?"

"I—I don't know."

Jamie stepped back but didn't take his eyes from his mom's face. Mr. Benton pulled her in close and squeezed her tight. She grimaced, and he loosened his hold. He hummed and stroked her hair.

"Why are you always crying?" he asked her. He wiped a tear from her face with his thumb. "Every goddamned time I look at you, you're crying. Do you know how that makes me feel?" He looked offended and grabbed her by the shoulders. "Do you?" He shook her, and Jamie tensed.

She didn't say anything.

He pushed her away from him. "Go clean up your face."

She didn't move.

"Go!" he yelled.

She turned and left the room. For a few seconds I didn't know what to do, so I just stared at the doorway she'd left through. Mr. Benton read my mind.

"Do you know what you're doing over there?" he asked. "Did Ms. Josephine teach you how to cook?"

I nodded.

"You're not talking tonight?"

"Y-yes," I said. "She taught me how to cook."

"Then prove it," he said.

"She's going home," Jamie said. "I'll finish cooking."

"Don't tell me what she's going to do. I decide who does what in this house. But you can finish supper." He smiled at me. "I'm not done dancing." He grabbed me and pulled me to him roughly. "You've grown up pretty."

His hands moved to the small of my back, and I tasted bile in my throat. He was nothing like the man I used to know. His eyes were bloodshot. His skin hung loose, like he was wearing an ill-fitting Mr. Benton suit.

"You don't come around much anymore," he said. "You used to be over here all the time."

"Leave her alone," Jamie said.

I pushed against Mr. Benton's chest. "I'm really not in the mood to dance."

Mr. Benton ignored both of us. "You're almost as pretty as your mama," he said. "That Lillian was a looker. She never looked my way, though. Thought she was too good for me." His arms tightened around me. "Are you like your mama? You think you're too good? That why you stopped coming over?"

Jamie grabbed my arm and wrenched me free, shoving his dad back. "Don't touch her again," he said.

Mr. Benton stumbled, his speech really slurring now. "Oh, you're protective of her." He chuckled and righted himself. "Sorry, I didn't realize she was your girl. Wait, but she's not your girl. She goes with that Barrow kid. You twist yourself up for a girl that's not even yours? You know her mama was crazy, don't you?"

My face burned.

"And her grandmother is batshit crazy, too." His voice got louder with every word he spoke. "You're wasting your time on a screwed-up girl that's not even yours. You're just as stupid as your mama!"

Mr. Benton was so caught up in his rant that he missed his warning. I didn't. I saw in Jamie's eyes the exact moment he changed.

"I hate you," Jamie said.

"What?"

"I said I hate you."

It was the quiet way Jamie said it that scared me most.

"I hate your guts, and I wish you were dead." Then he charged, and his hands wrapped around his dad's throat.

They scuttled backward, bumping into the table.

"You're so stupid." He spit the words in his dad's face. "You're the meanest piece of shit in this town. We all wish you were dead." He squeezed his hands tighter around his dad's throat. "You're never going to touch her again."

He wasn't talking about me anymore.

"Do you hear me? Tonight was the last time you push her, or hit her, or scare her. Never. Again." With each word, his fingers tightened around his dad's throat.

"Jamie, stop!" I pleaded.

He ignored me. Mr. Benton's drunken state put him at a disadvantage, and he couldn't pry Jamie's fingers loose. He opened his mouth wide, his hands slapping at Jamie's body.

"Jamie, let him go. Let's just go," I said.

"Jamie?" Mrs. Benton came in the kitchen. "What are you doing? Stop it! Let him go!"

Jamie looked over at his mom, and Mr. Benton took advantage of his distraction to get out of his hold. He was breathing heavily and rubbing his throat.

"You think just because you're eighteen you're a man now?" he huffed. "This is my house!"

Mrs. Benton ran to Jamie's dad, putting her hands on his chest again. It was the wrong thing to do. He shoved her, then drew his hand back and brought it down hard against her cheek. The force of it knocked her to the floor.

"You're always in the way," he said, stepping over her.

"You're going to regret that," said Jamie.

Mr. Benton laughed and started moving toward Jamie. "You're gonna regret putting your hands on me."

Jamie pulled a knife from the block on the counter. "Stay away from me. Get out of here. Go be a stupid drunk somewhere else."

Mr. Benton didn't listen. He lunged for Jamie. Jamie's mom screamed from the floor, reaching for them. Mr. Benton pushed Jamie back against the counter, trying to knock the knife out of his hand. They were grunting, and I saw flashes of the knife and then blood. I started praying again, this time my plea *Jamie, Jamie, Jamie!*

"Stop!" I screamed.

They didn't listen. I grabbed the handle of the skillet, lifted it, and swung. It bounced off the back of Mr. Benton's head. I felt the reverberations down to my elbows.

"Stop!" I screamed again.

Mr. Benton stopped. The whole world stopped.

He slumped to the side. Then Jamie pushed him, hard. He fell, his temple smacking against the corner of the countertop with an audible crack. He collapsed to the floor, blood slowly seeping out onto the white linoleum—too much blood to be coming from the tiny tear on his scalp, and I remembered what my grandmother said about head wounds. Then I saw the knife sticking out of his stomach, only the handle visible.

"Tom!" Mrs. Benton scrambled across the floor to him, her face a picture of horror. "Oh my God." She took his face in her hands. "Tom?" She looked down at the knife, then patted his face. "You're okay. You're okay."

But he wasn't. He was on his back, unconscious, his blood spreading in all directions.

She cradled his head in her lap. "You're okay." She rocked him. "Oh my God, my God, my God," she prayed. "Call nine-one-one!"

Jamie dropped to his knees and leaned over his dad. He was praying now, too. "My God, my God," he said. He was sweating, and his hands and shirt were covered in his dad's blood—blood I was now standing in. It was seeping toward the cabinets, picking up dirt and tiny bugs. Jamie's hand went to the knife.

"Don't pull it out!" I yelled. "He'll bleed more."

"Call nine-one-one!" Mrs. Benton repeated.

But Jamie didn't call anyone. He stared at his dad's face, then stood and stared at me.

"Jamie?"

He turned and shot out the back door, the screen door bouncing off the jamb.

"Call nine-one-one!" Mrs. Benton begged.

I pulled my phone from my pocket and chased Jamie out of the kitchen. My head and movements felt funny, like I was underwater.

"Jamie!" I yelled.

He was running into the woods behind our houses, the white of his shirt flashing through the branches of the trees.

I ran after him. "Jamie, stop!"

I sprinted, pushing through the brush, the tiny branches clawing at my body, scratching my legs, pulling at my hair. My skin burned. I'd never catch him. A branch slapped me in the face, and I felt my skin rip, my eyes tearing.

"Please!" I begged, my voice loud. "Please stop!"

He stopped suddenly and whirled around. I crashed into him, knocking us both to the ground. I saw stars. I scrambled to sit up and grabbed him, scared he was going to take off again. We stared at each other, our breathing loud, Jamie's eyes wild. He tried to pull away from me, and I tightened my hold, the blood smearing between us, making it hard to get a good grip.

"No. Stay with me. Stay with me."

"I have to get out of here."

"We have to get your dad help. He's hurt. Bad."

Jamie shook his head. "No." He pushed himself up.

"We'll tell them he was hurting you. I hit him to try and stop him. He attacked you."

"I had the knife. I attacked him first. They won't understand." He was crying. "There are things you don't know."

"I meant what I promised the other day," I said. "I won't let anything bad happen to you."

"Then get me out of here."

I knew leaving was the wrong thing to do, but I'd do anything to protect the boy who always defended me.

"Okay," I said.

We snuck back to the edge of our yards.

"Stay here," I said.

I left him in the cover of the trees and sprinted to my grandmother's house. I ripped open the front door, deciding not to stop until I got to my mom's room. The back door was open, and I heard the creaking of my grandmother's rocker.

"Lillian? You're home early," she said.

I grabbed my backpack and started frantically shoving clothes inside. My hands were shaking; my entire body was shaking.

"Yeah, I just came back to get something," I yelled to her, the trembling in my voice now.

Beth Hunter's letters were spread on the bed from earlier. I didn't want my grandmother to read them. I stuffed them back in my mom's shoebox and shoved it down into my bag. I grabbed a piece of paper and scribbled a note saying I was taking a trip and not to worry. The bloody prints on the letter contradicted my words. I promised I'd be back before my birthday. I didn't know if I was lying. I almost signed my name, but knowing that'd upset her, I signed *Lillian* instead.

I heard my grandmother coming down the hall. "What did you forget?" she asked.

My breath was coming too fast, and my chest hurt. I left the note on the pillow and darted to the window, lifted it, and dropped to the ground. I ran back to Jamie.

He hadn't moved. My relief at finding him still sitting there made me realize I'd thought he might not be.

"Let's go. We have to leave now."

He didn't respond, not even a blink.

"Jamie?" I squatted down next to him. In the time it had taken me to get a bag and come back, there was already less of him. He was shutting in on himself, disappearing right in front of me.

A siren sounded in the distance. I didn't know if it was an ambulance or the police.

I grabbed him frantically. "Come on. We have to run. Jamie!" Just like that night I had kicked and clawed myself out of Max's truck, I felt a surge of power course through my veins. I might be able to pick him up and carry him.

It wasn't necessary, though, because at my yell he came to and stood on his own.

"We have to go." I grabbed his hand and pulled him along.

We ran. White-knuckling my phone, I called Max. He answered on the third ring.

"Hey," he said. He sounded out of breath.

"I need you. Where are you?"

"Magnolia's. What's wrong?"

"I'm with Jamie. We're almost at Ferdinand Street. Can you come get us?"

"I'm on my way."

The line went dead.

I squeezed Jamie's hand. "He's coming."

We were standing at the edge of Ferdinand Street when Max's truck came careening around the corner. It skidded to a stop, and Max jumped out. One of his eyes was swollen, and his clothes and hair were disheveled. Maggie was with him.

"I was at Magnolia's when you called, and Max said you sounded . . . ," she said, her mouth opening, her words dying.

"Holy shit," Max said. He looked from me to Jamie, at our held hands, at all the blood. "What happened?"

The sirens sounded closer. Jamie wasn't speaking.

"Jamie and his dad fought. We have to go."

"Jamie and his dad?" Max asked. "Have you seen *you*?"

Maggie turned her head in the direction of the sirens.

"We have to get out of here. Now," I said.

"Is that his dad's blood?" Max asked.

I nodded and opened the passenger door. Jamie slumped all the way down in the backseat. Maggie climbed into the front seat next to me, and we drove off. She glanced back at Jamie, her mouth still open. She tried to get closer to him, to understand with her eyes and hands. I put my hand on her arm and whispered, "Not yet." I was scared we wouldn't be safe if the truth slipped out before we were outside town limits.

There was only one road in and out of St. Francisville. I imagined roadblocks with megaphoned voices telling us to pull over and exit the vehicle with our hands up. But we drove out of town with no fanfare and no witnesses. The road swept under us, black and smooth.

Max reached into his pocket, pulled out his cell phone, and threw it out the window. Cell phones had GPS. Maggie and I instantly did the same.

I turned to Jamie. "Do you have your phone with you?"

No response. He lay there motionless. I reached back and felt his pockets, but there was no phone.

"Where are we going?" Max asked.

"Just drive," I said.

"What happened?" he asked.

"Later." The truth could wait.

Twenty miles outside of town, the tears came. I already missed Fidelity Street and my grandmother. I wondered if the sirens had scared her. I was worried about my dad in his one-room apartment. I was afraid for the still boy in the backseat, and of a monster who wasn't coming back.

Chapter 5

The sun was rising, and I reflexively turned my face away from it, my cheek brushing the seat. I noticed its smell—leather mixed with Max's cologne. Dobie Gray was singing softly from the radio, asking for the beat. For a few seconds I didn't know why my chest was tight. Then I saw my hands. The blood had turned brown in the night and darkened the creases and lines in my fingers. A raw burning throbbed in my throat, like someone had crawled down it and lit a match. My hand kept going to it, trying to soothe the burning from the outside.

Without looking, I knew Maggie was asleep to my right. Max was facing forward, his hands on the wheel. His swollen eye was now black and bruised. I looked back at Jamie. He was crumpled on the backseat, folded at an odd angle, too long to fit comfortably. My throat tried to close, and I had to inhale deeply through my nose. I expected him to have aged during the night. I didn't know how it was possible, but he'd gotten younger, his sleeping face conflicting sharply with his bloodstained body. I turned forward.

We were surrounded by an abundance of trees on either side of the road, thick as a forest. "Where are we?" I asked.

"We're on the Natchez Trace."

That wasn't what I expected to hear.

"I didn't think it was smart to stay on any of the main roads. For a few hours I was just driving around on back roads, but then I remembered the Trace. My dad and I used to go this way when we took hunting trips. This road runs all the way up to Tennessee. Not a lot of people use it. There are no red lights, not much through traffic."

"That's smart," I said. I was glad to hear somebody had a plan. Looking at the side of his face, I noticed someone did look older in the light of this new day, and wondered about my own face.

"What happened?" I reached up to touch his eye, but he flinched away from me. "Who hit you?"

He didn't answer.

"Do you want me to drive?" I asked. "You have to be tired."

He looked at me, then down to my hands. "We need to get you and Jamie cleaned up."

I felt ashamed he didn't want my hands on his steering wheel. I slid them under my legs. I was careful not to look at the backseat again, or too closely at the worry in Max's face; I pretended this was all normal, just a summer road trip. I did this for a while and felt better. Then my hands pulsed beneath me, reminding me I could only sit on the truth for so long. Just like my grandmother, I latched onto fantasy at the first sign of trouble.

Max glanced over his shoulder at Jamie in the backseat. "That's a lot of blood," he said.

"It was a bad fight."

"Are you gonna tell me what happened?"

I nodded, and Max slowed the truck. He came to a stop on the side of the road and slid the gear shift home to park. He sat still, looking forward through the front window, and then bowed his head, waiting. A sudden heat hit me in the stomach. Max and Maggie were accessories to my madness.

"We were in Jamie's kitchen. His dad wasn't supposed to be there, but he came home early from work. He was drunk."

I watched the back of Max's neck, noticing the slope of his shoulders and ignoring the tears that burned my eyes when he covered his face with his hands.

"He was mad, so mad, because we'd made a mess in the kitchen. And the music was too loud. We'd been dancing."

When Max lifted his head to look at me, my eyes dropped, and I looked at his throat instead.

"It was bad," I said.

"How bad?" Max asked.

"Knife-in-the-stomach bad," Jamie said from the backseat, his voice thick.

We turned to look at him. He'd opened his eyes but not sat up.

"Shit! Is he okay?" Max asked.

Jamie and I shrugged at the same time.

"Are you okay?" Max asked me.

"No," I said.

Max pulled me closer to him. "You will be. We'll figure it out."

"His dad was trying to hurt him. Jamie fought back—"

"I don't want to talk about it now," Jamie said. His look said he meant it.

"All right, man," said Max.

Jamie rolled over, and we turned around. Maggie was awake. She looked at me, and I knew she'd heard. She slid her hand into mine, not caring about its brown stains.

"We're going to be okay," she lied.

Because we didn't know what else to do, we just kept driving on the Trace, kept moving forward. Jamie sat up after a bit and looked out the window, no noise and no fuss. He had trouble staying still, though, like he couldn't find a comfortable spot. I kept facing forward, watching the road as it came to us, even though the only place I wanted to look was at him. He started softly tapping the window, and I heard his breaths coming faster.

Whenever he shifted or moved in any way, I felt my body itch to move with him, like we were connected gut to gut with invisible string. His tapping fell into a regular rhythm. I tried staying still, but as he moved, the string between our bodies pulled tight, making my body move with his. My pulse raced and my chest heaved, trying to match Jamie's. I took a deep breath through my nose, and wasn't surprised when Jamie blew it out.

I couldn't stand it any longer. I climbed over the seat. I sat as close to him as possible, my body immediately relaxing, the string between us now slack. He looked in my direction, but he wasn't seeing me. The events of last night were playing on a loop before his eyes, over and over. His breath was still coming fast. Lining up with him, hip to hip, I concentrated on breathing slower, hoping his breath would slow to match mine. It did.

If I'd had my way, Jamie could have gone to sleep somewhere in the corners of his mind, and I'd wear his body like a suit. I'd feel everything he wasn't ready to and answer all the questions coming his way. He wouldn't have to wake up until he was ready. I knew that wasn't possible, though.

I replayed what Jamie had said the night before about me not knowing everything. "I know all I need to know about it," I whispered to him now.

Jamie didn't say anything, just reached for the ends of my hair and started twirling them. I dropped my head onto his shoulder, ignoring the eyes I knew were on us. I couldn't imagine how we looked from the front seat, wearing the same man's blood.

Max was right, there was hardly any traffic, but even so, every car that passed us was a threat, making my hands sweat. Each one made my throat burn. By noon, I couldn't stand it any longer.

"I need some water," I said.

Max met my eyes in the rearview mirror. "We're gonna need gas soon, too. How much money do y'all have?" he asked.

I shrugged. I'd given no thought to money. We all pooled our cash, and came up with maybe enough for one tank of gas and a bottle of water. I thought about food but didn't mention it.

Max pulled over at the next gas station. It was brazen to pull up to the front of the store like we didn't have anything to hide.

"Do you think it's safe to do this?" I looked at the front of the store but didn't see any cameras. The convenience store was old, but surely there was security.

"How else are we supposed to get gas?" Max asked.

"Aren't they looking for your truck by now?" My breath caught and my throat wouldn't stop burning.

Max kept his voice calm. "We have to have gas." He motioned to the store. "There's not a lot of places to stop around here. We need to take advantage." He spoke softly, like he was talking to a baby.

"Let's just do what we need to do and go," said Maggie. "The more time we spend here, the riskier it is."

Jamie whispered from beside me, "I want to clean up."

I did, too.

"It's not safe for you to get out," Maggie said. "Stay here, I'll get some wet wipes or something."

Jamie started shaking his head. "I can't wear this anymore." He pulled at his shirt. It was stuck to him in places, caked with dried blood. Some blood had soaked into the seat in the night, staining the stitches in the leather.

Max reached under the seat and pulled out a wrinkled T-shirt. "Put this on."

"Thanks," Jamie whispered.

I looked away as Jamie changed. When I looked back, he was balling his old shirt up tight, twisting and turning it. I put my hand on his shoulder.

"Here," Max said. "Give it to me."

Jamie immediately handed it to him, and Max put it under the front seat.

Max turned to me and said, "Try to clean up the best you can. Maggie will get you some water and something to help get the blood off Jamie. Don't take too long. I'm gonna stay out here with Jamie and pump the gas. Maggie, you pay for it."

"All right," she said, taking the money.

There was a wrinkled woman behind the counter watching me as I walked toward the restroom. I kept my hands in my pockets and was glad I was wearing jean shorts. The dried blood looked like mud on the denim, and muddy, scratched-up kids were nothing new to see in places like this. I was likely coming off some woods adventure. Once in the bathroom, I changed into some clean shorts. I mirrored Jamie's earlier actions and rolled the bloody ones up tight before tucking them into a corner of my bag. I didn't want them touching my clean clothes, but I couldn't risk leaving them in the bathroom.

Washing my hands in the sink, I kept my head down, avoiding the mirror. I watched as the last of Tom Benton's blood swirled around and around, then down the drain. I should've felt bad, but the only feeling that came was relief.

Hands on the edge of the sink, I risked a look at the

mirror. I was kind of expecting to see Lillian. There was a pounding on the door. My hands were shaking again.

"Olivia, let's go," said Maggie.

"I'm coming," I said.

Two deep breaths later I opened the door. Maggie was walking out the front door, and I looked to the woman behind the counter. She hadn't moved.

Outside, Maggie was sitting in the driver's seat. Max was standing in front of the open passenger door. I was almost to him when another truck pulled up. It looked like a work truck, a layer of dust and dirt covering it. The driver hopped out. His eyes were on me, and then he glanced back at Max's truck. He stared at it for a long time, and then looked at me again. *This is it. He knows.* I stopped in my tracks as he passed me, and then I turned to watch his back. *He's going to tell the clerk,* I thought, but I couldn't move. Someone took my hand. It was Max.

"Come on."

"I think he knows," I whispered. *He knows, and my life won't be my own anymore, and no one will save Jamie.*

Max looked in the direction of the store. "He's buying beer. He doesn't know. Let's go."

Max pulled me to his truck. I risked one more look back at the store. The guy was putting a six-pack on the counter. I wondered if I'd be like that with every person that passed us by.

Jamie was in the front seat. Maggie looked toward the road.

"Are we still in Mississippi?" she asked.

"Yeah," Max said.

"So, we're gonna just keep going? Don't we need a better plan?" Maggie asked.

I dropped my bag onto the backseat. Beth's letters were in it. Maybe she'd help us. If I explained to her what Jamie's dad was like, she'd understand. Maybe she'd do it as a favor to my mom.

"My mom's best friend lives in New Orleans," I said. "I think she might help us."

Jamie turned to look at me. "Yeah?" he asked.

"Yeah."

Max's face brightened at the idea. I didn't tell him I'd never actually met her.

"I don't know exactly where she is, though."

"New Orleans is a pretty big place," Max said.

Maggie spoke up. "Wait a minute. There's this artist on Oak Street. His name's Steve or Steven or something. My mom used to sleep on his couch every once in a while. I met him once when my dad took me to New Orleans to see my mom. He seemed like a good guy. If he's still there, maybe he'd let us stay with him until we found your mom's friend."

"Are you sure you don't mind asking?" I asked.

Maggie shrugged.

"That's a good idea," Max said. "We can dump the truck when we get to New Orleans."

I must've looked nervous, because he added, "Nowhere near Oak Street."

"There's a map in the glove box," Max said to Jamie. "Let me see it."

Jamie pulled out the map and handed it to Max.

Max unfolded it and studied it. After a time he said, "We could make it to Maurepas by tonight. It's not that far outside of New Orleans. There's a lake. I went camping there once." He showed us the route with his finger. He handed the map to Maggie.

"Don't take the most direct path," he told her.

"Got it," she said.

"I'm beat," Max said to me, and lay down in the backseat. I climbed in next to Jamie.

"Did I get it all?" Jamie asked. He turned his face from left to right. I took the wet wipe from his hand and wiped at a spot next to his ear.

"Now you did."

He grabbed another one and started wiping at his arms.

Maggie cranked up the truck, jammed it into drive, and sped off. She flipped through the radio stations, relaxing as Janis Joplin started up from the speakers, crooning about the pieces of her heart.

We got off the Trace and cut across Mississippi before hooking a right and coming back down through Kentwood, Roseland, and Amite. Max slept solidly. At Tickfaw we took a left, wanting to avoid the bigger town of Hammond. We went through French Settlement twice, as Maggie often came to a crossroads, shrugged, and took a right. She drove like there was no concern for gas money, and the needle slowly made its way down toward empty.

Max woke up after a few hours. He reached into the

front seat, hooking me under my arms and pulling me into the backseat. It took my breath away. He always took my breath away. He reached for my hand. I didn't know why at first, but it was an inspection; he was making sure all the blood was gone.

He traced the scars on my palm as he spoke. "I love you," he said.

My stomach flipped, and I didn't know if it was from what he said or his soft touch. He didn't wait for me to say it back. He'd stopped doing that.

We sat for a while in comfortable silence. Then Maggie, who couldn't stand quiet for too long, thought it would be a good time to play one of her favorite games: she asked a question, and you had to answer with the first thing that came to your mind.

"No thinking, just speaking," she said. "Max, what's your favorite color?"

"Black."

"President?"

"Woodrow Wilson."

"Band?"

"The Beatles."

She nodded, seemingly pleased with that answer.

Max smirked and added, "Justin Bieber's cool, too."

Maggie swerved and almost ran the truck off the road.

Max laughed, making me do the same. Then Maggie started laughing, and even Jamie chuckled. I caught his eye, and it felt so good for two seconds, but then his face changed, seeming to say that laughing was wrong the day after you stabbed your dad, and we promptly stopped.

Max got in a few questions of his own.

"Have you always hated living in a small town?"

"No," Maggie said. "But it seems like it got smaller as I got older."

"Is that why you want to go to New York?" Max asked. Maggie nodded.

"You're not scared of anything," he said.

Maggie smiled instead of answering.

"How did you get your black eye?" I asked Max.

He didn't answer. The questions stopped. My hands kept going to my stomach, trying to keep it quiet. Maggie noticed.

"Grab my purse," she said to Jamie. With one hand on the steering wheel, she opened the purse, revealing an assortment of candy bars and fruit. Without explaining, she divvied up the loot. I got a peach and a Snickers bar. I held the peach gingerly.

"Did you buy this stuff at that gas station?" I asked.

"Um, that's where I got it." She smiled, proud of herself. "We gotta eat."

I was hungry enough to be proud of her, too. Maybe this was why Maggie wasn't worried about gas; maybe we were going to steal that, too. I wondered how that would work. I thought this must have been what Deputy Daniel meant when he visited our class in fifth grade to preach against the life of crime. It was the best peach I ever ate.

We drove on, one town bleeding into the next. It was well into the night when we got to Maurepas. After that it was no time before Maggie parked the truck on the shore of the lake. It was the only vehicle in sight. Without saying anything Maggie stepped out of the truck and peeled off her clothes, making her way toward the water. This was normal for Maggie. She splashed in the water. Jamie stepped out of the truck, mumbled something about relieving himself, and walked toward the woods, leaving Max and me alone in the truck.

It was quiet for a long minute. "I got in a fight with Lyle outside of Magnolia's last night," he said.

"Why?"

"It's stupid."

"Was it about me? Did he say something?"

"It doesn't matter." Max reached up and touched the corner of his bruised eye. "He only got one in. It really wasn't his fault. I'd gotten into it with my dad earlier. I was looking for a fight."

"What did you and your dad fight about?"

"He thinks I'm pissing away my future. He said I needed to stop dicking around and take life seriously. Whatever the hell that means. I told him I was trying to be good, to make up for what I did. He said I had to try harder, that my behavior wasn't good for my future career. I said some things, some below-the-belt things. So did he. And then I tore out of there. I got to Magnolia's and Lyle asked where you were. That's all he did, but I didn't like how he said your name, and I was pissed you weren't with me. I sort of lost it and lit into him. I'm pretty sure I would've been arrested for assault if you hadn't called."

I crawled into his lap and kissed the side of his bruised eye. "What am I going to do with you?" I whispered.

He shrugged. "What am I going to do with you?" he whispered back, pushing the hair behind my ear. "You look like you got in your own fight."

He ran his fingers across the scratches on my legs, then turned my head so he could get a better look at the one on my face. His lips rested on my temple, and I closed my eyes and wished I could go back two days, to when one of my biggest problems was that he loved me too much.

He leaned down to get something from under the seat and pulled out a bottle. This was a new nightly custom, since the wreck. He never drank from it, just held it, testing himself.

"You want some?" he asked. "Just because I stopped drinking doesn't mean you have to."

He unscrewed the lid and lifted the bottle to my lips. I knew he needed me to take the drink as much as I needed him not to. We balanced each other out, a screwed-up yin and yang. I opened my mouth, and he poured a little in. Some dribbled down my chin, and his mouth went to it.

"That doesn't count," he said.

I took the bottle from him, and his arms wrapped around my body. I brought it to my mouth and took a long gulp. I felt his eyes on me, and my stomach muscles tightened in response. The burn from the whiskey trailed down my throat and settled in my belly. I gave the bottle to him. My body immediately hated me. I wiped the sweat from my neck, and my eyes teared. Maybe I should've stopped after the first sip.

"Come on. I know that wasn't your first whiskey drink," he laughed, low and rough.

"I'm out of practice."

"You want another?"

I shook my head.

I watched him for a while, but he seemed to be looking at some faraway place. He rubbed his thumb over the bottle's label. It was worn from this. My stomach knotted, because I was about to make the next move in the push-pull game I played with Max every day, but I needed his comfort, his strength. I tamped down the guilt and pressed my face into his neck and breathed him in. He smelled of St. Francisville, if someone can smell like a town. It was a mixture of sun, river, and boy. It was a pleasant smell, and I pressed my lips to him.

This had been one of our nightly customs. I'd missed it.

"I'm sorry," I said. *For so much.*

He squeezed me closer to his body.

"I shouldn't have called you. Getting arrested for assault would've been a lot better than this."

"Don't say that. Don't apologize. I'm glad you called. If y'all had left town without me, I don't know what I would've done."

My fingers played with his hair where it curled up at his collar.

"You were with him when he stabbed his dad? You were in the room?" he asked.

"I was in the room," I said.

"I'm sorry you had to see that. I didn't think his dad messed with him."

"He didn't usually. He never had before."

"What made last night different?"

"I don't know," I said. "It—it wasn't just the knife."

"What do you mean?"

"It wasn't just the knife that hurt him," I said.

"Yeah, you said they fought."

"They did."

"What else, then?" he asked.

I swallowed the knot in my throat. I couldn't say it.

Max exhaled loudly. "You always protect him."

He didn't know I was protecting myself.

He shifted in the seat, then slid me off his lap. "Fine, you don't have to talk about it." He was mad.

I excused myself from the truck and walked to the water's edge. Maggie was spending more time underwater than not, her head bobbing up every now and then. Watching her, I felt a sudden tightness in my gut and realized that Jamie still hadn't come out of the woods. The distance between our bodies was expanding, making the invisible string pull so tight it was painful. I didn't know what would happen if it broke. I was facing the woods, ready to charge, when he appeared at the edge of the trees, looking down, careful not to trip on the underbrush. At the sight of him, my breath began its cycle again, and I exhaled.

Jamie walked over to me and dropped down to the water. He reached his hands in and washed them, getting off what the wet wipes had missed. From this angle I noticed he had some blood on the back of his neck, too, and my stomach lurched.

I threw up on the bank, and Jamie stood. I quickly wiped my mouth. "I'm okay. It's not— I had some whiskey in the truck." I wanted to reassure him that it wasn't him making me sick.

"Are you okay?"

"I will be." But it felt like a lie.

The look on his face said he didn't believe me. He walked to the truck and came back with his bloody shirt. Max came to stand next to us. He looked at the vomit but didn't comment on it.

"I don't think it's a good idea to leave this in the truck," Jamie said. "I think we should burn it."

Max pulled a lighter out of his pocket and handed it to him. Jamie tried to light it, but his hands were shaking too badly. I grabbed it from him. I wanted to be the one who burned it, to get rid of this thing that scared Jamie. It took three flicks before it lit. I looked to the water to see that Maggie had stopped swimming and stood watching. The shirt took longer to burn than I thought it would, its light bright in the black night. I wondered if we should burn my shorts, too, and then I thought about Jamie's pants, and the bottom of my shoes, the seams in the backseat of Max's truck, and that spot on Jamie's neck. We couldn't burn everything, so just the shirt burned, until it was nothing but ash floating in Lake Maurepas.

A moment of silence later, Maggie ducked under the water and Jamie went back to his refuge in the backseat of the truck. Max walked around to the truck bed and opened his toolbox. He pulled out a sleeping bag and mosquito spray.

"I'm going to sleep out here," he said.

From his tone, it seemed I wasn't invited to join him.

"I guess I'll stay in the truck."

He shrugged.

It wouldn't be comfortable, but it would do. Sometime later Maggie emerged from the lake, and we tried to go to sleep. We each took a side and propped ourselves up against the doors, our legs tangling on the seat. What I wouldn't have given for a pillow. Jamie was already asleep. I was exhausted, but each time I closed my eyes I saw Tom Benton's face. Jamie whimpered, and I wondered what he was seeing in his dreams.

Maggie started talking about her dad in a low voice, telling me about a mural they were working on together. She spoke about the colors and brushstrokes like she was telling me a story, and I listened like it was one. I knew she was talking about him and art because doing so comforted her.

"I can't wait to see how it turns out." She stopped abruptly. I guess she realized it might not turn out. She closed her eyes and feigned sleep.

The only person who comforted me was my grand-mother. I craved her, but I knew if she saw me now, she'd only be glad to see Lillian. At least my dad, with all of his faults, was probably missing me at the moment. I was sup-posed to meet him for lunch tomorrow. We had monthly meetings at the diner. It had been my idea. We met the first Saturday of every month, our very own support group. I'd dubbed us "Lillian's Left-Behinds." I always felt like my dad didn't want to meet but thought he should, since he wasn't raising me.

We'd been meeting at the diner since I was little, but that didn't mean it was easy to talk to him. Any talk with my dad was awkward unless we talked about Lillian. Then he'd loosen up. He couldn't help but smile when he talked about her. Sometimes we'd play twenty questions.

"Where did you take her on your first date?" I asked him one time.

"We took the ferry to New Roads to see a band. We al-most didn't make the last ferry home. I found out how fast my truck would go."

"Did you kiss her?"

He'd smiled. "Yeah."

"How'd you like her hair best?"

"I liked it when she wore it down." He'd motioned to me. "Your hair is just like hers, exactly, down to that little wave." He reached across the table like he was going to touch me. He thought better of it, though, and dropped his hand.

"Did you guys ever fight?"

"Yes."

"About what?"

"We fought about everything—how to get out of this town, what to do on a Friday night. Your mother was a fighter."

"Why did you stay together if you were always fighting?"

"When Lillian was good, she made everything around her good. I can't explain it. I'd do anything to be around her."

"What's your favorite memory of her?" I asked him another time.

"Our senior year we went to the Gulf instead of on the senior trip. It was just the two of us. Your mom loved the beach. She wore a bikini. She didn't care that she was pregnant with you. I didn't, either. We only had a couple of days, because I had to get back to the garage. We stayed on the beach from sunup to sundown. Your mom was almost always moving, but as the sun set she stopped and stayed still. Watching her watch the sun, she was so pretty it hurt."

He'd fiddled with the sugar packets on the table. "You probably think that's stupid," he'd said.

"No, I don't."

It was our only family vacation.

"How did you feel when she told you she was pregnant?"

"Scared. Young."

"How did she feel about it? Was she happy, terrified?"

"Yes."

"You always say everything without saying anything."

"What do you really want to know?"

Did she kill herself because of me?

That was the one question I'd never ask him, though. I was too scared the answer would hurt him or me. So I asked him everything but, collecting evidence, finding out more about her life so I could retrace her steps to see where it all went wrong, hoping all signs didn't point to me.

She saw *Olivia* etched on a tombstone in the graveyard where she was eventually buried and decided that would be my name. She and my dad used to cut through the cemetery on their way home from school, but he said my mom often found other excuses to be there, not just to walk through but as the destination. She told him there was something beautiful about the trees, the history, and the quiet. I guess that's where I got it from.

In her last year my dad often found her walking from grave to grave, looking at the names on the headstones and wondering aloud what had happened to each person. One day he found her sitting in front of a tombstone, holding her very pregnant belly and reading the name over and over again: "Olivia, Olivia, Olivia." Rolling it out of her mouth and rubbing her belly as she spoke, like she was trying it out on the baby inside. When she noticed my dad standing there, she looked up at him, gave him a nod, and said it once more: "Olivia."

After my name was decided, Lillian spent more and more time in the graveyard. She walked the rows, her fingers trailing over the headstones, with my dad watching from afar. There were times he found her sleeping on the grass, lying between the tombstones like she was already resigned to her fate. He was scared to question her ease and ability to slumber among the dead, so he'd simply wake her and take her back home. It was never long before she made her way back, though, looking for a comfortable spot.

The crammed cab of the truck was uncomfortable. I disentangled from Maggie and got out. I walked to the sleeping bag.

Max rolled over and reached his hand out to me. I went to him.

"You don't have to talk about it now," he said. "I get it." He pulled me down to him. "Let's just go to sleep."

We spooned, the sleeping bag offering no real relief from the hard ground. His hand went around my stomach, fingers lightly touching my navel, and all I could think of was how my name must've sounded coming from her mouth. . . . *Olivia, Olivia, Olivia.*

Chapter 6

The next morning I sat up with a loud gasp, disconnecting from Max's body and looking out at the lake. It wasn't a nightmare. This was real life. I saw the sky's reflection bobbing on the water. It was a perfect blue-sky day. I heard someone's boat but didn't see it. Judging from the sound of the motor, it wasn't a fishing boat, but it wasn't a big boat, either—someone's ski boat, maybe. My eyes strained toward the horizon, looking for it.

Max lay asleep on the ground, his face peaceful, like he was used to not sleeping in a bed. The truck showed no signs of life. I walked to it and saw that Maggie and Jamie were still sleeping. I got my bag out of the back and opened it. I grabbed a clean shirt and unrolled it, and a ten-dollar bill fell out. I dug through the rest of my clothes to see if I could find any more money hiding, but that was it.

I knew we were almost out of gas and remembered we'd

passed a convenience store not too far down the road. I jumped in the back of the truck and looked for a gas can. I found one hiding under Max's toolbox. I looked in my bag for some paper so I could leave them a note telling them I'd gone to get gas. The only pieces of paper I had were Beth's letters to my mom, so I pulled out the shoebox and opened it.

All of Lillian's treasures fit inside this box. The sunlight bounced off of one of her necklaces. Besides my father's class ring, it was the only piece of jewelry she had put in the box. The rest she kept in her jewelry box on her dresser. I could figure out why my father's ring got the special placement, but not the necklace. The chain was white gold and delicate. It was a name necklace, *Lillian* spelled out in a pretty cursive font. From the photos on Lillian's bedside table, I knew she wore it.

I picked it up and undid the clasp, then brought it around my neck and fastened it. Then I picked up an envelope and pulled the paper out. It was one of the earlier letters, from when Beth was still angry. I reread one sentence over and over before writing my note on the back, the words *you left me* loud in my head. I placed it under one of the windshield wipers.

The sun was already in full effect as I walked down the road. By the time I got to the store, I was sweating. There was only one car parked outside the building. The store was old, with a sign out front reading *Live Crickets for Sale*. I didn't see any security cameras. The ding of the bell greeted me as I opened the door, and the man behind the counter looked in my direction. His eyes met mine, and he gave me a slow nod. I did the same. I decided I might as well take advantage of the facilities before pumping gas, and walked to the back of the store.

Walking out of the bathroom, I saw a TV mounted on the wall above the checkout counter and came face to face with Tom Benton's picture, splashed all over the screen. I stopped in the aisle; my cheeks instantly burned up. Just like that, I was back in Jamie's bloody kitchen. My breath came faster, and I felt dizzy. I reached out to the side for balance and knocked something to the floor. Dropping down, I put my hands on the ground and blinked hard. With the news story loud in my ears, I looked around for the fallen item, saw a candy bar, and picked it up.

Four teenagers, wanted in connection with the death of a forty-six-year-old St. Francisville man, are missing.

My hand gripped the candy too hard. He was dead. I'd thought he was, but it was one thing to suspect and another to know. Tom Benton would never hit his wife again.

Tom Benton was pronounced dead in his home two nights ago, the victim of an apparent beating and stabbing.

I stood, my legs trembling, and put the candy back on the shelf. I felt the clerk's eyes on me and willed my hands to stop shaking.

A witness reported seeing the victim's son, eighteen-year-old Jamie Benton, fleeing the scene with seventeen-year-old neighbor Olivia Hudson.

Someone saw us. I tried not to react to the sound of my name. Keeping my head forward, I flicked my eyes to the

TV. It showed a split screen with Jamie's and my pictures on it. Mine was my senior class picture. I looked at the man behind the counter. His back was to the TV. He was only watching me.

The victim's wife, Louise Benton, who is believed to have been home at the time of the assault, is not cooperating with police. The circumstances are unknown.

The clerk frowned at me in concern, and I forced myself to move forward.

At this time the extent of Hudson's involvement is not known, but a local resident described her as unstable.

My ears burned and my eyes pricked with unshed tears as I walked to the counter.

Eighteen-year-old Maggie Harrington, a known associate of the two, is also missing.

I knew I shouldn't, but I looked up to see Maggie's smiling face hit the screen.

A fourth teen, eighteen-year-old Max Barrow, went missing the same night, though his connection to the events is unknown. Police are asking for any information on the whereabouts of all four teenagers. Barrow was last seen driving—

"Can I help you?" the clerk asked.

My tongue thick, I swallowed and said, "Yes, I need ten dollars' worth of gas." I put the bill on the counter.

I took one more look at the TV and saw Jamie's house. I stared at it for two seconds too long, and the man turned and followed my stare.

"Yeah, they've been playing that story all morning." He

turned back to me and took the money. "They're saying they think that kid killed his dad. Can you believe that?"

"It's hard to believe," I said. I waited for him to recognize me.

"I'll put you on pump one." He looked down at the gas can like he was waiting for an explanation.

I choked out, "Thanks. I ran out. I'm always pushing my car to the limit."

He chuckled. "You and my wife both. She thinks when the gas light comes on, it's just a suggestion."

I fidgeted with Lillian's necklace, and he looked at it.

"Lillian—that's a pretty name," he said. "I have a niece named Lillian."

"Thank you," I said.

"How far'd you walk?"

"Not too far. My car's just up the road."

He nodded. "That's good. It's already a hot one out there."

"Yeah, thanks."

I walked out of the store and toward the pumps, worried that any moment now he'd realize who I really was and come charging after me. He was old; I could probably take him. *As if that was a thing I would ever do.* I bet he had a gun.

I put the gas can down and lifted the nozzle. The pump started, and I lowered the nozzle into the can, reading the warnings on how not to create static electricity and blow oneself up when pumping gas into a can. Explosions were the least of my problems. The pump clicked, and I put the nozzle back. As I lifted my eyes to the store, the man gave me a little wave—he had no idea he'd just dealt with someone unstable.

On the walk back I had to keep switching hands to carry the gas can. My body was coated in sweat, and the news story replayed in my head. Down the road I saw Jamie walking toward me. As I got closer to him, he looked worried. He noticed me struggling with the can, ran up, and took it from me.

"Are you okay?" he asked.

"There was a TV at the store," I said. "We were on it. All four of us."

The gas can slipped, but he caught it and asked, "What did it say?"

"I'm so sorry, Jamie."

"Why?"

"He's dead."

Jamie stopped in his tracks. "What?"

"He died. We killed him."

Jamie snapped his head to me. "*We* didn't do anything."

"What do you mean?" I asked. "Yes, we did."

"You didn't do anything," he said.

"I hit him on the head with a cast-iron skillet!"

"That didn't kill him. I did it." He started walking. "I killed him."

I walked after him, grabbing his arm. "They want you for questioning, Jamie. We have to tell them what happened. We didn't mean to kill him."

He whirled around, dropping the gas can. "*We* didn't

kill him. I did it. *I* wanted him dead. *I* wished him dead. I'm so fucking happy he's dead, but *you* didn't do it." He was breathing loud, and his eyes were wild. "I love you, Olivia. But you're not taking any part of this blame. This is mine. Tell me you understand."

"I understand," I lied.

"What did they say about y'all?" he asked.

"They don't know what our involvement is yet, but they're looking for us, too."

"Did anyone recognize you?" he asked.

I shook my head. "There was only one man there, the clerk. He had his back to the TV. But he'd seen it before. He said they've been playing the story all morning."

"He didn't place you?"

"No. He thinks I'm Lillian." I touched the necklace.

Jamie looked at it but didn't say anything. Then he picked up the gas can and gripped it with both hands. A car came down the road and slowed as it got near us. The car was old, and so were the people in it, a man and a woman. The driver stopped and rolled his window down, Patsy Cline's voice spilling out, singing about falling to pieces. My eyes stung and my chest tightened. It was my grandmother's favorite song.

"Do y'all need help?"

"No," Jamie and I both said at the same time.

"Run out of gas?"

I wanted to scream at him to leave us alone, to get out of here, because I couldn't be held responsible for what we did next.

Instead, I answered, "Yep, I thought we had enough to make it to the next town, but obviously we didn't." I pointed to the can as evidence.

"Where's your car?"

"It's just up the road a ways," Jamie said. He said it with so much confidence that I almost believed him.

We looked in the direction of the car that didn't exist. The man turned his head to follow our stare.

"How far up the road is it?" he asked.

"Not too far," I said.

"Why don't y'all get in? We can take you back to your car."

"That's okay," Jamie said.

"We don't mind walking," I added, my voice cracking.

The driver looked like it was going against all his Southern-man principles, but he sighed, "All right, y'all be careful," and slowly drove away from us.

My heart was hammering so hard I wouldn't have been surprised to find bruises on my chest later. We walked the rest of the way in silence, the only sound the sloshing of the gas inside its can.

Max and Maggie were both standing next to the truck, facing the water. Jamie put the gas can down and we joined them. The four of us lined up along the edge of the lake and watched as the water lapped at the shore, tiny waves caused by some boat. How long before somebody recognized us? Maggie reached out to hold Jamie's hand. Jamie reached for mine, and I leaned slowly into Max. We stayed like that for some time, connected.

"He's dead. I killed him," Jamie said.

Max's eyes shot over to mine.

"There was a TV at the gas station," I said. "The news was on. They said Mr. Benton died from his wounds. They're looking for all of us."

"Holy shit," Max said. His hands went to his hair, and he started pacing.

"Well, it's not murder," Maggie said. "It can't be murder," she said to Jamie. "He hit your mom. It was self-defense."

Jamie didn't answer.

She looked at me. "I mean, come on. We all know Jamie's dad," she said.

We all knew his dad.

"They know we're together," I said. "They showed our pictures. They're gonna find us."

"I need to call my dad," Max said. "I bet this town doesn't have pay phones. I'll call him when we get to New Orleans."

"What? You can't," I said.

"Maybe your mom's friend can help us, and I'm not saying we shouldn't find her, but I know my dad can help us. He's good. He's gotten a lot of bad people out of a lot worse, and what Jamie did was justified."

He waited for me to agree with him.

He looked at Jamie. "I know my dad would represent you. I mean, how long had your dad been beating up your mom?"

Jamie flinched. "A long time," he said.

"Right, and nobody ever did anything about it. It's gonna

be okay," Max said. "You'll see. I'll talk to my dad. He can help us."

I wanted to believe him.

"How much gas did you get?" Max asked.

"Ten dollars' worth."

"We'll need more than ten dollars' worth of gas if we're gonna make it the rest of the way to New Orleans."

He unscrewed the truck's gas cap and emptied the can. "I'm gonna walk back into town. See if I can find a day's work."

"People are looking for us," I said. "Shouldn't we just go?" I looked to Maggie and Jamie for backup, but they kept quiet.

Max walked over to me. "We need to get to New Orleans. Obviously this town is too small for us not to be noticed. The worst thing we could do right now is get on the road in the middle of the day and run out of gas. We'd definitely get caught. At least this way, we *might* not." He reached for my hand. When he squeezed my fingers, I felt stronger. "It'll be fine. No one's looking for just one guy."

I knew he was right.

"Y'all will be okay here," he said.

"All right."

Another squeeze, and he picked up the gas can and was gone.

Jamie came to stand next to me. He handed me the note I'd left them. I carefully folded the letter and put it back in its envelope and inside Lillian's shoebox.

"What if Steven watches the news?" I asked Maggie. "It might not be safe for us to go there."

"I doubt he'd make the connection," she said. "Besides, Oak Street is mostly artists and hippies. They're not usually up on current events."

She plopped down in the grass.

"But what if my mom is at Steven's?" she asked. "I'm not scared of her calling the cops or anything. It's not like she'd watch the news, but I'm not sure I could handle seeing her."

"Don't you want to see her?" I asked. "How long has it been again?"

"Three years."

We each took a different spot on the ground, and no one talked for a long while.

Jamie was next to me in the grass. My tongue felt thick, and I was regretting not grabbing my toothbrush. "I feel like crap," I said. "Do I look like crap?"

Jamie gave me a once-over. "Remember that time we went camping and we found out just how allergic you are to poison ivy?"

"Oh my God, my eyes swelled shut."

"My mom didn't recognize you."

"I had to sleep with socks on my hands."

Jamie snort-laughed. "You look a little better than that."

I slapped him halfheartedly. "Well, you look like crap, too."

"Noted. Will my mom forgive me?" he asked.

The look on his face bent my heart in painful ways.

"Give me your hands," I said.

I studied his palms. "Yes, she'll forgive you. She'll realize you saved her."

"You're a palm reader now?"

"Yes."

"When did you learn how to do that?"

"While you were sleeping."

"I waste so much time sleeping. What else do you see?"

"I see food. Max is going to bring food."

"Do you see cake?"

"No, no cake."

"Let me see your hands," he said.

I raised an eyebrow.

"I learned while you were talking." He studied my palms. "Your scars cross over the lines in your hands, like you have two lives."

"Or one that canceled out the other," I said.

"No, I see two lives. One to mess up and one to get right."

"That's convenient. What else do you see?" I was whispering now, in case Maggie heard. I trusted Jamie's sudden psychic ability.

We were sitting cross-legged, facing each other. We used to sit like this on my grandmother's living-room floor when we played gin rummy, or odd one out, or talked about school, music, our families. We'd talked out all of life's problems in just this position.

"I see you happy," he said.

"Yeah?" I asked.

He nodded. "And I see you."

When we were younger, Jamie started having this recurring nightmare. In it we were lost together, somewhere in the dark, somewhere we'd never been. In the dream the darkness was so black that I couldn't see him or him me. As in most childhood nightmares, someone was chasing us, and we had to be quiet so we wouldn't be found. Jamie was always afraid that because it was so dark I wouldn't know it was him, and I'd leave him there. So we'd sit like this, and I'd close my eyes and trace his face, reassuring him I'd always know him, even in the dark. Then I lost my name to Lillian's, so Jamie returned the favor and traced my face, too, reassuring me there was at least one person trying to remember me.

My fingers itched to reach out and touch his face, to make sure I'd still know him in the dark.

"I see you, too," I said.

At dusk Max came down the road carrying food and the gas can. From the look on his face, the can was a lot fuller than it had been this morning. He put it down and dropped the grocery bags at my feet. He took my hand and walked toward the lake, stopping at the water's edge. He started taking off his clothes.

"What are you doing?" I asked.

He was standing in his boxers. "I've spent the day loading dirt into the backs of trucks, and I want to swim. I want you to swim with me."

His hands went to my shirt and lifted, his fingers grazing my elbows. His eyes didn't leave mine. I wasn't the kind of girl to wear matching bra and panties, so when I kicked my shorts off, he smiled at my contrasting choices. He took my hand and led me into the water.

Despite the heat of the day, the water was cold. Once we were in up to our waists, something brushed against my leg, reminding me we weren't alone.

"What kinds of fish are in this lake?" I asked. "Are they big?"

Max didn't answer, just dropped under the water and came up splashing. It took my breath away. I splashed back. He picked me up and threw me, and I squealed. I didn't know how it had happened, but we were playing and laughing like this was the end of a normal blue-sky day, with no time for anything but fun and easy smiles.

After a time we circled each other in the water, then got still—too still. He looked at me like he was trying to see inside me. I felt burned by his stare and tried to swim away from him.

"Come back here," he said.

He grabbed me, pulling me to him, our legs tangling in the water.

"I'm not ready to let you go yet."

The water was dripping off his chin, and my eyes were glued to it. He touched the chill bumps on my shoulder, then traced the freckles there.

Even though the water was cool, I was burning up.

"Your lips are blue," he said. "We should probably get out."

I nodded, but neither one of us made a move. He leaned in toward me like he was going to kiss me.

"Did you know he was dead before we left town?" he asked, his lips so close to mine. "Is that what you didn't tell me last night?"

"No."

"It wouldn't have mattered." His eyes were so sad. "If you'd known. I'd do anything for you."

That should've made me feel better, but I felt crushed by it. I was scared of the *anything* he'd do. Judging by the look on his face, he wasn't happy about it, either.

"I know," I said.

I pulled back again. "I'm hungry. Let's see what you brought."

We set about fixing dinner: hot dogs and chips. We ate the hot dogs cold, because we were scared a prolonged fire might draw attention. It was like summer camp—but a dark and twisted version. Max pulled the map out of his truck and showed us we were closer to New Orleans than we'd thought, less than an hour away. We decided we would sleep part of the night and then get up and on the road in time to get there before the sun came up.

Maggie started her questioning game again.

"Quick: what's your favorite body part?" she asked nobody in particular.

Max answered first. "My right arm."

Maggie asked, "Why?"

"Because I've broken it three times."

She looked around to Jamie. "What's yours?"

"My feet, because they get me where I'm going."

"Olivia, what's your favorite body part?"

I quickly answered, "My belly button." Jamie and Maggie laughed, which was what I wanted. I got up and walked to the truck for more chips.

Max didn't laugh, but instead said, "Because that's where you were connected to your mom."

That stopped me, but I didn't turn around. I just shrugged and said, "It's proof I had one." I stayed on my path to the truck, only coming back when I was sure the mood was light again.

After dinner Max laid his sleeping bag on the ground. We all lay on it together, not really fitting, but no one cared. The others went to sleep quickly, and I pretended to. Maybe they were pretending, too, because there was awkwardness in the air. Some time later sleep did come, though, and it must have knocked us all out like bricks, because the next thing I noticed was this feeling of being baked, the sun bright and beaming down on us, unrelenting.

It was Max who moved first. "What time is it?" he asked.

He jumped up and went to the truck. Jamie and Maggie started stirring.

"We have to go. It's ten o'clock. We overslept by a lot." He scrubbed his hands over his face.

I felt like I'd been cooked to the ground, my skin tight.

"Let's go," Max said. He reached down and pulled me up, unsticking me.

We stumbled to the truck. I sat in the back with Jamie. It felt brazen driving in the stark daylight, like we had nothing to hide. Neither Max nor Maggie made a move to turn the radio on, and the silence sat on us heavily. When we saw a sign that said there were only five miles to the city limits, Jamie looked over at me, and I could tell something was wrong.

"Are you okay?" I whispered, careful not to break the silent fog in the truck.

"I'm okay," he quickly whispered back, but he wasn't. He leaned into me. "There's something I need to tell you. I just can't do it yet."

"Okay. I can wait." I didn't know what it could be. I figured I already knew the worst. He nodded, and I scooted next to him so we'd face New Orleans as a united front. We'd find Steven's, and in a little while Max would call his dad and everything would be better. But then I snuck a quick look at Jamie sitting to my left, and couldn't bring myself to believe it.

Chapter 7

We drove into the city in a convoluted way, trying to avoid the interstate. We came into the east part of town, where the street corners were full of people and the sidewalks dotted with mothers swaying barefoot babies on their hips. We didn't expect the drive through New Orleans to be hard. We didn't expect a lot of things. We stared out the window, watching the scenes change from street to street, some houses completely remodeled with bright paint and new windows, others with cracked paint and no windows. Some of the houses looked like Katrina had just happened, with visible watermarks on the sides; many were still too broken to be lived in. The streets were lined with men, though some of them could have been boys; it was impossible to tell their ages by their faces, because everyone looked old, all carrying scars that couldn't be painted over.

Max rolled his window down, and then Maggie did, too,

making sure it was all real, not a scene from a movie. Nothing separated us from them, the smells, sounds, and stares. My stomach clenched at the amazing aroma coming from a dive on a nearby corner. I didn't know if it was hunger pains or some other pain, but tears sprang to my eyes and I felt too young to be in this place. *Welcome to New Orleans.*

The roads were all torn up, seeming worse now than right after Katrina. Things still looked to be in transition of some sort, each street at a different level of repair. We took the bumps and detours, no one saying anything. It was easier to walk in New Orleans than to drive because of all the one-ways. Thanks to those and the road construction, we somehow ended up in the French Quarter. Then again, that could all have been a plan hatched by the city officials, because even if you tried not to go downtown, somehow all roads led to Bourbon Street.

Driving through the French Quarter was like entering a new dimension. Everything had been restored to its pre-apocalyptic-hurricane state. It was only noon, but people were already partying in the streets, wearing smiles and beads and carrying ridiculously tall drink cups. It didn't feel real. It was like we had wandered into some play intended to convince the tourists that everything was back to normal. The shop owners were in on it, with their too-wide smiles, pointing and directing everyone's attention away from anything unpleasant.

But we were from Louisiana, and we had just come from one of the places they didn't want us to see. Downtown quickly lost its appeal, so we exited stage left. We made our way uptown through back alleys and side streets. My dad hadn't been to New Orleans since the storm—not that he had ever been there much anyway. He said it was better to remember it the way it had been. He didn't care that it was being rebuilt. He said, "Some things you can't get back."

We parked the truck on a side street uptown. Walking away from it proved harder than I expected—almost as hard as the drive out of St. Francisville. We were leaving one more comfort behind and stepping farther into the deep end of whatever was coming, and no matter how discreetly the truck was hidden, it would eventually be found. Leaving the truck felt like starting a countdown to being caught.

We had taken everything that might be useful out of it—a flashlight, Max's sleeping bag, the map. We walked for a while and then stopped to get something to eat. We spent the last of the money Max had earned the day before. Only in south Louisiana can you buy seafood gumbo from a convenience store and know it will be good.

When we made it to Oak Street, Maggie studied the houses, trying to remember which one might be Steven's. They all looked so similar. Looking around, I decided my dad was wrong. Some things you could get back. Shops were interspersed with shotgun houses with real people sitting on real porches. There was life and creativity everywhere, from the design of the buildings, to the smell of the food, to the sway in people's walks and the sound of their talk, to all the colors of all the different faces. There was even a man painting the scene from a street corner. None of this escaped Maggie, who was standing decidedly taller. A woman with paint splatters on her arm walked by us. Maggie smiled, and I knew these were her people.

Steven seemed glad if somewhat confused to see all of us, once Maggie reminded him who she was. He hugged each one of us tight to his chest like this was a planned visit and we were all old friends. He didn't give Max's bruised eye a second glance, and didn't seem to notice that Jamie didn't hug him back.

"Wow, Vicky's daughter. Look at you. This is amazing," he said.

We were standing on the sidewalk outside his house, where he'd found us lingering near his mailbox, Maggie still unsure we were in the right place.

He studied Maggie, even turning her all the way around. "I haven't seen you in so long." He shook his head like he couldn't believe it. "She talks about you all the time."

Maggie gave him a *Really?* look, but he didn't notice.

"Are you here to see her?" he asked.

Maggie nodded. "Yeah, I wanted to see her before I left for school." Her voice didn't crack, like there was no lie in what she was saying.

"I haven't seen her in a couple of weeks, but she always comes back around. In fact, my band is playing tonight across the street at the Maple Leaf, and she almost never misses a show."

Maggie had mentioned, on the walk to Oak Street, that Steven was a well-known artist, at least locally, but she hadn't mentioned he was a musician as well. It seemed that was a prerequisite for artists, like being talented in just one way wasn't enough. Steven led us up the front steps and into his house, which looked more like an art studio than a living space. There was little furniture, and none of it matched. I was relieved not to see a TV anywhere. A large easel took up most of the living room, and canvases lined the walls. There were paint splatters everywhere, even on the ceiling. Maggie didn't mask her appreciation, walking straight up to the artwork. As for Steven, he sat back and watched Maggie like she was the art.

He offered us the use of his two bathrooms, and we relished the hot showers and toothpaste. I felt bad for the others, who'd have to put on the same dirty clothes as before, so I asked Steven if he had a washer and dryer we could use. I started to explain why the others hadn't brought clothes, but he cut me off immediately.

"Of course. You, beautiful friend of Vicky's daughter, can use anything here you need."

I could tell he meant what he said, like he was used to travel-weary kids stopping by his house, looking for people he occasionally let sleep on his couch. It didn't bother me that he was another person who didn't know my name.

As it turned out, Steven opened his home to a lot of people. For the next couple of hours, I watched as an array of visitors wandered in and out, opening doors and disappearing behind them, or opening the refrigerator to take out some food or drink. They were all met with ready smiles from Steven, who only asked them in return if they were coming to the show later on tonight. They all were.

It was easy to pick out the drop-ins from the live-ins. A guy who looked about our age took the seat next to me on the couch. He kept looking at me like he recognized me, and I started sweating.

"I'm Luke," he said.

He smelled like incense, and it hurt my nose. He put his hands on his knees. His hands looked old. I wondered what had happened to them. Luke was one of those people who you couldn't tell right away if they were good-looking or not. I kept waiting for him to do something that'd reveal what he really looked like.

"I'm Olivia." I wondered too late whether I should have given him a fake name, but Steven already knew who we were, so there was no point in lying.

Luke reached for the cigarettes sitting on the table next to the couch and pulled a lighter from his pocket. I watched the fire spark from his hand, and as he smoked his cigarette, I felt like I was watching something intimate. He brought the smoke slowly into his mouth, then closed his eyes as he released it through his nose. He did this over and over in a way I'd never seen anyone smoke a cigarette, and I blushed.

Looking into Max's face, I could tell he was suspicious of Luke. There weren't boys like this in St. Francisville, and Max was still getting used to the unknown. Max reached for me and pulled me from the couch. He led me out to the front porch.

"I saw some pay phones a couple of blocks back," he said. "I'm gonna call my dad."

"And you're sure that's the right thing to do?" I asked. I couldn't stop my voice from coming out high-pitched. "We could just find Beth. She could . . . she might—" I didn't know what I was trying to say. I just knew I was scared of him reaching out to his dad.

"We'll find Beth. We'll take all the help we can get, I promise. But my dad's a defense attorney. This is his job. I won't tell him where we are, just that we need help. Believe me, Jamie needs him. I wouldn't be surprised if my dad can make all this go away."

I worried Max might be overestimating his father's powers.

"Will you come with me?" he asked.

I looked back into the house. "I don't want to leave Jamie."

"Right," he said. "I'll be back as soon as I can." He leaned in and kissed my cheek, and my hand went to the spot his lips had touched.

A minute later I walked back into the house, just as Maggie asked Luke, "Do you live here with Steven?"

Luke nodded.

"Then you might know my mom, Vicky."

"Yeah, I know your mom." He leaned all the way back on the couch, stretching his arms out. "She's a really great person. She keeps trying to talk me into going back to school. She also doesn't think I should live here."

"In New Orleans, or at Steven's?" Maggie asked.

"Um, both." He laughed low-like and reached over to put out his cigarette.

Maggie just stared at him. "How old are you?"

He seemed surprised by this question, like he couldn't believe that of all the questions in the world she could ask him, she'd picked this one trivial thing.

"I'm not sure. My parents didn't keep up with that sort of thing."

I couldn't help myself. "Do your parents live in New Orleans?"

"Um, no . . . they don't. As it turns out, they couldn't keep up with me, either."

"Oh." It was the only thing I could say. Luke's eyes made me sad, so I looked away from him.

Maggie looked pissed all of a sudden, and she stood and stormed out the front door, leaving me alone with the boy with worn-out hands. I realized it bothered her that her mom was mothering this strange boy in this even stranger house.

Jamie came out of the bathroom, and I sighed in relief. He sat down on the couch, on the far end from Luke.

Luke said, "Do I know you from somewhere, man?"

Jamie shook his head. "I don't think so."

"Where did y'all say you were from?"

"We didn't," I said. I looked into his face. "We didn't say where we were from."

I was ready to give him a hard look, or threaten him—anything to get him to stop asking questions. But I didn't have to do either of those things. A boy who didn't know or

111

even care how old he was wasn't one to get caught up in the details of other people's lives. He just nodded again.

"I get it. Where are any of us from anyway? Right?"

"Right."

An hour later Max still wasn't back. I'd started watching the clock thirty minutes after he left. He'd said the pay phones were only a couple of blocks away, and I was worried about what might be keeping him. Maggie offered to go looking for him.

"No," I said. "I don't think we should separate any more than we already are."

"Do you think he was picked up?" Jamie asked.

I should've gone with him.

"There's at least half a dozen bars between here and the pay phones," Maggie said. "Maybe he got lost in one of them."

I glared at her. I wanted to say he wouldn't do that. "He'll be back," I said.

Jamie looked worried.

"Soon," I added.

❧

The sun was setting, and still no Max. I jumped anytime someone came into the house, hoping it'd be him. My muscles were coiled tight, and my hands were sweating. Steven was in the kitchen cooking supper. He started talking to Maggie from the kitchen, his voice loud. As the day had gone on, he had remembered more about Maggie and her mom.

"You know, your mother is so proud of you. She tells anybody who'll listen that you're going to SVA in the fall. Hell, she's told me a few hundred times, because she forgets who she tells what." He laughed at that, and then stopped suddenly, I guess realizing that Maggie might not think that was funny. "Congratulations, by the way. That's amazing. My nephew went there. He was a sculptor, but he didn't do so great once he got there. New York isn't for everybody. But you . . . you'll be okay. You've got Vicky in you."

I looked at Maggie, because I knew it was the Vicky in her she was worried about. Maggie met my gaze, but didn't say anything. The smells coming out of the tiny kitchen were making me homesick. I'd been trying not to think of my grandmother, and I was getting pretty good at it, but at the moment, with Steven not talking anymore and the only sound coming from the kitchen an occasional clink from a pot, the smells . . . the smells took me away. It was no longer Steven in the kitchen but my grandmother, making dinner for my friends and a few odd extras. She was wearing the stained apron she always wore when she cooked, and her hair was pulled halfway back in a messy gray bun with loose hairs around her face. I closed my eyes and I heard her calling to Lillian that it was almost ready.

Steven stuck his head back into the living room, to tell us that it was in fact ready. He was not my grandmother. We went into the kitchen. There were no chairs, but there was a table in the middle of the room. There was some sort of chicken casserole and rice and French bread. The live-ins came out of their hiding spots and grabbed bowls. I grabbed my own bowl. Steven started to leave the room.

"You're not eating?" I asked.

"No, I never eat before a show." He went into the living room and greeted a group of people that had just come in the house. "Hey, boys, we're in the back." Then he and the rest of them disappeared down the hall.

I'd pushed the homesick feeling away until I brought the food to my mouth. The taste brought tears to my eyes, embarrassing me, so I put my bowl down and excused myself from the room.

I walked back into the living room to find Max sitting on the couch. The relief at seeing him was immediate and sharp, a literal pang in my chest.

"Where've you been?" I whisper-yelled. "What took you so long?"

"I needed some time."

"You needed time?"

I had expected him to look relieved after calling his dad, but he seemed agitated or restless or something else I couldn't name. He stood up and moved around the room like an animal pacing inside its cage. There was a faint whiskey smell in the air. He abandoned the living room for the front porch. I followed.

The night was falling down around Oak Street. Max put both hands around the railing on the front porch. He held on to it hard, like he was afraid someone or something was going to come along and try to knock him off the porch. He wouldn't look at me.

"Where have you been?" I asked again.

Nothing.

"Fine, don't answer me. I can smell where you've been."

He glared at me. "I'm sorry. But I needed a drink. You'll need one, too, in a minute."

"You scared me." My voice caught. "I've been sitting in this house, imagining the worst. And you've been getting drunk." I hated that Maggie was right about him.

He dropped his head. "I'm sorry," he said.

"What did your dad say?"

"I thought I could make one call and everything would be better." He lifted his face to mine. His look said everything wasn't better.

I kept swallowing, my mouth drier than it had ever been. He opened his mouth to say something else, but no sound came. I stepped closer to him, as if having less space between us would soften the blow of whatever was coming next. I looked into his chest, my nose almost touching him, and asked, "What did your dad say?"

I felt him looking down at me with tired eyes. I felt the breath from his mouth moving above my head, but still he said nothing. Instead, he put his hands on my back and pulled me into him, making me turn my face to the side. I wanted to look up at him, but I only held on. I wondered at his silence and what he was holding so hard to. I wondered why everything wasn't better. Maybe his dad wasn't as good as he thought, or maybe we were in more trouble

than we thought; maybe we wouldn't be forgiven or justified; maybe there would be no way out. I was grateful for
this silence that allowed me not to know what he knew. I
felt his heartbeat against my forehead, and I concentrated
on the rhythm of it.

My reprieve wasn't long. He took me by the shoulders,
and I took a deep breath. When I looked up at him, he
asked, "Did you know about the journals?"

I replayed his question over and over again in my head,
fast and then slow, trying to make sense of the words. There
were journals on the shelf in Jamie's bedroom, and there
were two underneath his floor. My first instinct was always
to protect Jamie. I kept quiet.

"Sure you did," Max said. "You guys know everything
about each other." He didn't try to hide his frustration. "So
you know he planned it."

"What? No, he didn't plan it. I was there. I was in the
room." *I hit his dad with a skillet.* "There was no plan."

Max's face said he didn't believe me.

"I need to talk to Jamie," I said.

"Now is the time to talk to *me*. Jamie is screwed. You
need to trust me now. Please."

"I have to talk to Jamie." I pulled away from him.

"My dad has a friend in the DA's office. He says the journals change everything."

I was pretty sure that whatever Jamie had needed to tell
me earlier had to do with his journals.

There are things you don't know. It didn't matter, though.

There was nothing Jamie could say that would change my mind about him.

I went back in the house, but instead of going to the kitchen, where Jamie was, I walked down the long hall, looking at all the art that hung there. My mind needed a minute to process what I'd heard before I said anything to Jamie, or maybe I wanted to put off what I knew was coming next.

At the end of the hall, a door was open. Steven and the people that had just come in were sitting around a table doing lines of cocaine, the sound of the drug going up their noses louder than I thought it should be. I'd never seen anyone doing that—in person, that is—and I knew I should look away, but I couldn't. I stood frozen to the spot, shocked. The people at the table turned to look at me. A girl was with them, not at the table, but standing up, facing the window. From behind she looked young, my height with short hair. When she turned around, I saw that her eyes were ninety years old.

"Hey," she said to me. "Do you want to come in? Do you party?"

"No, she doesn't party. This one's a baby," Steven said. He came to the door and shut it, his eyes never leaving mine.

On my way back to the kitchen, I bumped into Luke coming out of one of the other bedrooms. He reached out to touch my face. I hadn't had time to put my expression back in its everything-is-normal place, so I thought he might ask me what was wrong. If he had, I just might have told him that everything in my life was out of control. I wanted to tell him I was too young to be in this place, and that I wanted to go back to St. Francisville, where no one looked at me. I wasn't used to being seen. But he didn't ask me what was wrong.

"I know who you are now," he said. "You don't have to be afraid of me. I won't tell your secret."

"I don't have a secret."

He pulled his hands away from my face. "Okay. Just know I'd never judge anybody, because I've made a few bad choices myself."

I didn't know why he was telling me this, but I knew I didn't want to talk to him anymore. When I tried to pass him, he reached out and grabbed my arm.

"Be careful where you go. Your photos are everywhere. I went downtown earlier. Y'all are splashed all over the TV."

I stopped breathing and my eyes filled with my stupid guilty tears. I waited for him to say something else, but he didn't, so I just said, "Okay, we won't."

He nodded.

I wanted to offer him something in return for his warning. "There's food in the kitchen. Steven cooked; it looks really good."

He shook his head. "I don't go into the kitchen." At first he didn't offer anything more, like what he'd just said was normal, but then he said, "Once I was on a really bad trip. I went into the kitchen and the cabinets started to breathe."

"Oh." And then I added him and that girl's eyes to my growing list of reasons not to do drugs.

Luke walked into the living room, but I wasn't ready for that yet, so I stayed put, pretending to analyze one of Steven's paintings. I stayed there until I was convinced I understood what was in front of me. When I came back down the hall, everyone was in the living room watching Luke, who was sitting with a guitar. Jamie and Max were standing together against a wall, and Maggie was nowhere to be seen. Max looked at me inquisitively because he knew I hadn't said anything to Jamie. They moved apart when they saw me, giving me room to slide in between them. I went to my own corner instead. It was while I watched Luke move his hands on the guitar and listened to his voice that he revealed himself as beautiful.

People with break-your-heart voices could afford to say strange things and avoid kitchens. And as I listened to Luke, I reached my limit of surprises for the day and felt the tears sting my eyes again. I wanted to stop them, so I did something to surprise them, thinking that maybe if I caught *myself* off guard I'd stop crying.

I plucked a pack of cigarettes from a nearby table and put one in my mouth. I realized too late I didn't have a lighter, and then a light appeared in my face, like magic, offered to me by one of the live-ins. I took a pull on the cigarette and nodded him a thank-you. I inhaled it and my lungs squeezed tight inside my chest, trying to keep the smoke out, but I won, making the smoke move down my throat, then back up and out my mouth, exhaling with my cool, not-my-first-time face. Jamie's and Max's surprised looks got on my nerves, so I stared back at them as a new

Olivia, a cool, crying, smoking Olivia, one who appreciated good art and didn't get scared when people started doing drugs in front of her or told her they knew who she really was. I was nothing if not adaptable.

Two puffs in, I remembered why I don't smoke. I turned and walked out the front door before the coughing started. It was Jamie who followed me. He didn't say anything; he just stayed three steps behind me as I made my way down Oak Street. When I stopped, he stopped, and when I walked, he walked. It was the same thing he used to do when we were little, when I was angry for some reason or another. He'd see me walking down Fidelity Street, come out of his house, and follow me down the street, never saying anything but always there. Just in case I wanted to turn around, he'd be there.

When I finally turned to face him, I cried harder because I'd promised him if he came down out of my tree, I wouldn't let anything bad happen to him. I was scared I couldn't keep that promise.

"What's wrong?" he asked.

"You mean what else?"

"Yeah, what else is wrong?"

I wanted to ask him what he'd put in his journals that changed everything. Instead, I said, "Max talked to his dad."

"Yeah, he told me, but he wouldn't tell me what his dad said. He said I should ask you."

"They found your journals."

Jamie looked down at his feet. His shoulders tensed up.

"I'm guessing they're not talking about the ones on your shelf."

Jamie didn't say anything, just walked to me and sat down on a bench. I sat down next to him. He turned his face away from me, and a heat settled in my belly.

"Jamie?"

"I watched him," he said. "For so many years I just watched. He threw her around like she was weightless."

I felt more tears burning beneath my eyes, and the heat from my stomach worked its way up my throat. His voice had lowered so much I had to strain to hear him.

"When I was younger, I looked up to him." He glanced at me, ashamed.

"When you were younger, he was someone to look up to."

"But then he kept losing his job," he said. "He couldn't provide for us anymore, and I could tell, even then, how ashamed he was. I guess he drank so he wouldn't have to feel it. Then everything turned to shit. He'd look into her face, the face of the wife he was supposed to love, the mother of the child he was supposed to love, and he'd hit it. He'd beat her face like her face meant nothing. I watched him hurt her, but he never hit me. He'd walk past me like I wasn't even there." He wiped his nose, and then he looked at me with tears in his eyes. "I started provoking him, just to see if he'd hit me, too. He wouldn't, though. He just kept looking through me. I knew I'd really have to push him."

"Why did you want him to hit you?"

"I wanted him to see me. I wanted to take the heat off of her. That night was the first time he had looked at me in a really long time. I hated him so much. Every day I imagined how I could stop him," he said. "I wrote down all the ways. I filled up two journals."

He stopped talking for a while, and I was grateful. I scooted right up next to him. I laid my head against his shoulder and leaned into him to get as close as possible.

"The journals made them think you planned it," I said. "You might've fantasized about it, but you didn't plan it the way it happened. We have to tell them the truth."

Jamie tilted his head toward mine, his face resting on my hair. "I wrote about killing that prick every day for the last two years. They're not gonna believe I didn't plan it. It doesn't matter that I never thought I'd do it. What matters is that I'm not sorry I did."

"But if I tell them my part in it, they'll realize—"

"She had to be perfect. He'd blow up with no warning. Nobody can be perfect. Sometimes she never saw it coming. I ran away every time."

I pulled away from him. "That doesn't matter. You didn't mean to—"

"Every time," he said. "When I was younger, I didn't feel guilty about it. I guess it was a survival instinct. I was so scared of him. The guilt came later."

The street was busy, but it felt like we were the only two people in the world. I couldn't hear any of the surrounding noises, only Jamie's words.

"But you didn't mean it to happen," I said. "He was threatening you. If we tell them I was there, that I hit him with the skillet, they'll know you didn't plan it."

"I'm not implicating you."

"Jamie—"

"Let me be the one who finally stopped him," he said. "By myself. Please? Let me be that for her."

"Your mom knows what I did."

"She knows you hurt him, but the knife in his gut is what killed him. *I* did that. Don't take that away from me." His eyes were begging.

"I won't take that away from you."

I looked up to see Max standing down the street, a whiskey bottle hanging from his hand. He was officially off the wagon, and it no longer mattered. The world as I knew it was over, so who cared if Max had a drink? His face was tired and sad. I didn't have to be a lawyer's son to know the journals showed intent, and if we went home, it was certain Jamie would be tried for murder. I tried not to think of what that meant for the rest of us.

I closed my eyes and imagined St. Francisville, recalling every little detail: the way the moss hung in the trees, the way the sun felt when I stood next to the river, the slope of my grandmother's backyard under my feet. You never knew when you were going to see someone or someplace for the last time.

When we walked back to the house, Max offered the bottle to Jamie, and Jamie surprised me by taking it. Maggie was sitting on the front steps. She stood as we walked up the steps to the front porch swing. Jamie and I sat down.

"Everyone's gone across the street to help the band set up," she said. "Steven said we could sneak in the back if we wanted to see the show." She pointed at the alley that ran next to the bar. There was a side door.

"Not now," I said.

She looked at me and could tell something was very wrong, because her face dropped. When Max stepped up onto the porch, he opened his mouth to tell us his dad's news, only barely parting his lips, but that was all the room his dad's words needed to seep out and up into the air. They rose high above us before hitting the roof of the porch and falling down on us.

I didn't want the words to enter my head, so they hung outside my body in a whisper that played over and over again. *Intent, first degree, change of venue, life sentence, death sentence, accessories, plea deals . . .* I was angry at the last one, because there were no deals worth having being offered to Jamie. They were reserved for Max, Maggie, and even me, but not Jamie. If we went home, Jamie would be judged, tried, and sentenced by strangers who didn't know the monster his dad was, strangers I wouldn't be allowed to get close to so I could explain that Jamie was still a boy.

"With the journals, the DA's office is pushing for a first-degree murder charge," Max said. "My dad says he can get it down to second degree with a plea. If you agree to the plea deal, then the death penalty is off the table. My dad can make sure you're not sent to Angola."

Angola, Louisiana's state prison, where 90 percent of inmates died behind the walls. Even if Max's dad could make it so Jamie wasn't sent there, he'd still be sent somewhere to wait until he died, because even a second-degree murder conviction carried a mandatory life sentence, something we all had learned in our Louisiana government class. A life sentence in Louisiana was just that.

Max's dad, who was using his power and position, trading in every favor to separate his son's fate from Jamie's, had convinced them that because we weren't mentioned in Jamie's journals, this wasn't a conspiracy. He'd even convinced them that we weren't accessories, just caught up in teenage instincts, flawed friendships, and poor judgment.

"If you don't take the plea, you can take your chance with a jury," Max said. "But then all bets are off."

At first Max spoke confidently, but as he continued, the words tripped out of his mouth, like he was only now hearing them. He was only now realizing there were things worse than death.

Apparently Louisiana wouldn't be understanding or forgiving, but instead required Jamie to trade his life for his dad's in some way or another.

"Tell your dad thank you," Jamie said, "but I won't need a deal." He got up and handed Max the whiskey bottle, then walked down the front porch steps. He turned back to us. "I'm not going home." He walked across the street and then down the alley before disappearing through the side door of the Maple Leaf.

Max stood and turned to me, his face deflated, the lines in his forehead making him look much older. There was fear in his face as well, like he was afraid I blamed him for being the one to tell Jamie his dad's news, that I blamed him for not being able to save us. Part of me wanted to go to him and make him feel better, to tell him all of this was out of his control—a hard concept for someone like Max to understand.

"Olivia—" he said.

I sighed. "I'm not leaving him."

"Jamie's dad was a bastard who deserved what he got," Max said. "If Jamie goes home, he'll go down for it. I get why he wouldn't want to go home. But not you. My dad can make it so we don't go to jail. We'll have community service and records, but we won't do time."

"You don't know everything. You don't know what I did."

"What do you mean? What'd you do?" he asked.

"I hit him with a skillet."

Max just stared at me, like he was waiting for me to make sense.

"They were fighting. Jamie had a knife. His dad lunged at Jamie, and I tried to stop Mr. Benton. I hit him in the head with a skillet."

Max gaped. I didn't take that as a good sign. He recovered and said, "You hurt him. You didn't kill him." It was the same argument Jamie had made. "My dad didn't say anything about a skillet."

"But it'll come up. Won't they do an autopsy? It'll show a head trauma."

"Why can't Jamie have done that, too? They were fighting. Jamie hit his dad with the skillet. He grabbed the knife. He stabbed him. End of story," Max said.

"But Jamie's mom was there. She saw."

"She's not talking to anyone. She's not saying anything. My dad says she's traumatized or something."

"My fingerprints are in the kitchen; they're on the skillet," I countered.

"Jamie invited you over for dinner. My dad can say you were helping Jamie's mom cook." He paced on the porch. "This doesn't have to be your crime. You can come home." Max sounded almost hopeful, like he'd found a way out for me.

I hated to crush his hope.

I guess he could tell from my expression what I was about to say, because he twisted his face up. "Olivia—"

"No," I said. Jamie hated being alone. Whatever Jamie's fate was, it'd be mine, too. "I'm not leaving him," I repeated.

"Of course you're not," he said.

Where does that leave you and Maggie? I thought it, but didn't say it; I already knew what the answer should be, what it needed to be. I needed to let them go home, back to their lives.

"I'm sorry," I said.

"Don't be. I should have known better. If it's a choice between him and me, I always know who you'll choose."

"Max—"

"I know you love him, and I know it's different from the way you feel about me." He started pacing on the porch again, his hands going to his hair. "I know I shouldn't be jealous of him, but I am. I'm so fucking jealous of him."

"No, don't—"

"He has you. You're only on loan to me. Everybody knows you're his girl."

"It's not like that," I said.

"I know. I know it's not like that. You know what I mean."

"You're drunk."

"Yeah, I am. That doesn't make what I said not true."

"I can't talk about this right now," I said.

"When do you want to talk about it?"

I wanted to say, *Never,* but I stayed quiet.

"I hate you sometimes," he whispered.

I knew that, too. I looked over at Maggie, who'd stopped moving after Jamie went across the street. She didn't look at me, didn't act like she'd heard anything we'd said. She just stared in the direction that Jamie had gone. I called her name, but there was no response. It was like she was stuck, her body not able to absorb what was happening around her. I wanted to go to her, to hold her, or hug her, to help her understand. But I needed the practice in walking away from her, so I followed Jamie's steps across the street.

I looked back at the porch once I got to the bar. Max was talking to Maggie, but her eyes were on me. He was wringing his hands as he no doubt explained to her the deals dividing us, and she kept shaking her head. I knew that, like all of us, she'd been holding on to the idea that the stakes weren't this high, that we'd be allowed to go home together, that somehow we wouldn't be punished.

I turned from them and slipped through the side door. The band was onstage, tweaking their instruments. "Check one. Check two," Steven said into the microphone. My eyes adjusted to the darkness of the room. The crowd was already standing and swaying, their bodies moving in anticipation of the music they knew was coming. I looked around for Jamie. He was sitting at a table. We locked eyes.

"Here." Luke appeared next to me and handed me a shot glass. "You look like you could use one," he said.

I needed something. Maybe this was it. Jamie was looking at me with a question in his eyes. *Do you need my help?* they asked. I shook my head. I didn't need him to defend me from this strange boy.

The liquid was pale yellow. I didn't know what it was, and I didn't care. I slammed it back and forced myself to swallow.

"Thanks," I said.

"No problem," he said, and disappeared into the crowd.

Jamie was still staring at me.

"I'm okay," I mouthed.

He nodded and turned to face the stage.

A few minutes later, Maggie and Max walked into the bar. Maggie and I had so much to say to each other, but I could tell she didn't want to talk now. Neither did I. She went to sit on a barstool near the entrance, looking carefully into the faces of the people coming in. Maybe one of them would be her mom. She tried to look aloof as she studied each person, but she mostly looked vulnerable.

Max had followed me to the back of the bar, where I could keep everyone in sight. I didn't want any more surprises today.

"I'm sorry," he said.

"Me too. Do you still hate me?" I asked.

"A little."

"I don't want you to be mad at me," I said.

"I'm not mad."

I rolled my eyes.

"Okay, I'm mad. But not at you. Not at him. Just at the situation." Max pulled me into his arms and buried his face in my neck. "I'll help you," he whispered into my hair.

I put my arms around him, hugging him tight. I needed Max's help, even if it wasn't fair of me to take it. I had guilt stacked upon guilt. I didn't deserve him.

"You break my heart every day," he said. "Loving you hurts so much." He squeezed me tighter to him. "I'll help you leave me. Whatever you need. Me and Maggie won't turn ourselves in until you and Jamie can get away safe."

I knew it wouldn't be that simple, that he wouldn't make it easy to leave him, but I said, "Thank you."

He reached out to brush my cheek, touching the spot he'd kissed earlier. "You're welcome."

I planned on staying hidden at the back of the bar, but when the music started I found myself moving toward the stage with the crowd, my body drawn closer to the sounds. Max followed. I wanted him to come closer. I stopped abruptly, making his body almost touch mine. He still smelled like home. I missed home so much. I leaned back into him, laying my head back. His hands were on my stomach, pulling me tighter against him. He dipped his head down, his mouth brushing my neck. He kissed my shoulder. I thought he'd turn me around to face him, but he didn't. He just held me to him, pressing his face into my hair and inhaling, making me wonder if I smelled like home, too.

I closed my eyes and then turned to face him. I already missed him, so I reached for him, pulling his face down to mine. Our lips touched, and I tasted whiskey. The alcohol tasted sweeter on his tongue. My body sagged into his, and I allowed him into my bloodstream.

I was drunk from the shot and Max's kiss. His eyes were heated and his hands were everywhere. My breath came fast, and I felt desperate. I reached for his face again, because I wanted more, more of him and more time. I plastered myself to him, sealing my lips to his. Max pulled me even closer. I raised up on tiptoe. I might climb him. The song ended, and the crowd applauded. For a second I thought it was for us. I pulled away, and my lips felt bruised.

"Goddamn," Max said quietly.

Luke came up to us, his hands full. He offered me another shot. The look on Max's face said he didn't appreciate being interrupted. I took it without saying anything. That one went down easier. I was getting better at it.

"Is that tequila?" Max asked.

"Yeah, you want one?" Luke held up the other shot glass, but Max shook his head.

The band started a new song, apparently a crowd favorite, because people started yelling and whistling. I turned to see Jamie still watching the band. Then, as if he felt me watching him, he turned his head to me. His confession hung heavy in the air between us. *For so many years I just watched. . . . I watched him hurt her, but he never hit me. He'd walk past me like I wasn't even there.*

"I'll take it," I said to Luke, who was still standing there, looking at the band.

I wasn't sure what I was doing, I just knew I wanted to forget our troubles and be someone else for a little while. This shot didn't go down as easy as the others. Jamie was still watching me. *I wrote about killing that prick every day for the last two years.* Swaying on the floor, I put my head down. I concentrated on breathing. Max's hands were on my back, rubbing up and down.

"I think you need to slow down," he whispered, his lips at my ear.

Eyes closed, I shook my head. There was no time to slow down, and I didn't want to.

I reached out and squeezed his hand. The music was louder now, pulsing in my ears, Delta blues spliced with zydeco. I wanted to get closer to it, to help drown out the sound of Jamie's words in my head, but there were too many people. Turning around, I bumped into a table. I pushed the chair back and used it to climb on top of the table, knocking over a glass. Max grabbed my legs, steadying me.

"What are you doing?" he yelled over the music.

"I don't know," I said.

My nose burned from the mysterious smoke clouds floating through the room, and I felt the music inside me now. Across the room Steven made eye contact with me and

132

smiled. I didn't know if it was the alcohol, but for a second I felt invincible. The room was bursting with people, their movements in sync with the music. Max didn't take his hands off me.

"Get down from there," he said.

Shaking my head, I pulled my legs from his reach, anchoring myself in the center of the table. I looked at the people standing around it. They looked back at me expectantly, like they were waiting for a show, and I felt obliged to give them one, my body moving to the music. Who was this girl? I didn't know, but I liked her. She wasn't afraid.

That's when the whistling started, making me feel high. I looked across the bar to see Maggie and motioned for her to join me. She looked back at me with worried eyes. A guy near me held up a shot—Southern hospitality at its finest—and I bent to take it. It burned down my throat. My audience cheered. I might be out of control, but it felt good.

Jamie was up on his feet and coming toward me. He looked worried, too, and I mouthed to him again, "I'm okay." He didn't believe me this time. I felt a hand on my leg, but this time it wasn't Max. It was my new friend with another drink, but Max pushed him out of the way. The guy put the drink on the table and pushed Max back, using both hands on his chest. He yelled something in Max's face and flicked his eyes up at me, then said something else. Max reared back and punched him. Blood burst from the guy's nose, bright red against the white of his face, like the blood on Jamie's shirt and on their kitchen floor, and just like that I was sober. People started pushing, their drinks spilling. Someone bumped the table, and I reached out to the wall to keep from falling.

There was yelling and shoving. I couldn't see Max anymore; a group of people surrounded him. The fight spread like a virus: elbows hit stomachs, feet were trampled, fists flew. I saw Jamie yell something at me, but I couldn't make it out. The crowd was moving like a current, and instead of bringing him closer to me, they carried him away like the tide.

"Jamie!" I yelled.

The table rocked again, and I squatted. I tried to get down, but there were too many people crowded around, everyone pushing, trying to avoid the commotion. I looked up to see Max, his face fierce, coming for me. He grabbed me and pulled me off the table, carrying me through the crowd, and by some miracle the people parted for us. The music never stopped.

We found our way out the side door, Maggie suddenly there behind us, the sound of sirens drawing close. Max dropped me to my feet.

Jamie burst through the door as a police cruiser came down Oak Street, its red and blue lights reflecting off the side of the building, and I couldn't breathe. It stopped in front of the Maple Leaf, and we flattened ourselves against the wall. Jamie reached out to grab my hand.

Seconds went by and we didn't move. I closed my eyes, thinking, *If I can't see them, they can't see me.* A few minutes later we heard a door slamming open, then yelling, the drunk and disorderly pissed they were being arrested and saying things to the cops they'd probably regret later. The arguing escalated. The sounds of handcuffs clicking shut mixed with the police radio.

We were pressed against the side of the building for maybe twenty minutes, but it felt like much longer. My fingers were numb from Jamie's grip. Finally we heard the car doors slam shut, and the cop car drove away. We exhaled collectively, Jamie dropping down to rest his hands on his knees.

"What the hell?" Maggie asked. She looked from Max to me.

"Do you really think it's such a good idea to bring that much attention to ourselves?" She glared at me. "What were you thinking?"

"I wasn't the one throwing punches," I said.

Max stared at me hard but didn't defend himself.

"Are you trying to get arrested?" Maggie asked him.

"You didn't hear what that guy said," Max answered.

"It doesn't matter what he said. He doesn't matter. He's not in hiding. You are." She looked back at me. "Seriously, what were you doing?"

"I don't know," I said.

"Are you sure?" Jamie asked, his voice almost a whisper. He looked down at Lillian's necklace before meeting my eyes. "Number nineteen, dance on a table in a bar."

Of course. When I wanted to escape myself for a minute, I became her. I felt the night crash into me, and my face flushed.

"I'm sorry," I said.

"Hey," said Maggie, her voice gentler now. "It's okay. It was a stressful day. Now that we've blown off some steam, we're gonna be okay." She looked at Jamie. "She just danced a little and maybe had too much to drink." Her eyes cut to mine. "She's fine." She said it like it was a threat, like I'd better be.

"We should probably go back to Steven's," Jamie said.

"I'm going to stay for a little while longer," said Maggie, "listen to the rest of the set; then I'll be over." She fidgeted.

I knew she wanted to see if her mom would show up. I stepped to her and hugged her tight. "I'll see you later," I said.

She nodded and went back inside.

Walking down the alley to the front of the bar, we found Oak Street still very much awake and full of people. The girl with ninety-year-old eyes was standing by the entrance. She was arguing with a guy, and they were getting pretty loud. We stepped around her and crossed the street to Steven's house.

She yelled out after us, "It's not safe for you there. You can't trust anybody in that house."

I didn't know what to say to that. Max herded us to the front door. I turned to look back at her just in time to see the guy she was fighting with walk away. She looked at me like she was used to being walked away from. "They're all liars," she said.

Because we didn't know what else to do, we went inside. Max pulled out his sleeping bag and opened it up on the floor of the living room. Jamie immediately dropped down on it, exhausted. Max walked into the kitchen, and I followed him. He ran the water in the sink and started washing his hands, which were bloody from the guy's nose. Standing next to him, I poured some liquid soap in my hands and reached into the water for him. The water was warm, and I cleaned his hands. I was getting good at cleaning blood off things.

For a while the only sound was the running water. "Two bar fights in three days," I said. "You should probably chill out."

"I'm sorry," he said, his voice serious. "My temper is obviously something I need to work on."

With my fingers running over his knuckles, I asked, "What did the guy say?"

He shook his head. "Maggie was right. It doesn't matter." He looked angry with himself. "After telling you I'd help you and Jamie get away, I almost blew it by starting a bar brawl."

I rinsed the soap off our hands. "Don't be too hard on yourself. I'm the one who started it. I'm sorry, too."

We dried our hands on a towel. "I'm exhausted. Come on," he said. He took my hand and led me into the living room.

I lay on the couch, and Max sat at my feet. Jamie was careful to leave room for Maggie on the sleeping bag.

Max said, "I'm gonna stay up, at least until Maggie gets back."

My lids heavy from the tequila, I closed my eyes, but sleep didn't come easily. Too much had happened. I kept replaying that girl's warning in my head. If we weren't safe here, then where would we go?

Between that and the fact that we were apparently the only three people in the city of New Orleans trying to go to sleep, I couldn't wind down. Listening to the sounds around me, I wished for a mute button so I could turn them off one by one. That made me think of my favorite childhood book, *Goodnight Moon,* and the nightly ritual my grandmother had performed. She'd read the book, and then we'd say good night to everything in the room. It had always made sleep come, so I tried to channel her, wishing each noise and the day's memory a good night.

Good night, Jamie, sleeping soundly within my reach, and good night to your confession. Good night, Max, our bodyguard, and good night to your temper and your whiskey kiss. Good night, Maggie, sitting on a barstool waiting for your mom. Good night, people pushing and fighting and the music never stopping. Good night, people walking down the street with your too-loud laughs. Good night, artists who do not sleep. Good night, New Orleans.

Chapter 8

It was three days before they found my mom's body. The river's current had carried her downstream for several miles before depositing her on the shore near some dockworkers, who were never able to forget that day. They told the story to anyone who'd listen, their versions eventually making it back to St. Francisville. They told how her nightgown had clung to her still body. They told how her hair had moved in the water like it was alive. They told that she was still beautiful. For three days the townspeople searched for her. Some of them suspected foul play, but not my dad. He said as soon as he saw my grandmother's back door, left wide open, he knew where she'd gone, and he went to the graveyard and waited for them to bring her to him.

Waking up on Oak Street, I was disoriented. How did I get on this couch? For just a second I felt like I'd been washed downstream. Looking around Steven's living room, I saw Max's sleeping bag rolled up tight in the corner, but everyone was gone. I heard music coming from the front porch. My head was pounding—my punishment from the night before.

Luke was sitting on a stool on the front porch, his hands on the guitar doing strange things to my early-morning senses. *They're all liars.* I wrapped a blanket around my shoulders, a gift from someone in the night, and walked out to join him. With my bare feet planted on the splintered wood of the porch, I looked out on a still-sleeping Oak Street as Luke serenaded it. I watched his bare back, so tan it seemed used to no shirt, and how the muscles moved and pulled as he made the notes. He belonged nowhere and to no one, a perpetually homeless, stateless being. His hands were so worn. Maybe that's what happens when you walk away from your life, by your own choice or someone else's. The price of abandonment is wearing out, one piece at a time. That made me think of the people and place I had deserted, and I brought my eyes down to my own hands and wondered when the decay would begin.

I felt a familiar tug in my belly, and I saw Jamie coming down the street, reminding me I'd always belong to someone, to Jamie, my much-needed anchor. He'd keep the decay away. He walked right past Luke, neither one seeming to notice the other.

"Max is out looking for Maggie," he said. "He said she

never came in last night. I told him to give her a little while and she'd be back, but he wanted to go look for her."

I guessed Maggie's mom had never showed up at the bar. Jamie knew, like I did, that Maggie would need time to heal in private. She rarely backslid in her I-don't-care-about-my-mother recovery plan. When she did, it always took her a while to regroup. I knew she'd want to call her dad, her sponsor in her addiction to her mom, so to speak, who was always ready to talk her down and prevent her from going back for more. That stopped me. If she called her dad, he'd know where we were, and Jamie and I wouldn't have a chance to get away. *Please, Maggie, don't call your dad.* If she'd only come back to me, I'd tell her what I had always secretly hoped: that there's nothing wrong with a child being addicted to her mother. It's only a natural craving.

Jamie and I went back inside, and I tried to distract myself by taking care of basic needs, finding Cheerios and almost-bad milk. We sat on the countertops and ate breakfast.

"Max said he'd help us get away," I said.

Jamie stopped chewing and stared at me.

"Us?"

"Always."

We heard the front door open. I put my bowl on the counter and walked into the living room. Max was standing in the doorway. When he moved into the room and shut the door, the sunlight dropped unceremoniously from him. Luke was still playing on the porch, our very own soundtrack, the music slow and lulling.

"No Maggie?" I asked.

"No. I've been looking since before dawn. I don't know where else to try. I was hoping she came back here."

"She will . . . eventually. You look tired." And he did, his face drained and weary from too much worry, too much alcohol, and too much living beyond his eighteen-year-old expectations.

He reached out to take my hand and said, "I'll sleep later. Right now we need to find her."

He pulled on my hand, his body leaning toward the front door, wanting me to join him in his search. I stood my ground, making him look back at me.

"Maggie doesn't want us to find her, not yet."

He frowned.

"Don't worry. She'll be back, but be ready. When she comes back, she'll be angry and looking to take it out on anyone who gets in her way."

Max understood addiction. He looked sad, sadder than he'd looked since leaving St. Francisville, and I wanted to comfort him. For just a second, I wished I was a normal girl in a normal place with the boy she loved. I wanted to take advantage of the sounds coming from the front porch and be bold and pull him into a dance, the slow-moving, spinning kind; we'd dance and smile and he'd see me as spontaneous and Lillian-beautiful. But I was not a normal girl, and this was no normal place.

Jamie came into the living room, and Steven exited his bedroom in nothing but a very short bathrobe, ending our conversation.

"I've got some errands to run today," Steven said. "Y'all just make yourselves comfortable."

I worried about where he might be going. I imagined there were many places in New Orleans with televisions and headlines spilling our secrets by now. He walked by me, headed to the bathroom, and my arm shot out to him. He stopped and looked at me quizzically.

"What kind of errands?" I asked.

His brows went up, and so did Max's behind him.

"I was bored and thought about getting outside for a while today," I said. "I was just wondering where you were going."

"I need to get some more paint supplies. The store's just up the street, and then I was going to visit with a couple of friends down the block. You're more than welcome to join me."

I relaxed and then wasn't sure what to say. "Oh, okay. Maybe . . ."

"I'm gonna grab a shower. You let me know."

"Okay, thanks."

Steven nodded and walked into the bathroom. Max and Jamie immediately came to stand next to me.

"What was that about?" Max whispered.

"Luke told me last night that our photos are everywhere. You know we're on TV. Oak Street seems like the only place that doesn't watch the news."

Jamie asked, "What were we going to do if he said he was leaving the street? Tie him up in the back?"

"Of course not," I said. *Well, maybe—whatever was necessary.*

We entered into a staring contest. Jamie was the first to turn away.

When Steven came out of the bathroom, dressed and ready, I said, "I'm just gonna hang out here and wait for Maggie to get back."

"Okay, try not to get into any trouble," he said. "Well, any *more* trouble." He walked to the front door before turning back to face us. "Just because I don't have a television, doesn't mean I don't hear things," he said. "I knew your story yesterday." He pointed to Jamie. "What you'd done."

Jamie tensed.

Steven laughed. "Relax, sweetie. I'm no rat. I don't want cops at my house." He opened the door, but before he left he said in a singsong voice, "But nothing comes for free."

The screen door bounced off the jamb. We hadn't moved from our spots.

Nothing comes for free.

"We can't stay here," I said. I started pacing.

"We can't leave without Maggie," Max said.

"I know that," I snapped.

"We need time to figure out what to do next," Max said. "Where can we go?"

"My mom's friend Beth. She'll help us."

❧

Maggie finally returned around lunchtime in a very special mood, announcing to the room, "I'm okay. I'm sorry if I worried y'all." She looked right at me. "I didn't do anything stupid."

We were the only ones in the house who were awake. The live-ins were still sleeping.

"Can I use your sleeping bag?" Maggie asked Max. "I feel dead."

"You can't sleep," I said. "We have to get out of here."

"Why?" she asked.

"Luke knows about us, Steven knows, this whole house probably knows."

Her jaw dropped.

Max said, "Steven said he wouldn't call the cops, but then he gave us this cryptic message about nothing being free. I have no idea what his idea of payback is, and I don't want to find out."

"We have to risk it," Maggie said.

"Why?" I asked.

"Because we need my mom. Which sucks for us, because she's a terrible person. But it's true. You guys can't get any-where without good IDs or passports, and I know she'll be able to hook us up. She'll come back here. I know she will. Steven said she's singing at the bar tonight."

I guess we didn't look convinced, because she said, "Trust me, guys. We need her. We have to stay put for now."

She grabbed the sleeping bag and disappeared into one of the rooms down the hall. Max was looking at me like I should go talk to her, but I shook my head.

"We won't be able to change her mind," I said. No one

could convince Maggie that her ideas weren't great. And she was probably right. We probably did need her mom.

"Then we're gonna need money," Max said. "Nobody in the ID business is going to donate their services. What are the chances your mom's friend would give you money?"

"In addition to harboring fugitives? I don't know. Maybe." *If she even knows who I am.* Maybe I could use the letters I'd brought with me as proof I was who I said I was. "It wouldn't hurt to ask her."

"We'll need to find her," said Max. "Any ideas where to start?"

When I told him no, the weariness in his face amplified. He'd taken on the responsibility of keeping everyone safe, and he only truly relaxed when we were together. Maybe that was why he'd gone looking for Maggie. He was trying to keep us all in one place—a task that was becoming increasingly difficult.

I grabbed my bag and opened it. "I have these letters."

I went into the kitchen, and Jamie and Max followed me. I reached inside the bag and pulled out my mom's shoebox, then spilled Beth Hunter's letters out on the table. I laid them from left to right, lining them up so the envelope corners touched. They took up the length of the table. The older ones were yellow and worn, having spent many years in the graveyard before I found them. After all this time I wasn't just going to find Beth Hunter; I was going to convince her to save Jamie and me.

"Beth leaves them at Lillian's grave. I've never actually met her," I admitted.

"The last one came a couple of weeks ago," Jamie said. "It said she was moving to New Orleans."

I leaned against the counter and watched Max as he looked down at the letters, reading the name on all the envelopes. He reached down to pick one up, and I shifted uncomfortably. Up until that moment only three people had ever touched them: me, Jamie, and Beth Hunter. He seemed to sense my discomfort and put it back down.

"She just leaves them at your mom's grave?" he asked. "But she never comes to see you?" He looked from me to Jamie for confirmation.

"She doesn't come see me. I don't think she sees anyone. Her parents moved away a long time ago."

"You said her name is Beth?"

"Yeah, Beth Hunter."

Max frowned. "Why didn't you ever tell me about the letters?"

I shrugged.

"Just another one of your and Jamie's secrets," he said.

"Max," I sighed.

"I'm sorry. I'll stop." He exhaled loudly. "It's just that if you'd told me about the letters, I could've told you that my mom gets letters from her, too. Not this many, though. I found them once."

Jamie and I traded looks. Max's mom was at least nine or ten years older than Beth and Lillian, and I had a hard time imagining how they were connected.

"My mom and Beth's older sister, Marie, were best friends growing up," Max said, as if reading our minds.

147

"Marie spent whole summers at my mom's house. There are a lot of photos of them together. There are pictures of Beth and your mom, too. Apparently Marie was always left to babysit Beth, who was always with your mom, so the four of them spent a lot of time together."

I really wished Steven's kitchen table had some chairs, so I could sit.

Max came around the table to me, tentatively. He lowered his voice. "I found a box a while ago. It was in my parents' bedroom." He looked down at my hands. "After the wreck, my dad started hiding his whiskey from me. He said he didn't want to leave it out and tempt me. Like I was some goddamned addict or something. I told him it wasn't necessary, that I could be around it and not drink. I found his stash in his closet."

I wondered if it was the whiskey bottle from his truck, the one with the worn label. "Why were you looking for it if you didn't need it?"

He didn't answer.

"I kept looking around the room after I found it. I'm not sure why. That's when I found the box. It was under my parents' bed, on my mom's side. The letters were inside. The return addresses were from all over. I didn't read them, but I'm positive Beth's name is on all of them. There was a photo album, too. I looked at that first. My mom came into the room and busted me. I thought she'd be mad, but she wasn't. She just sat down, ignored the bottle, and started looking at photos with me. She got really quiet when she showed me the pictures of your mom. I could tell it made her sad to see them."

His eyes were noticeably softer, like the memories of his mom had taken away some of his earlier fear. It was hard to believe the things he was telling me. In all the time I'd spent at Max's house, his mom had never talked about my mom. Max's mom, the woman whose belt always matched her shoes, was a woman who hid letters and pictures in a box under her bed, like I did. And there were pictures of my mom I hadn't seen. What other parts of my mom were hiding in the other houses of St. Francisville?

Jamie cleared his throat. "So what's the plan? You're going to introduce yourself to Beth and say what?"

"I don't know yet," I said. "Something along the lines of, 'Hey, we've never met, but I'm your dead best friend's daughter, and I need money.'"

"That should do it." He came to the table and picked up a letter. "I'm sure she's seen the news. What if she turns us in?"

"Then it's over."

I found the last letter and reread it, hoping for some clues as to where in New Orleans she might be. She mentioned she was going to try to get a job at this restaurant she and Lillian had once visited when they were in high school, a place called the P.M. Café.

Max, who was reading the letter over my shoulder, said, "That's on Napoleon Avenue. I passed it when I was out looking for Maggie. We'll start there."

Just like that, we had a plan and a new direction.

I had butterflies in my stomach. I wished I was going to see Beth without needing something from her.

Max walked out of the room and came back in with a couple of baseball caps. He handed one to Jamie. "Steven won't miss them."

They pulled the bills down low over their foreheads. I grabbed sunglasses from my bag and put them on.

The walk to the trolley was silent. I kept my head down. As soon as we rounded the corner, I saw the trolley stop. I started walking faster, but Max reached for my hand and jerked me back to him. Jamie's eyes went round at something, and he turned and sat on a bench, his head down. I looked up at Max and his mouth was on mine. The kiss was desperate, and it scared me. His hands were on my face. He pulled his mouth away but kept his face close.

"There's a cop over there," he whispered.

My body immediately tensed.

Max's eyes bored into mine. "Don't move."

I started to say something.

"Shh," he said.

His lips touched mine again, and I closed my eyes, tears coming because this was it. Max felt them on his hands and wiped them away, trailing his fingers across my face.

"Shh. It's okay," he lied.

One kiss, two kisses, three.

He brought his hands down and looked over my shoulder. His lips at my ear, he whispered, "He's walking around the corner. He's almost gone."

Max straightened up and cupped my face, his thumb

wiping at another tear. "He's gone. Let's go." He grabbed my hand and pulled me to the trolley stop, Jamie following. We paid with money we'd swiped from Steven's house and took seats in the back. Now I was desperate.

I caught Jamie's eyes, and they looked old, like the sight of the cop had aged them. Old eyes in a young face, like the girl from last night.

Two trolley stops later my heartbeat still hadn't slowed. Beth Hunter had to help us.

When we got off at Napoleon Avenue, I was shaking. Jamie grabbed my hand, holding it still.

"If you're going to Greece, you better start packing now," he said.

It was a line from a seventh-grade play neither of us had been good enough to be cast in. In other words, a big thing was about to happen, and I'd better be ready. We ran the lines from time to time when the situation fit, or when something needed to be said but we didn't know what it should be.

Jamie looked at me expectantly, waiting for me to respond with my line. I knew he was trying to distract me, keeping my mind off cops and my fast-beating heart.

"There's too much I want to take," I said. "How do you fit everything you want to bring?"

Jamie looked both ways and pulled me across the street. "You don't bring everything, only what you really need."

"What do I really need?"

I was feeling better, less desperate.

He looked me in the eyes. "Me."

151

"Will I love it?"

"You will," he said. "The water is a blue you've never seen in real life."

Max walked quietly behind us, watching the play.

The café was easy to spot. My mom had a matchbook from this place in her shoebox. I was surprised it was still here after all this time. We stood across the street from it. It had outdoor seating, but all the seats were empty.

"I see people inside," Max said.

We crossed the street as the front door opened. A couple of men came out, and one held the door open for us. The place was empty, and the bartender looked at us expectantly.

"We just closed the lunch shift. We won't open back up until five o'clock," he said.

"That's all right," Max said. "We're actually not here to eat. We're looking for someone."

I removed my sunglasses, and we walked up to the bar.

"Oh yeah?" the bartender asked.

"I'm looking for my mom's friend," I said. "She just moved to New Orleans. She mentioned she was going to try to get a job here."

"Who's your mom's friend?" he asked.

"Beth Hunter."

"Yeah, Beth started here a few days ago. She's not working tonight, though."

"Do you know where she lives?" I asked. "We're only in town for the day, and I was really hoping to see her."

He looked suspicious of us and leaned across the bar,

coming closer to me. "Why don't you know where she lives?"

"She never told my mom where she was staying. I just thought since we were here . . . but it's no big deal. Sorry to bother you."

We turned from the bar.

"Wait," the bartender said. He looked conflicted, like he was trying to decide whether we were dangerous. That was the million-dollar question.

"She's subletting an apartment. It's about five blocks down on the left. It's an old walk-up with a wrought-iron gate. I don't know the apartment number."

"Thanks," I said.

∾

Someone was coming out of the apartment building just as we walked up, and he held the door for us to walk through. I found Beth's name on a mailbox by the door. Her apartment was 3C. Max took off in the direction of the stairs, but I stopped him.

"Wait," I said. "I need to do this alone."

His brow furrowed.

"I need to be alone the first time I meet her."

I couldn't explain it, and they didn't make me try.

"Okay. We'll wait here."

Jamie said, "Look at you, going to meet Beth Hunter." He grinned, proud of me.

Beth was the biggest clue to who my mom was. She'd never fit inside my box. The excitement was back, like my mom might be just around the corner. If only I walked fast enough, I'd catch her.

As I stood outside Beth's door, the million reasons not to knock ran on a loop in my head. She might not understand. She might not be home. She might call the cops. But the door opened, and just like that the girl from my mom's walls was suddenly standing in front of me.

There was no breathing, only stares. I could tell she recognized me. I was sure *Lillian* would be the first name she said. But instead she said, "Olivia."

I didn't move.

"Olivia?" she repeated.

I nodded. Yes, I was Olivia.

Chapter 9

Sitting on her couch, Beth Hunter and I stared at each other. Whenever she moved or shifted in her seat, it was alarming at first, because all my life she'd been sitting still in photos. It seemed like any minute now my mom might walk out of the kitchen and sit down to join us.

I decided Beth hadn't changed all that much since the pictures in my mom's bedroom were taken. Her hair was shorter and not as shiny but still blond. Her face was basically the same, only slightly more lined.

"Would you like something to drink? I have iced tea," she said.

"No, thank you," I said. I wondered if I sounded like Lillian to her, too.

"What brings you here?" she asked. She looked nervous.

I wanted to say, "Dead moms, dead dads, and old

letters," but instead said, "I'm in trouble." I hadn't planned on blurting it out like that, but there it was.

"I know," she said. "You're all over the news. The police know you're in New Orleans. They found your friend's truck."

"Jamie—" I stopped myself, terrified to spill my secrets to someone I might not be able to trust. "He's my best friend," I continued. "He didn't . . . he's not . . ." I exhaled loudly. "He's good. It's not murder. Not really. There are things no one knows."

Beth put her hands on mine. "I know Tom Benton. Well, I knew him." She didn't say anything else, but her look said she knew exactly what kind of man he'd become. "But, Olivia, you're an accessory after the fact. Do you realize how much trouble you're in?"

"That's why we've got to get away. Jamie can't go back home, ever, and I can't leave him. I won't. We need help. I'm sorry to just show up here, but we don't have a lot of options. You and my mom were friends, best friends, so I thought maybe you'd help me. It's not safe where we're staying. We're not safe."

Beth stood and went to her window. Looking out of it, she said, "How can I help you? What do you need?"

I felt bad, but I said, "Money. My friend Maggie thinks her mom might know someone who can get us fake passports, but we'll have to pay him. I don't even know how much he'll charge, but we don't have anything. And if we can just spend a night or two here, just enough time to make a plan."

Silence followed, and I shifted in my seat.

"Wait here," she said.

She disappeared down the hall. I worried she was calling the police. There was a calendar pinned to the wall next to her desk. We'd been gone less than a week. It had taken just a few days for life to flop on its head and become unrecognizable. Time continued to move forward in its day-to-day way, one day closer to whatever was next for Jamie and me—one day closer to my eighteenth birthday, I realized.

Beth returned to the living room, her arms full of a huge photo album. She sat next to me and opened the album to a picture in the middle. She pointed to it and said, "This was the last time I saw you."

It was a photo of my mom sitting up in a hospital bed. In her arms was a baby wrapped in a pale pink blanket. My mom wasn't looking into the camera but into the baby's face, and she was smiling. Beth showed me the picture with no hesitation and no warning, like I was used to seeing such things. She seemed unaware that she had just shown me the only proof I had ever had that my mom once looked at me.

I didn't move or breathe, only stared at the picture of the two of us. My mom's face was pale and tired, but happy, too. My fingers went to it, to the smile on her face.

"You've never seen this picture before? I know your dad has a copy, or at least he did," she whispered.

I shook my head; I couldn't take my eyes off it. I had only shared three days with my mom. The time we spent together, the space we shared, my crib in the corner right next to her bed. What if it was the sound of me breathing that sent her into the water?

"She wouldn't let anyone else hold you that first day. She just stared at you and kept saying how perfect you were. She told me that she'd been staring at your face for so long that she could see it even when she closed her eyes." She smiled a sad smile at me.

"If she thought I was so perfect, then why did she leave me?" My voice was a small squeak, and I hated it.

"I don't know. If she loved me like I loved her, then why did she leave *me*? Why did she leave your dad or Ms. Josephine? Some things we're not supposed to understand."

She touched the photo again.

"This was also the last time I saw her. Last times are funny things, because you rarely know it's a last time until it's too late. I was going to come see both of you again once you were released from the hospital, but your first day home I was scrambling around trying to get packed. I was leaving for college the next week. I called and asked to speak to your mom, but Ms. Josephine said she was sleeping, so I told her to tell Lillian I'd come by the next day." She went quiet, because we both knew there was no next day for my mom.

She flipped the pages in the photo album. It was full of the two of them and St. Francisville. Most of them were the same ones my mom had on her bedroom walls. She reached out to touch some of them.

"Everyone who knew your mom fell in love with her. That was her true gift. If you spent even a little time with

158

her, you loved her and wanted good things for her. When she died, the whole town was devastated. Everyone came to her funeral."

She looked from the pictures to me. "It's strange, the things you remember. From the funeral, I remember how quiet everyone was. With that many people there, you'd think there'd be noise, but there was no noise, only the sound of the preacher talking."

Since she'd said the last time she saw me was at the hospital, I asked, "Wasn't I at the funeral?"

"Ms. Josephine didn't think it was any place for a newborn. Her friend Mrs. Cavalier kept you at her house."

I looked back at the photos and turned to the last page in the album. In the center of the page was a picture of Lillian as a little girl. She was sitting on a stone bench with a woman who, on closer inspection, I recognized as my grandmother. They were in my grandmother's backyard, back when it wasn't sad.

"This is my favorite picture of her," she said. "Ms. Josephine gave me a copy. Lillian was seven."

In the photo my grandmother's hair was down, something I'd never seen in real life. The wind must have been blowing, because their hair had wrapped and laced together. My grandmother was looking into my mom's face and smiling the smile mothers reserve for their daughters.

"This is my favorite picture, too," I said.

Beth pulled it out of its sleeve, then turned to the photo of me and my mom in the hospital and did the same. She handed them to me. "You should have these."

I was too desperate for them to disagree with her.

I held them gingerly. "Were you surprised she did it?" I asked.

"I was devastated, but I wasn't surprised."

"Why weren't you surprised?" I tried to rein myself in.

"No one who really knew Lillian was surprised."

She looked down at her lap, and then back up at me, like she wasn't going to offer anything more.

"I've never known anyone, before or since, who felt things the way your mom did. She absorbed too much, you know?"

I had no idea.

"She couldn't shake things off. Your grandmother monitored how much news she'd let Lillian watch, because a sad story might keep her in bed for two days. I once opened the newspaper at your grandmother's house and sections of it had been cut out, the parts Ms. Josephine was scared to let your mom read.

"But when she was happy, she was electric. I'm not saying that flippantly. I felt electricity when I was near her. She could shock you with her energy. It made up for all the bad times. I'm pretty sure she was bipolar, but we didn't know that then. There was so much we didn't know."

"What else didn't you know?"

"How tired she was. How much she was hurting. She tried to tell us."

"How?"

"There were days when she wouldn't get out of bed, when she'd stop talking. For days she wouldn't talk. And during the good times, she'd be so reckless with her life. She never knew how important she was."

"But you did," I said. "I have your letters. The ones you left at her grave." I pulled out the shoebox and opened it. I laid a handful of the envelopes between us.

Beth's fingers went to them, but she didn't pick one up. She stared at them for a long while and then said, "So that's where they went. I thought maybe it was your dad, or your grandmother, or the wind. I never imagined it was you."

I wanted to tell her that neither my grandmother nor my dad ever went to the grave, but decided that might make her sad.

"I've read them." I looked at her apologetically. "I couldn't *not* read them. They're how I found you, actually. The last letter . . ." My voice trailed off.

She nodded, like now she understood. "The hardest part was not being able to talk to her. So I wrote letters. It was the best I could do. We made all these plans, your mom and me. I made her write a list of all the things she wanted to do, so she could look at it when she was sad. I guess I hoped it would be an incentive for her to get better. I have my own copy."

"I thought it was your list, too. I thought you made it together."

"No, it was just hers. I have my own list. I've been working on both of them for a while now."

"My mom's list is hanging on her bedroom wall."

"It's still there?" Beth asked.

I nodded. Everything was still there.

161

"All the signs she gave us, and we didn't do enough. There's a price for something like that."

I thought about the cost. My dad's happiness; my grandmother's sanity; the rest of Beth's life, which she'd given over to working through my mom's list.

"I'm sorry I didn't come see you," Beth said. "It was painful to even go back to that town, but to walk back into Lillian's house . . . I couldn't do it."

"Did you ever see my dad?" I asked.

"No. After Lillian died, something in him did, too. Looking at him was hard after that. We kept in touch, though. Somewhat. We talk sometimes. I always make sure he knows where I am." She touched my knee. "I told myself you both were okay, that at least you had each other."

"Not really," I said.

She cleared her throat. She had noticed Lillian's necklace, and she went still. Then she met my eyes. "I gave that to her," she whispered. "I got it from one of those street festivals, for her seventeenth birthday. She loved anything with her name on it. You would've thought I'd given her diamonds. She wore it every day.

"I looked for it, after she died." She exhaled loudly. "Ms. Josephine called me the day before the funeral. She wanted me to come over and pick out something for Lillian to wear. She said she knew Lillian wouldn't want to be buried wearing anything her mother had chosen. I thought Lillian would want to wear the necklace, but I never found it."

"I'm sorry," I said. *For so much—your picking out your*

162

best friend's forever outfit at the top of my list. "It was in her box." I motioned to the shoebox in my lap. "It was under her bed. These are her mementos."

Beth looked down at the box. "Do you mind?" she asked.

"No." I put the box in her lap.

She fingered through the items, slowly, one by one. She picked up a movie ticket stub and grinned. "We got kicked out of the theater for smoking in the back row."

I widened my eyes in surprise.

"We were the only ones in the theater," she explained. "Who was it going to hurt?"

I laughed, and so did she. She put the ticket stub back and picked up the ski-lift ticket, looking closely at my mom's picture. "We had no business on snow skis. We almost died that first day." Her smile got bigger. "We dropped out of ski school after a couple of hours. That was our first mistake. Lillian was convinced that since we could water-ski, snow and a mountain wouldn't be a problem. One has very little to do with the other, by the way, but you couldn't talk her out of something once she got the idea.

"Our next mistake was deciding to forgo the bunny slopes because we wanted a real rush. We ended up walking down that mountain carrying our skis. There are pictures somewhere."

She put down the lift ticket and perused the other items in the box. She touched everything. Picking up my dad's class ring, she said, "I remember the day he gave this to her." Beth slid it on her finger. "She loved him so much."

I soaked up her comments, each word a gift. I wanted

her to keep picking up different things from the box and tell me something else I didn't know about my mom.

She laughed and picked up a piece of paper. It was folded in four and had the words *Top Ten* written on it. "I can't believe she kept one of these."

Unfolding the paper, she looked at me with a smirk. "Okay, so Lillian had this thing where she ranked everything. She'd leave top-ten lists everywhere. And they were ridiculous: top ten reasons not to marry a farmer, top ten reasons to drink Strawberry Hill before football games, things like that."

We laughed. She looked down at the paper, and her smile died. I read the words on top of the page, words I'd read over and over again: "Top ten reasons never to leave St. Francisville."

I watched her face as she read it. "I guess you've read this," she said.

I could recite it. Lillian listed all the things she loved about the town, like my tree and the cemetery. Numbers two and three on her list were names, Beth Hunter and my dad. Her number one reason: *The world is too big.*

Beth folded the list and put it back in the box. She put the lid on it and gave it back to me. There were tears in her eyes, and I felt hot.

"I want to help you," she said, her voice thick. She wiped her eyes. "But as much as I'd like you to stay here, I don't think it's a good idea. If your dad comes to New Orleans, this'll be the first place he'll come."

"You don't know him anymore," I said. "He won't come to New Orleans."

"I disagree."

My face fell.

"But I have some money saved. You can have it."

"I don't want to take your savings. I wish I didn't need . . . I wanted to come see you anyway. I've wanted to see you for a long time. It's just, me and Jamie . . ."

She touched my knee again. "I'm glad you came. I want to do this. Besides, it's on her list: help someone who really needs it."

Number eighty-two.

"Thank you," I said.

"I have almost five thousand dollars saved."

My eyes went round at that number.

"You'll need it," Beth said. "Who knows how much this guy's gonna charge? And then you'll need money to get around. Can you trust this guy?"

Could we trust a friend of Vicky's? Probably not. "I don't know."

"If you get caught . . ."

"I won't tell anyone you helped us."

"Of course not," she said. "I can't get the money until tomorrow. The café on Napoleon, can you meet me there tomorrow afternoon, around two?"

"Yes."

I was desperate to spend more time with Beth. I wanted to play twenty questions, like I did with my dad, but I thought about Jamie and Max in the lobby of the building like sitting ducks.

Beth stood up.

I guessed it was time to go. She walked me to the front door.

"It's going be you that meets me tomorrow and not the police?" I asked.

"It'll be me."

"Thank you for the pictures, and for everything."

"You're welcome, Olivia."

She looked like she wanted to hug me, but instead she reached for my hands.

"All my life I was worried it was me," I said. "That her life was perfect until me."

She squeezed my fingers hard, too hard.

"It wasn't you."

My fingertips pulsed.

Max and Jamie were sitting in the hall outside her door. "People were looking at us funny, just hanging out in the foyer," Max said.

Jamie stood. "I heard you laughing. Did it go okay?"

"She's gonna help us," I said, massaging my fingers.

"Are you okay?" Jamie asked. "You look weird."

I was drunk on her memories and words. "Yeah, I'm fine. She's going to give us money, a lot of money. But we can't stay the night here. They found the truck and everyone knows we're in New Orleans. She's afraid my dad might come to see her. She said to meet her at the café tomorrow at two."

"Can we trust her?" Max asked.

"We can trust her. She's doing it as a favor to my mom."

The look on Max's face said he wasn't sure, but he said, "Good. Let's go."

Once we were back on the street, Jamie fell in step with me.

"She's just like we imagined," I said. "I showed her the box, and she told me some really funny stories. She gave me these." I reached into my bag and pulled out the pictures.

Jamie took them. "Wow. Look how tiny you were. . . . Is this your grandmother?"

"Yes."

"She was beautiful." He handed them back to me, then dipped his head to me and whispered, "Did you find your mom?"

"No, but I'm getting closer."

It wasn't you.

When we got back to Steven's, Jamie took a seat on the front porch swing. I went to join him, but Max reached out, stopping me. He leaned down, and his lips brushed my ear and I stayed still, listening, but he didn't say anything. His face was so close that I closed my eyes, but that didn't matter because I could still see him. Suddenly, the weight of what Max wasn't saying hit me in the chest: *Don't go with him. Stay with me.* I felt like I was losing my way to the swing, and if I didn't move now, I might never get there. I gently pulled away from Max and walked to Jamie, sitting down to take my seat next to him. I turned my hand over, palm up, and Jamie slid his hand home to me.

Chapter 10

Vicky Harrington walked up the steps to Steven's front porch, looking at me like she knew me but couldn't quite remember how or where from. Max looked from me to Jamie, figuring out who she must be from our expressions. It had been three years since Maggie last saw her mom, but it had been much longer for me. We were all still in elementary school. Maybe that was why I had such a hard time making the person from my memories be this woman standing in front of me. She looked so much like Maggie, the same height and the same eyes, but whereas Maggie's petiteness was endearing and then easily forgotten because of her magnified personality, Vicky Harrington looked like a dying child. It seemed possible that Vicky was working harder on her drug addiction than her singing. She gave me a smile when she finally placed me, but it was a fearful one. She moved past us to the front door.

Maggie was still napping in one of the bedrooms, but no one could sleep through the happy noises that came from Steven when he saw Vicky standing in his living room. Maggie came down the hall and stopped when she saw her mom. It was easy to see from her expression that her mom didn't look like she had three years ago, and not for the first time I wondered what it was like to have a mother with a changing face.

Steven, oblivious to any tension in the room, took Maggie's hand and then grabbed Vicky's, and then he twirled them around in a ring-around-the-rosy kind of way, not noticing that he was the only one smiling. After a few twirls he caught on and stopped. Vicky kept up the momentum, though, spinning around the room in slow motion, taking in all our faces. It was easy to see she was able to place everyone in the context of Maggie. She began dispensing pleasantries.

"This is a surprise." She reached out and touched Maggie's arm. "Look at you. Wow." She turned to me. "You look so much like your mother. You even scared me a little bit on the porch." Looking at Jamie, she said, "I bet you're still as sweet as ever, and, Max Barrow . . . You've grown up really nice. I can't believe you're all here."

"They're here to see you, sweet Vicky," Steven said, wrapping his arm around her and giving me a wink before leaving the room.

She looked around, and her face dropped, like she was sad there was no one else to be surprised to see. Then she perked up. "I'm singing across the street tonight. I don't really have a band at the moment, but the group that's playing lets me sing a couple of songs. Y'all should come check it out."

We all nodded politely, and then a long stretch of silence laid itself out. Vicky looked back at Maggie and said, "Are you still singing?"

Maggie nodded.

Her mother ventured, "We could do a duet."

The way she said it, childlike and hopeful, made my eyes tear up. Maggie nodded again, and then a silent but unanimous decision was made by the rest of us to exit to the porch, leaving Maggie alone with her mom.

I was the last one out. Reaching back to close the front door, I saw Maggie becoming a child again with Vicky standing in the room, her face losing its bravado and growing younger minute by minute. When the door clicked shut, I was envious of Maggie, because she was getting her face-to-face fix.

It felt awkward with the three of us standing on the porch together, so I suggested to Jamie and Max that we take a walk. It was completely dark now, and there were only a few people on the street. We came to a section of the sidewalk where some homeless people were sleeping and had to go around them. I imagined the homeless people in New Orleans were very different from the ones in other cities. We were likely stepping around poets, artists, and musicians, who had all left wherever they were from to come to this city. I liked to imagine it wasn't so they could make it but so they could be near each other.

We walked several blocks, looking into the store windows, no one saying anything. We stopped at an antique shop and looked at all the stuff: a mirrored table, a silver tray, a hairbrush. If I didn't know better, I'd have thought it was all taken from my grandmother's bedroom. I closed my eyes and saw her face. It wasn't the one she had when I left, but a new one, an older one. Her wrinkles were deeper, the lines sagging around her eyes, their color dulled. We had aged her even more, first Lillian and then me.

I wondered how Maggie was doing with her mom. I wondered if she'd asked her about the guy who could get us passports, and then I felt guilty, because they had so much other stuff to talk about. But she'd have to get around to it. We hadn't talked about what she should tell her mom we needed new identification for, and I hoped Maggie could come up with something believable.

It was probably wrong to leave all that up to Maggie, but I knew she wanted some time alone with her mom. Then the truth hit me, the way it does sometimes, and I opened my eyes to the realization that sometimes what we want is not what we need, and maybe the last thing Maggie needed was to be left alone with a mother like Vicky.

I felt like my heart had caught on fire. Without explaining, I turned away from the shop and ran back to Steven's house. Jamie and Max followed.

We found Maggie sitting on the couch alone. She was the fourteen-year-old version of herself, and she was crying. All my life, I had never seen her cry. I'd always believed

172

having a part-time mom was better than having no mom at all, but seeing Maggie now, I thought it was probably better to lose your mother all at once.

"What happened?" Jamie asked.

"Where's your mom?" I asked.

Maggie didn't say anything. I sat down next to her on the couch. Maggie fell into me, her arms around my shoulders, her face pressing into my neck, her tears falling onto me, but she made no sound. There was no wailing to make up for all the crying she had never done, only voiceless tears.

I could tell when Maggie's emotions switched, her body tensing and the heat in it rising. I could tell when she stopped being sad.

"We talked for a little while. She asked when school started. She even asked about my dad. Then this guy came in and they went to the back room. I'm pretty sure he was her dealer." She looked down at her lap, and the heat in her body rose so high it burned my skin where we were still connected at the knees. The heat dried up her tears from the inside.

"She told me to wait right here for her, and even though I knew who he was and what she was going to do, I just sat down and said, 'Yes, ma'am.'"

Maggie stood up now, disconnecting from my body, leaving me cold. She walked toward the back room, and we got in line behind her like dominoes. I could hear Luke playing his guitar in his room, the music seeping out from under the door, dark and sad.

Maggie went inside, and we followed. Vicky and a man

were sitting at the table in the middle of the room. The man looked like what I thought a drug dealer would—the kind of person who always seemed dirty, no matter how clean they were.

I wasn't exactly sure of everything I was looking at on the table, but I recognized the needle. Vicky stood up, looking shocked, and backed away from the table as if distance would convince her daughter there was no wrongdoing. Maggie looked from her mom to this man, back and forth. I expected her to beat him and scream at him, or scream at her mom—something loud. Instead, she walked to the table and sat down. She was so calm it terrified me. She put her hands on the table. She turned over her arms, laying her veins open to the man, and said, "Make me understand."

The burning in my heart started again. All eyes fixed on the two people in the center of the room. I looked at Vicky, waiting for her motherly instincts to kick in, but she just stood there and stared, as if waiting for Maggie to cross over to her side. I looked back at the door, hoping Steven would burst in and say, "No, this one's a baby," rescuing us all, but there were no interruptions. The man looked at Maggie and shrugged, like it didn't matter to him who sat across from him. He reached out to touch her arm, stroking it from the crook of her elbow to her wrist, up and down, over and over. The man's thumb pressed in at the crease of Maggie's elbow, and I swear I felt it. My hand went to my own arm.

Max and Jamie stood on either side of me, and even

though our feet were planted side by side, Max's body leaned forward at the same time as Jamie's leaned back. Through the wall, Luke's music picked up speed, and my breath did the same. When the needle touched Maggie's skin, the fire in my chest moved upward, burning my face. I kept waiting for the heat to thaw me so I could move and do something, so I could stop Maggie from proving her point. Yet I could only watch and wonder if we'd lose her as soon as the drug entered her veins, or if the loss would be gradual.

The room came alive when Maggie grabbed the needle and threw it at her mom.

"Fuck you!" she screamed at Vicky. She jumped up from the table, knocking the chair back. "Fuck. You."

It was a test, and her mom had failed. Vicky ran out of the room. The dealer picked up his needle and followed her. The four of us looked at each other, breathing hard, like we'd just come to the end of a race.

There was so much sorrow in Maggie's eyes. They filled again, tears spilling down her cheeks. The sight of them made me feel a hundred and two years old. I reached out to her, my hand going to her arm. I rubbed the dot of blood away from the place where the needle had pricked her.

"I'm sorry," she whispered before going out the door.

I looked at Jamie, his eyes too big in his face. I had to get him out of this place. I had to get him somewhere where it was safer to be lost, but Maggie needed us first.

I followed her down the hall. "Where are you going?"

She turned and looked at me once she got to the front door. "I'm going to sing."

I left Max and a too-quiet Jamie sitting on the swing on Steven's front porch and walked over to the Maple Leaf. Sneaking in the back door, I was worried I'd be recognized as one of the troublemakers from the night before, but no one seemed to notice me. As promised, Maggie was already standing in the center of the stage, forgetting about the duet and taking her mom's spot completely. Vicky sat on the same barstool that Maggie had sat on the night before, and watched her daughter. I made my way over to Vicky. The band began to play, not seeming to care who was there. For just a second Maggie didn't move, only looked at her mom. Then she leaned in to the microphone and opened her voice to the crowd.

When the song was finished, there was clapping and whistling, noises that always followed Maggie's performances. I looked back at Vicky to see her staring wide-eyed at her daughter. Anybody could see the pride in her eyes. Maggie wasn't looking in her mom's direction but instead into the crowd and at the band members, who were asking her to sing one more. She complied.

Once she was finished, she hopped down off the stage and walked over to me and Vicky, leaving her new fans disappointed. Her mom looked scared, even leaning back on her stool as Maggie approached.

"You used to know a guy who could get fake IDs, right?" she said. "I need a couple."

Vicky seemed shocked that this was what Maggie wanted to talk about. "My friend Louis, he does good ones," she said. Her voice was small, like she was the child now.

"Can he do passports?" Maggie asked.

Vicky's eyes went round. "Yeah. They're expensive, though."

"How much?"

"I think they run a grand apiece. Maybe more."

Maggie looked at me, and I nodded.

"We want 'em."

Vicky looked from Maggie to me and back again. "Who are they for? Are you in trouble?"

"That's not something you need to worry about, and let's not pretend you really care."

Vicky was quiet for a long moment. "He'll need to meet you. He decides who he works with."

"Can you set it up?"

"Yeah. I'll come by Steven's tomorrow evening and tell you when and where."

"Sounds good." Maggie grabbed my hand and pulled me off the barstool. "Let's go."

"Wait," Vicky said. "We could still do the duet."

Maggie went stiff. "I don't *ever* want to sing with you."

We left the bar, Maggie still holding my hand. Hers was shaking, and I squeezed it.

Jamie and Max were still sitting on the swing. The two boys scooted over, making room for Maggie and me. With all four of us on the swing, it was reminiscent of being crammed in Max's truck, and I wished we could go back to that small world, when I thought there was a way out for all of us.

The music from the bar carried across the street to us. The voice was haunting, and Maggie turned her head to it.

I stood and faced Max. "Dance with me," I said.

And he did.

The wood creaked under our feet, harmonizing with our movements. Max looked into my eyes and whispered, "You're beautiful."

I loved this boy. Seconds ticked by. I felt my heartbeat in my ears, and my lips twitched to tell him.

Instead of making declarations, I whispered back, "So are you."

He smiled and brought his lips to mine, a soft kiss, and I didn't mind that Jamie and Maggie saw.

"I'll miss you," he said, his voice quiet.

"I'll miss you, too."

A lump formed in my throat, and I swallowed around it. I looked back at Jamie and saw that his eyes were on Maggie, and they were sad. He pulled her down to him so her head rested in his lap. She closed her eyes as she hummed along with the song playing across the street. I recognized her mom's voice. Jamie rubbed his hand over the crook in Maggie's arm where the needle had stuck her, slowly, over and over, like he could wipe it all away.

I looked back to the bar as Vicky hit a high note. Her voice hadn't changed all that much from how I remembered it a long time ago, back when she was singing in St. Francisville. My dad had always made a point to see her sing. He said voices like that were rare. He never missed a show.

Parents were curious things. For the first time since leaving home, I missed my dad. I'd always held so tight to my resentment of the choices he'd made, but looking into Max's eyes, I felt some of it loosen. My dad was only Max's age when my mom killed herself. He wasn't the grown man I imagined him to be in all the stories he told me about him and my mom. He was a boy's size and a boy's age.

The wind picked up and tried to blow my thoughts around, but they stayed wrapped up in a small town and my dad's eighteen-year-old face. I squeezed Max tight. My dad went to the cemetery the night my mom went missing from her room. He spent days there, waiting for her. He didn't go back home until the day after the funeral, spending Lillian's first night in the graveyard with her.

Max squeezed me back and asked, "Are you okay?"

I didn't answer him. My dad once told me a secret. He said the hardest thing he ever did was walk away from the cemetery and leave her there. Maybe that's why he never went to the graveyard with me. Maybe he was afraid that if he did, he wouldn't be able to leave her again. My body went still, only my hair moving in the wind, like it was alive. With Max's question hanging in the air, I wondered where my dad was waiting for me.

Chapter 11

I always believed there was a heaven and a hell, but when I was a little girl I didn't think my mom was in either of those places. I imagined her spirit floating above her tombstone, caught in the leaves of the oak trees. I spent much of my childhood in the graveyard on the off chance she could see me. Jamie and I spent countless days playing among the trees, hiding behind tombstones, treating the cemetery like our very own backyard. I'd walk the rows as my mom had and tell Jamie the stories my dad had shared with me, even showing him the tombstone where she found my name. Some of my earliest memories are of tiny fingers tracing the letters carved into the marble and wondering what my own tombstone would look like someday. You might think that morbid, but for me, the daughter of Lillian Matthews, it was normal. What other thoughts could a child who spent hours playing in the presence of a ghost be expected to have?

There were moments when I didn't feel like playing, lonesome moments when I craved closeness to her. It was times like these that Jamie had looked at me and said, "I'll run away with you," a phrase we traded when things in our lives got scary or sad.

❧

Later that night all four of us were lying on the king-sized bed in Luke's room. We'd been upgraded, Steven's only explanation as he moved our bags into the room being "Luke left. He's not coming back."

We exiled ourselves there and began a marathon of sitting and staring, the day's events too much to digest. The bedroom door was open, and Steven walked by every once in a while. He looked in on us each time, and each time he frowned when he saw we hadn't moved from where we sat, our backs warming the headboard.

The need for sleep came, but we tried to fight it, too scared to close our eyes on this day.

Maggie was the first to succumb, her body sliding down to rest between Max and me before she turned on her side to sleep. Max looked like he was prepared to wait out the night, always the bodyguard, but as more time passed, sleep won and he closed his eyes. Jamie went next.

Our bodies were tangled and overlapping, legs over legs,

arms wrapped over arms, stomachs, hips, and sleeping faces warm and almost touching. I lay still, appreciating it, and listened to the sounds of our breathing. I smiled at the sound of Maggie's; even her sleeping breaths were musical.

Eventually I allowed the soft, sleeping rhythm of our bodies to close my eyes, and I wondered how I'd ever sleep without them.

I'm not sure how much time passed before my eyes opened. I untangled my legs from the group and crawled from the bed. I was instantly lonesome. Cold, uncomfortable, anxious feelings crept in now that I was no longer connected to them.

Jamie shifted on the bed, and I saw that he was awake.

"Can I see something?" I asked.

He nodded, and I went to him. My hands went to his hair, soft and dirty blond. I watched it slip between my fingers. The color had changed over the years, growing darker over time. When we were little, it was the kind of blond you could practically see through. I smoothed his hair back to reveal the baby-fine hairs at his hairline. I wanted to see if they were still white blond, proof that the little boy I remembered was still inside him. They were. I closed my eyes to the feeling and the memories that came with it, the two of us together, always together. When I dropped my gaze back to Jamie, his eyes were on me. I saw the silent request in them, but I shook my head.

"You have to leave me," he said. "You have to take the deal. Go back home, back to your life."

Jamie, whose hands fit mine and breaths matched mine,

and who had always been mine, hoped there was a way I could exist without him. My eyes filled, and I shook my head again. I dislodged a tear, and it fell onto my face. I didn't wipe it off.

The boy who always knew how to pick his words said, "I had dreams for us. They didn't look like this."

He got up and walked out of the room. I followed him to the sidewalk in front of Steven's house.

"I know your dream for me," I said. A future with choices, and a future that allowed me to go home, to the place I loved, back to my grandmother, my dad, my mom's grave, and my tree, not to mention Max. I wanted those things, too, but not at the cost of losing Jamie. "It's not too much to give up."

"Yes, it is. You can't give everything up for me."

"They're all better off without me—my grandmother, my dad, everybody in St. Francisville. If I don't go home, everybody can stop being reminded of the girl they couldn't save, and my grandmother can keep waiting for Lillian to come home."

I convinced myself the waiting wouldn't kill her, and imagined I was even proud of myself, that I'd given her that hope that her daughter was just away on a trip but would be home someday.

"What about your dad?" Jamie asked.

"My dad can stop feeling guilty for me coming in second to his grief. It's not too much to give up."

"I don't believe you," he said.

Now Jamie thought I was a liar, too.

There was a long silence. "Are we not supposed to talk about Max?" he asked.

"Max understands," I lied.

"Yeah, right. You can't do this for me."

In his eyes was only his dream for me.

"Do you want to go alone?" I asked.

"Go where? We don't even know where we'll go."

"We'll take a bus across Texas. We'll cross into Mexico."

I didn't flinch as I said it, like I'd made this plan a long time ago. We'd find a place with people who didn't see drowned mothers or drunken fathers when they looked at us.

"Remember when we were little and your mom bought you that cat?" I asked. "It followed you around like a dog, and my grandmother wouldn't let me play with you, because Lillian was allergic to cats."

Knowing where I was going with this, he started shaking his head. "Of course I remember, but—"

"You gave that cat away. It made your mom so mad, but you didn't care."

"I gave a *cat* away! Not my life. No matter how screwed up they are, you can't give up your family for me."

"How many black eyes and busted lips have you gotten for me?"

"I don't know," he said.

"I don't, either. I've lost count. How many times did you correct my grandmother when she called me Lillian in front of you?" I asked.

"I don't know."

"Every time. You corrected her *every* time. How many times did my dad do that?"

"I don't know, Olivia."

"Never. Not once. For a long time you were the only one who called me by my name. My dad barely spoke to me. It was just you and me on Fidelity Street. You are my family."

He exhaled loudly. "Olivia . . ."

"I'll run away with you."

He closed his eyes.

"I had a dream for you, too," I said. I'd wanted him to be able to go to LSU, to have a life that he chose, to live in a house where he didn't have to tiptoe.

Eyes still closed, he said, "I know."

Silence followed—the respect given to dead dreams—and because neither of us knew how long the mourning period should be, we stayed quiet.

Jamie turned and went back inside, and I followed. We climbed back in the bed, our movements disturbing Maggie. She made a noise and frowned, reaching one hand out for me, grabbing my shoulder, the other one reaching for Jamie. He gave her his hand, and her face relaxed. I understood the gesture. In light of recent events, a physical reassurance that we were still together was necessary.

Jamie settled down into the pillow, being careful not to let go of Maggie's hand, and after a few minutes he was asleep.

I closed my eyes and imagined Jamie and me in Mexico. I saw myself there, but not him. Taking deep breaths, I tried again to see him. I closed my eyes and imagined the ocean, the sand under my feet, and the breeze on my face. I heard the seagulls, but I knew he wasn't there. I shut my eyes again, but he wasn't in the desert, or in the mountains, or anywhere beautiful. I imagined him in a different future, the one that terrified me. I tried to see Jamie someplace with locked doors and scheduled visits, a place with isolation and no windows, because they wouldn't even let him have the sun. I saw the building, inside and out, but I didn't see Jamie there, either.

I knew no amount of worrying would change the way things turned out, but I scooted my body down between Jamie and Maggie, their still-held hands resting on my chest. I turned my head to him, brought my mouth close to his face, and whispered, "Where are you going to be?"

I noticed first the feel of the Spanish moss moving and bumping against my face. Then the breeze blew over me, slow and warm, carrying with it the scent of flowers and the river, and without being completely awake, I knew I was in St. Francisville. I felt the tree beneath me, hard yet smooth from many years of my sitting in its seat, and I opened my eyes to a still-sleeping Fidelity Street. Waking up in the seat of my tree was not a new occurrence, but it was rare and a surprise, being that I fell asleep in a tiny shotgun house a world away in New Orleans.

My new surroundings threw me off balance, and I grabbed the branch in front of my face, my fingers wrapping around it tightly. For a while I looked at my grand-mother's house. The windows were dark, and if I listened closely I was able to hear my grandmother inside. She was sleeping, and I heard her breathing and the occasional turn she made in her bed. That's when I was sure I was dream-ing. I possessed great powers when sleeping.

I risked a quick look in the direction of Jamie's house, but there was nothing to see, no light, no noise. The house's front windows were black, making me think of Mrs. Ben-ton's face and the many times it had carried bruises. It was fitting: my grandmother's house always looked abandoned; Jamie's house always looked battered.

A light came on in my grandmother's house, and I turned my head in its direction. It came from my mom's bedroom, illuminating my mom through the window. She looked past me, down at the river below. It was not the real her. It was the ghost version of her, the one who occasionally vis-ited me in my sleep, always looking out of that window. She looked like she did in the photos from her room: so young, so pretty. She turned her face to the side, the way she always did, tilting her ear to the window and closing her eyes, like she was listening to some sound coming from the river. I turned my head in the exact same way, like I always did, and tried to hear it, too, but I couldn't.

My mother disappeared from the window, and I relaxed my grip on the branch and prepared to wake up back in New Orleans, because this was usually where the dream of her and the window stopped. But a few moments passed, and I was still there. I heard my grandmother's back door open, but there was no sound of it closing. Then Lillian was in the backyard, and I watched her move across it, away from the house and toward the river. The wind picked up and tried to blow me out of the tree. It made her nightgown hug her hips as she walked down the slope and through the trees. I tried to wake up, because I knew this was the night, and I didn't want to see it. But my body, acting of its own volition, climbed down and followed her.

I stayed two paces behind her, never catching up to her, never wanting to. The sound of the leaves crunching under our feet was loud in the quiet of the night, and the wind blew her hair behind her, toward me. Once she was at the water's edge, I knew I should close my eyes and cover my ears, so I wouldn't have to see or hear any of this, but I couldn't move.

My mother stayed still for a moment and then walked into the river. My chest burned as I watched her wade out until the water came up to her knees. Once she was in up to her waist, she turned her face back toward my grandmother's house. She looked right through me. She was crying, and she looked lonesome, like she already missed us. Her face was so much like my own.

It started to rain, and it was warm. I turned my face to the sky. It fell softly at first, gliding across my cheeks and down my body. I looked back out at the river, but there was no Lillian, just me and the river and the rain. She'd gone under. Even though it was only a dream and it wouldn't change anything, I ran down the bank after her. The rain turned the dirt into mud; my running turned into sinking and slipping. The rain came down harder, and I fell and went into the river headfirst, the river's fingers, wet and lapping, pulling me out farther. Then the current had me, and in no time I was almost completely submerged, only my face still above the water. I opened my mouth to scream for her, but I just swallowed river. The rain pushed my head under, and the current pulled me from below, the rain and the river coconspirators.

I was dying, I knew it. But right before I died, I felt the ground against my feet. I'd somehow found my way back to the bank, only it wasn't the muddy bank my feet touched but concrete, and it was warm. Sound flooded my ears, but it wasn't the river. It was car horns.

I heard my name, and the voice was loud and scared. Then Max was flying down the steps of Steven's front porch, his shirt open and flapping. I was in the street. He was running. Cars were coming, but everything played out in slow motion.

I woke up one part at a time. I turned my head toward the cars trying to stop, their horns hurting my ears. Max crashed into me, knocking my head back, making me look at the sky. It was bright blue, cloudless. Then his arms pulled me into his body. He spun us around, the cars' honking not stopping this slow dance as he carried me to the other side of the street without putting me down.

His heart was beating fast against my side, and his voice matched its rhythm. "What were you doing? What were you doing?" he asked.

I wanted to answer, but I didn't know what I was doing

standing in the middle of the street when only a moment ago I'd been drowning in the Mississippi River. I sometimes sleepwalk, the only discernible trait I inherited from my dad. But the only place I had ever walked to before was my tree. Maybe that was where I was headed, but I was a hundred miles from my tree.

The people passing in the cars squinted at me through their windows and shook their heads slowly, like they were chalking me up as yet another person not able to handle the effects of too many days in New Orleans. Max still hadn't let me go. Did he not trust that I wouldn't dart back into the street? I looked at his face, but he wasn't looking at me; something up at the street corner had his attention. I followed his stare.

At the intersection policemen were lining up barricades, preparing to close off the street. We looked down to the other end of Oak Street and saw that another policeman had started directing traffic away from the street.

"Is it over?" I breathed.

My eyes shot to Jamie and Maggie, who were standing on the porch. Max pulled me closer in to his body, like there was a way to tuck me inside him, to shield me from their eyes. I was terrified, but also grateful that Max was on my side. I'd never seen anything fiercer than the look in his eyes.

"It's not over," he spit out.

Chapter 12

Jamie and Maggie looked at the cops and then back at us. For some reason the cops weren't making a move for us; they just continued closing off the street at either end. Max slowly released me, but he grabbed my hand and pulled me tight against his body. He never took his eyes off the policemen standing closest to us as we made our way back across the street. Once we were on the porch, Max herded all of us inside. We split, two of us at each of Steven's front windows, looking out.

Steven came into the living room. "Are they closing the street off?"

He took in our panicked stares and said, "Calm down, the police aren't going to come bursting through the door. Well, probably not." He laughed. When he saw that we weren't going to join him, he continued, "There's a festival today and a street dance tonight. The setup starts pretty early, because people here love an excuse to start drinking before noon."

Steven went through the house, pulling art from walls and stacking the canvases up in the living room. Apparently he had plans of setting up shop somewhere on the street. He came back into the living room, his arms full.

"Will you boys go around to the storage room in the back?" he asked. "I need my easels. You'll see them as soon as you open the door." He didn't wait for an answer before going into the kitchen.

Maggie said, "I'll go."

"I'll go with you," Max said.

They walked out and slunk around to the back of the house, then returned a few minutes later and helped Steven set up his display down the street, not too far from the house. He brought a folding chair and a bottle of wine with him, his provisions for the day. The street was completely blocked off now, and we were trapped in the house.

A couple of hours later, people started filling the street. I watched from my spot in the window. This festival wasn't so different from the festivals in St. Francisville, in that it had art, food, and people, but there was a different flavor to this one. It had something to do with the variety of people crammed into one narrow space. I'd never seen so many faces, and even though it wasn't likely the people knew each other, they seemed to trade smiles and laugh together like old friends. The policemen were at every cross street, walking around and talking to each other and the people passing by. They laughed, and some even danced to the music floating in and out from different places. After a time they became less scary and more like decoration.

"It's time to go meet Beth," Max said. "And I'm coming with you."

We'd been watching the festival for so long that it was hard to peel my eyes from the window. I was scared it would turn into something else if I turned my back on it, like a police raid. I knew it was irrational, but I was worried the festival was just a front to lure us into feeling safe enough to walk outside.

Jamie looked out at the street and then back to me. "I wish you didn't have to go. Be safe."

"I will."

Max took my hand and pulled me to him "Relax," he whispered to me as we went out the front door. We walked against the stream of people and had to hold each other tight to keep from being pushed apart. Once we were off Oak Street, we both breathed a sigh of relief. Three cops were standing next to the trolley stop. One of them pointed in the direction of Oak Street. Max grabbed my arm, and we ducked down a back alley.

"We'll have to go the long way around," he said.

Our detour brought us to the riverside. The Mississippi River spread out before us, wider and more imposing than I was used to, making the stretch we had in St. Francisville look like its little sister. I stopped and leaned against the railing that ran along the length of the boardwalk. The breeze felt good, alleviating the sticky humidity of the day.

Max stood behind me, caging me in with his arms, his head lowering to kiss my shoulder.

A song came from the direction of the water. It was one I'd never heard before, and I couldn't make out the lyrics—something about a boy and the river. The tone was sad but beautiful, and I couldn't help myself from humming along.

"Are you worried about seeing Beth again?" he asked.

"No, not really," I lied. "Are you worried?"

"What if it's a trap? What if she called your dad or the police?"

"All I can do is hope she didn't."

Wanting to put off the possibility of Beth failing me, I ducked under the railing. I wanted to get a closer look at the river. Maybe I'd be able to hear the song better. I walked to some steps leading down to the water's edge. I took them carefully. I watched as the river moved and lapped against the rocks at its shore, my eyes stopping on the elaborate riverboats docked next to it. They were huge, lining up along its edge like ladies-in-waiting.

Max followed me down the steps. "What are you doing? We need to go."

"Do you hear the music?" I asked.

He frowned and cocked his head toward the water. "I don't hear anything."

The wind gusted. The music seemed to be coming from the river, its melody seeping out of the water, rolling along the current to me, drawing me forward. It was like the dream of my mom sitting in her bedroom window, turning her head to a sound coming off the river. Was it a sound only I could hear? Did it mean I was going crazy like my mother? Instead of being scared, I was curious.

Even though the music was muffled by the sound of the current and the barge now moving down the middle of the river, I was hypnotized by the song. I walked closer to the water, but Max stopped me.

"What are you doing?" he asked.

It was the third time he'd asked me that today. And I still didn't know how to answer him. I tilted my head toward the music. There was a lullaby quality I hadn't noticed before.

"You really can't hear that?" I asked.

"I can't hear any music."

Maybe hearing the music was proof I was getting closer to finding my mom.

The wind shifted again, and the song drifted away. I tilted my head again, trying to catch its sound, but it was no use. Soon I couldn't hear it at all, and I was forgetting its tune.

Max took my hand and squeezed. "We need to go. Beth will be waiting."

"Okay. Sorry," I said.

His eyes looked worried, and I hated it.

"I'm fine," I lied again.

He led me back up the steps and onto the boardwalk. Fifteen minutes later we were standing on Napoleon Avenue across the street from the café. Beth Hunter was sitting outside on a bench, her back to us. Max looked around cautiously, like there might be cops hiding behind the bushes, ready to jump out and get us. He looked at me like he wasn't sure what I was going to do next.

"Wait here. I'll be right back," I said.

I left Max standing under the streetlamp and went to her. When she saw me, she clutched her bag to her chest. She motioned for me to sit next to her. I sat down and looked over my shoulder at Max. Beth followed my gaze.

"Is that Judy Stephenson's kid?" she asked.

"Yeah. He was with me yesterday, too."

She turned back to face me. "He looks kind of . . . intense."

"He's worried I can't trust you."

"I see." She put the bag in my lap. "You can, though." She fiddled with the straps. "That's as close to five thousand dollars as I could get you."

I put my hands on the bag. "It's too much. We found out we need two thousand for the passports. I don't want to take more than that."

She put her hand on top of mine. "I want you to have all of it. Please, take it. You'll need it." She looked sad all of a sudden.

"Okay," I said.

"Yesterday it didn't sound like you could trust the guy who's doing them."

I thought about Maggie's mom. She wasn't the most trustworthy person.

"I know," I said. "But we don't have a lot of options. We need to leave the country, and this is our best bet."

"Please be careful. I plan on sticking around New

Orleans for a while. So maybe when you get where you're going, you could email me or write me a letter. So I know you're okay."

"I can do that." After reading her letters all my life, I loved the idea of writing her one.

"Maybe you could let your dad know you're okay, too."

I'd been trying not to think about what it'd do to my dad when I didn't come home, what it would do to him for me to leave him, too.

She dug in her purse and pulled out a small bag. "I have something for you."

In it was a necklace, its chain silver and delicate. It was a name necklace, with *Olivia* spelled in a pretty cursive font.

"I wanted you to have your own," she said. "I got it at the Riverwalk." She unclasped it and reached around my neck to fasten it. My name sat on top of Lillian's.

"Thank you," I said.

I tried to think of another excuse for her to touch me, or something to ask her. All my life I'd wanted to talk to her, and now I was running out of time and things to say.

I reached up to take off Lillian's necklace. "You should have this."

Her eyes lit up, and she reached for it but then hesitated. "Are you sure?"

I nodded.

She wasted no more time and put it on. "There," she said, and then took a deep breath in and out, like Lillian was finally where she belonged.

I glanced at Max, and he looked back at me impatiently. "I need to go," I said.

Beth nodded, but before I stood, her hand went to the side of my face, stopping me. "I thought I had more time," she said. "With Lillian . . . I thought there'd be more time to figure it out. I'm so sorry. I'm sorry I waited until it was too late, and I'm sorry I didn't come see you."

Tears pricked my eyes. "Me too."

She dropped her hand from my face.

"Do you think I'm like her?" I asked. "I mean, do you think I'll be like her?"

"You look just like her, but you know that."

That wasn't what I wanted to hear. "I don't know why I asked you that. It's not like you know me well enough to know if I'm like her." I rolled my eyes. "Well, maybe you do. I am a fugitive from the law. That's probably not the best evidence that I make good choices."

"I wouldn't say that," Beth said. "Besides, the situation you're in now, that's not something Lillian would've done. This has your dad written all over it."

I must have looked at her like she was crazy, because she smiled.

"You have a lot more in common with him than you think," she said.

"How so?" I asked.

"You love like him. You wouldn't be here if you didn't. You're loyal like him. Your friend Jamie is lucky to have you. But be careful. That kind of love can eat you up."

People walked by us, some of them paying attention to

198

us, others not, and I held the money to my chest and worried about being eaten up.

I knew I needed to leave. I wished I'd taken a picture of her, too.

"Goodbye, Beth."

"Bye."

I stood and walked away from her, leaving my mom's childhood best friend behind.

I didn't cross the street back to Max, but walked along the sidewalk, my head down and full of everything Beth had shared with me. The bag swung from my shoulder like it was an ordinary bag, not the thing that carried what Jamie and I needed to survive.

I didn't hear Max come up to me. He didn't say anything, just took my hand. I'd miss his hand in mine. When we got to the river again, he held it tighter, like he was keeping me from the water. The river was quiet this time.

I looked into the crowds of people standing on the street corners, and that's when I saw someone I recognized, someone who didn't belong in New Orleans. It was my dad, his face tired and sad. At first I thought it was because Beth had just talked about him. That I was seeing my dad in some other man's face. It couldn't be him. He wouldn't come looking for me. He wouldn't leave St. Francisville. He never left home. But then Max saw him, too.

"Holy shit," Max said as he pulled me behind him, and we ducked down an alley.

We ran, our bodies close to the building. We didn't stop until we came out on the other side, and I was dizzy.

"Does your dad know Steven?" Max asked. "Will he know to go to Steven's?" He grabbed my hands and shook me. "Olivia, did you hear me?" He took my face in his hands. "Are you okay?"

No, I was not okay. "He came for me," I said. "I can't believe he came for me."

On the way back to Steven's, I saw my dad's face everywhere. It was burned into my brain. A couple of blocks from Oak Street, Max stopped me.

"There's something I need to tell you. You should know that my dad will be here tomorrow."

"What? Why?" I asked. There was already one dad too many in New Orleans.

"I talked to him again. He wants to be here so he can be with me and Maggie when we turn ourselves in."

That sobered me. I guessed they wouldn't be able to travel home on their own, just casually strolling into St. Francisville and waiting around until somebody noticed them.

"When are y'all doing that?"

"I'm not sure. In a few days, I guess? We'll meet Vicky's friend and put you and Jamie on a bus after that. We'll make sure y'all are way out of town before we do it."

"So then why is your dad coming here tomorrow?"

"I couldn't talk him out of it. He said he'd feel better being close to where I was."

My dad had never been comfortable being close to where I was, which was why I couldn't believe he was here, in New Orleans.

Max sensed my discomfort and rubbed my shoulders. "He doesn't know where we are. I know where *he'll* be, and I told him I'd call him when me and Maggie were ready to go in."

"All right," I said.

He squeezed my shoulders tight.

"I can't stand that you're doing this," he said.

"You wanted me to pick a direction and go," I joked.

"You know this isn't what I meant."

"I know."

"Will I ever see you again?" he asked.

"I don't know."

He turned and walked to Steven's house. He never reached for my hand.

When we got there, Jamie and Maggie were on the front porch.

"My dad is in New Orleans," I told them. "We just saw him. He was on the street."

"Is there any chance he'll think to come here?" Max asked Maggie.

Maggie didn't get a chance to answer, because her mom walked up the porch steps. She stood across from us, arms hugging her body like she was protecting herself.

"My friend Louis said he'll do the passports, as a favor to me. There's this place near Audubon Park where he does it. He wants to meet tomorrow night. He said I should bring you."

She looked at Maggie expectantly.

"All right," Maggie said.

201

"I'll meet y'all here tomorrow at nine."

"We'll be here. You can go now," Maggie said.

Vicky went down the porch steps, then turned back to face Maggie. "I am sorry."

At first I thought she was apologizing for yesterday, but then she threw her arms out to her sides and looked down at her body. She was describing herself.

"Your dad has always been good. The only time I was good was when I was with him. I tried to keep up. I just couldn't. I know you hate me. And you should. But leaving you was the best thing I ever did for you."

She turned and walked away, disappearing into the meandering people on the street.

"Good, you're back," Steven said. He came outside onto the porch. "I have a favor." He motioned for us to follow him inside.

"I need you and Olivia to take a package to a friend," he said, picking up a red duffel bag and handing it to Max.

It looked heavy.

"What is it?" I asked.

"Do you really want to know?" He waggled his eyebrows at me. "He lives on—"

"No. We're not delivering drugs for you," Max interrupted, and dropped the bag.

"I think you'll do anything I ask," Steven said, smiling. "Everything has its price, remember?"

The smile was genuine. He wasn't angry.

Steven looked at me. "Like I was saying before I was

rudely interrupted, my friend lives on Dublin. It's six blocks down, one block over. It's a blue house with black shutters. You can't miss it. It looks like it might fall in on itself at any minute. His name is Mark, real scruffy guy, doesn't take a lot of baths. You give this bag to him, and he'll give you something in return. Make sure you make it back with it. Maggie and Jamie will stay here with me."

Steven started whistling and walked toward the kitchen. He seemed so upbeat and happy, like he wasn't blackmailing us.

"Maggie, come try this gumbo and tell me what you think," he said. "What are y'all still doing here?" he asked us. "Run along, children. Don't worry about the cops. They're too busy with the crowd." He waved us away with his hands.

I took the bag Beth had given me and put it inside my backpack, then gave it to Jamie. "Hide this under Luke's bed."

Max picked up the red duffel bag. "We'll be back," he said.

We walked in silence, the bag slung over Max's shoulder. Life had become unrecognizable. Every time we passed a police officer, I kept my eyes straight ahead, but my ears burned, and I felt like the bag on Max's shoulder was screaming that we were up to no good.

We found the house, no problem, and stood outside of it. Steven was right. It looked like it might collapse at any time. It even leaned a little to the right.

Max grabbed my hand. "Let's get this over with," he said.

I knocked on the front door. No answer. I knocked again.

"Hello?" I said. "We're friends of Steven's."

The door cracked open an inch. Max pulled the bag off his shoulder.

"We have something for you," he said.

The door opened the rest of the way. It was Vicky's drug dealer.

"Are you Mark?" I asked.

He nodded. He looked at Max warily.

"We just want to drop this off and get out of here," Max said.

"Steven usually sends Luke," Mark said.

I shrugged. "He sent us."

Mark moved out of the way and motioned for us to come inside. The place was filthy, much like the man. He went into the kitchen, and we followed.

"Put it on the table," he said.

Max did as he was told. Mark opened the bag and my breath caught. Inside were bricks of cocaine, like I'd seen in movies.

"Now, this is pretty," Mark said. He pulled a knife from the back of his pants. This was no pocketknife. The blade was long. He cut open one of the bricks and did that thing I'd also only ever seen in the movies, where he wet a finger and drew it across the brick, and rubbed it on his gums. My life was an unrecognizable, drug-dealing movie.

"Let me get something for you," Mark said, and exited the kitchen.

"Shit," Max said. "What in the hell are we doing?"

"Our first drug deal," I whispered.

The side door opened, and a guy walked in. "Where's Mark?"

"He's in the back," Max said.

"Who are y'all?" the guy asked.

"We're friends of Steven," I said.

"Ah. Where's Luke?"

"He's not staying with Steven anymore," I said. "He left."

"I bet Steven didn't like that," he said.

I shrugged.

"How do you know Steven?" he asked.

"What does it matter?" asked Max.

"Chill out, man. I was just curious."

The guy approached me. "I saw y'all there the other night, before Steven's gig." He stepped into my personal space. "Since you're Steven's new errand girl, let him know I have a few things you can take care of for me, too."

Max tensed next to me and straightened to his full height. "This is our last *errand* for Steven."

Mark came back into the kitchen with a stuffed envelope. He handed it to me. "Make sure that finds its way back to Steven. All of it," he said.

I nodded and handed the envelope to Max. Mark studied us for a second.

"Y'all don't look stupid, so I'm guessing you know what'll

happen if it doesn't," he said. He pulled the knife back out and set it on the table.

"We know," Max said.

"Good. Now leave."

"Gladly," Max said.

❧

"We're not doing anything like that again," Max said as he threw the envelope at Steven.

Steven caught it with a surprised look on his face. "You like to tell me what you're not gonna do. It's cute." He walked to his room. "The gumbo's done. Help yourself."

"Mark was the guy from the other night." I motioned my head toward the back room.

Maggie looked embarrassed. "I'm so sorry. I never thought Steven would use us."

Jamie exhaled loudly and ran his hands down his face. "Tomorrow, everything changes."

He looked at each of us for a beat. The music from the street was getting louder. He grabbed Maggie's hand and pulled her out the door and into the street. We followed. We watched as he spun her around and around, then dipped her back. I looked in the direction of the police, but they weren't paying any attention. Max and I were probably bringing more attention to ourselves by not dancing. Maggie and Jamie melted into the crowd, her face and body popping up every now and then, moving to the music the way only Maggie can. Because we were so connected, they could only go so far down the street before pulling us after them.

Somewhere between the porch steps and the middle of the street, it was silently agreed that the night was to be enjoyed. When we caught up to them, Max grabbed one of my hands and Jamie grabbed the other and they took turns spinning me. I wished I could keep both of them. We were immune to all serious things as we moved and danced, weaving in and out of people before finding our way back together again. Through all the dancing and laughing, there was a voice in the back of my head whispering, warning me that we were under some Cinderella spell, and that like all spells this one would be broken at midnight. But for the moment it didn't matter; nothing mattered but being almost eighteen on the streets of New Orleans with these three people.

Max stopped dancing, and he was sweating.

"I can't keep up with this one," he said, pointing to Maggie.

"I can," Jamie said, and he pulled her to him.

They performed their wedding-night dance, just like they'd done at most every function I'd ever been to that included music. The dance had been perfected over time. Max watched them with a look of awe.

I stood closer to him. He looked down at me, and for a time we stayed like that, bodies lined up, barely touching. The music wrapped around us, holding us close. Then Max brought his lips to mine, and the kiss was so soft. His hands went to my hair, his fingers playing with the ends, before bringing my hands to his lips. He kissed my scars, and I wanted to crawl inside him, the words *I love you* on the tip of my tongue.

Instead, I said, "This is a great night."

"This is the best night," he said.

❧

The night got away from us without our noticing, the way nights in New Orleans do. Exhaustion hit before long, and it was obvious it was time to go back to Steven's.

Max said, "Wait here. I don't see any cops, but I'm gonna go up ahead and make sure."

I said, "Okay," but Maggie wasn't having it.

"I can't wait, I'm going with him," she said. "I have to lie down right now, or I'm gonna pass out in the street." She charged after Max.

Jamie and I stood in our spots until Max motioned to us from the porch. He didn't wait for us but instead went into the house with Maggie on his heels. By the time we got there, Maggie was already asleep on the couch. Seeing her asleep and knowing that morning would come soon, I felt the sadness creep back in—the first sign the spell was breaking.

Jamie went to Maggie and gently lifted her head into his lap. He stroked her hair and watched her sleeping face. I said his name, but he didn't respond. He settled into the couch, like he was ready to spend the night that way, soaking up as much of Maggie as he could.

I opened the bedroom door carefully, not wanting to wake Max if sleep had taken him as soon as he lay down, like Maggie. But he wasn't asleep. He was standing at the end of the bed with his head bowed. He didn't move when I came in, as though he, too, felt the spell being lifted.

That night we'd gone cliff diving at Thompson Creek, I was scared, but I jumped anyway. I was always scared when I was with Max—mostly of the way he made me feel. I knew I couldn't let one more second go by without telling him how I felt about him.

"I love you," I said.

His face shot to mine. "You tell me now, the day before you leave me forever?"

"I'm sorry," I said.

He paced at the end of the bed, his hands going repeatedly to his hair and then sliding down the sides of his face. "I know. I've known."

I decided I wasn't ready for the spell to be broken, and I went to him. In the walk from the door to the bed, I only wanted to get closer to him, to get closer to the boy who carried home with him. When he touched me, my body fell into his, sending him off balance and bringing us both to the bed. I wrapped up in this boy.

Our breathing was loud, and his hands burned me where they touched me. Instead of being scared, I wanted to get closer. We pulled at each other's clothes like it was a race to see who could get the other one naked first. Relief hit me when we touched skin to skin.

He hovered above me, his elbows braced on either side

of me. His eyes looked deep into mine, and I wanted to die with him looking at me like that.

"You're beautiful," he whispered.

The feeling of drowning hit me again, and I started shaking. I felt like I was being pulled under, but then Max put his mouth on mine, and I felt my chest expand with him, over and over again, my own resuscitation.

He whispered, "I love you, I love you," into my ear, his breath hot, his fingers gripping my hips.

He loved me. I opened my mouth, but he sealed his lips over mine, making me swallow my words, so I showed him with my body.

Late in the night Max turned on his side and curled me deep into him. Every part of him was touching every part of me. We were so connected that it was hard to imagine a space without him. I'd read stories of people waking in the night to rub aching legs that were no longer there, lingering ghost sensations. That's how I would feel without him. No matter how far away I went, I'd always feel him.

"I know I'm supposed to step aside and let you leave," he said. "I said that's what I'd do. But how?" he asked. "How do I do that?" He was whispering now.

"I don't know," I said.

His fingers drew circles on my stomach. "Won't you be a little sad?"

"It's gonna break my heart."

"Good," he said. He was quiet for a long time. "You love him more than me."

I shook my head. "Just longer."

He held me tighter to him, then buried his face in my neck and hummed, a thing he did when he was sleepy. For the first time that night, I was scared, scared the dreams to come wouldn't be sweet, and scared his arms weren't strong enough to keep me still. All day I'd feared sleep, worried my subconscious would pull me back into the street like it had the night before and my body would head home.

As if sensing my unease, he said, "Trust me," and I did.

Chapter 13

My eyes opened to a still-sleeping Max, his face turned to mine. He looked younger in his sleep, his tanned skin contrasting with the white of the sheets. My fingers itched to reach out and touch him. I wanted to trace his face like I did Jamie's when we were little, to help me memorize him, but I was scared I'd wake him.

I wasn't sure how long we'd slept, but it felt late. He opened his eyes, and for a time we stared at each other.

"I didn't want to leave without saying it," I said. "I'm sorry if you think that's mean."

He rolled onto his back and stared at the ceiling. "I'm glad you said it. I've been in love with you since freshman year, so it feels good to hear you say it."

"You didn't speak one word to me freshman year."

Still not looking at me, he said, "I was scared of you.

When we were in Spanish class, you could conjugate your verbs better than anybody else. It was intimidating."

"Shut up." I pushed his shoulder.

He flipped over and came to rest on top of me.

"I love you," I said.

"Will you say it in Spanish?"

"You're so stupid."

He nodded.

Getting serious, I asked him, "Will you take care of yourself? Will you stop drinking again?"

"Will you stay with me to make sure?"

"No," I said.

"Then, no."

There was a quiet knock on the door, and Maggie's face popped in.

"My mom's here," she said.

Vicky wasn't supposed to meet us until later. We got dressed and met them in the living room. Vicky was sitting on the couch next to Jamie. She looked nervous.

"Hey," she said. "Louis wants to meet early. He's got something going on tonight, and he won't have time to get your passports ready. But he said he could do it now, if you could come now." She looked at all of us but Maggie.

I looked at Max, who was staring holes into Vicky. I knew he didn't trust her, but what choice did we have?

"Where are we meeting him?" I asked.

"He has an apartment on Pitt Street, near Audubon Park."

"Let me grab my bag." I went back into the bedroom and

pulled my backpack from beneath the bed. When I turned to leave the room, Jamie was standing in the doorway.

"Are you ready?" he asked.

I nodded.

"And you're sure? After this, it'll just be you and me."

"Most of my life it was just you and me," I said. "You're my family."

"And you're mine."

"Are you ready to go to Greece?" I asked.

"I'm all packed," he said.

The sun was shining brightly, the glint of it bouncing off street signs and highlighting the holes between the leaves on the trees. We walked down the sidewalk, Vicky leading the way to the trolley stop. Once we were on the trolley, Maggie sat next to her, surprising Vicky and me.

Maggie looked at her mom, opened her mouth, and then closed it. After letting out a loud breath, she said, "Thank you for helping us. Things are shit between us, but I really appreciate you hooking us up with Louis."

Maggie looked like it had been physically painful to admit that, and Vicky looked like she was about to cry.

"Don't thank me," Vicky said, her voice thick. She stood and walked to the front of the trolley, reaching up to grab a hand strap. She didn't look back at us.

I sat down in Vicky's vacant seat. Maggie shrugged and looked out the window.

We got off at our stop, a few blocks from the park. It was so quiet. There were no cars in the street. That should've been my first clue that something was really wrong.

We were almost at Pitt Street when Vicky slowed her steps in front of us.

She turned to face us. There were tears in her eyes. "We need to turn around," she said.

"What?" I asked. "No, the street's up that way." I pointed in the direction we were headed.

She put her hands on my chest and pushed me, forcing me backward.

"No, we need to turn around," she said again, her voice louder.

"Why?" Maggie asked. "What's going on?"

Vicky looked at Maggie. "I'm so sorry, baby girl."

I immediately looked around us. There was no one on the street, no cars, no people. Where were the people?

"What did you do?" Maggie asked.

"Y'all need to run," Vicky said. She kept pushing me back. "I'm so sorry, Maggie."

"Why? What did you do?" Maggie asked again.

Vicky started sweating, her words coming out in a stammer. "I—I owe Louis m-money. A lot of money. He was gonna subtract a thousand from what I owe for bringing him your business. But then he checked y'all out, to see if he could find out why you needed the passports. He found out about everything." She chewed her lip and tears spilled down her face. "There's a reward for any information that leads to your arrest. It's worth a lot more than I owe him. He was gonna wipe my debt clean."

We couldn't speak. The air had been knocked right out of us.

"You sold us out?" Maggie asked. "Of course you did."

"I'm sorry," Vicky said. "The cops are waiting up ahead, a swarm of them." She looked at Jamie. "They think you're dangerous. Y'all need to run."

We took several steps backward but didn't turn away from her.

Vicky reached out and grabbed Maggie's hand. "I'm so sorry," she cried.

And she was, I could tell. We couldn't speak. I couldn't believe what she'd done. Maggie's mouth hung open. There was no time for anything but to turn and run.

So we did. We were sucked into a vacuum as we ran, no noise but the sound of our feet pounding hard against the concrete sidewalk and our loud breathing. I didn't know where we were going. We made it a couple of blocks before we saw two policemen standing next to their vehicle. We skidded to a stop and turned and ran back in the direction we came from.

"Hey! Stop!" one of the policemen yelled.

Max took a right down an alley, and we followed. He reached out and grabbed me.

"Me and Maggie will try to lead them this way," he huffed, pointing to a side street off the alley. "Y'all go that way." He squeezed my hand. "Go!"

This wasn't how we were supposed to say goodbye. I hesitated. His lips crashed to mine for one brief moment. Then, with panic in his eyes, he yelled again, "Go!"

We turned and ran, Max's last-time kiss still warm on my lips.

My chest was on fire, but we ran. All of a sudden a man stepped out from the alley, and we crashed into him so hard that I saw stars. He grabbed me and wrenched me to him, turning me around so my back was against his chest. I felt something sharp poke me in the side: a knife.

I strained to look up at him. It was Mark, the drug dealer.

"I thought y'all were gonna get away from me." He was breathing hard, his chest heaving against my back. He squeezed my arm. "You're fast."

Jamie was standing in front of us. He looked from the man's knife to me and back. His eyes were wild.

"Louis was worried Vicky might change her mind, that she wouldn't be able to see it through, selling out her own daughter," Mark said. "Turns out he was right. I've been following y'all."

He squeezed my arm so tight I whimpered. Jamie's eyes went wide.

"The three of us are gonna walk over to Louis's apartment, and y'all are going to jail," Mark continued. "And then me and Louis are gonna split a big, fat check."

"No," I said.

He squeezed my arm again. "I really don't care what *you* do, but *he's* coming with me." He gestured with his head toward Jamie. "He's worth a lot of money."

He pushed the knife harder against my side. Jamie's eyes were glued to the blade.

"Do y'all understand?" Mark asked.

"Don't hurt her," Jamie said.

"I won't, if you come with me."

"Jamie, don't," I said.

"I'll go with you," Jamie said. "Just don't hurt her."

"No, Jamie. Run!" He had to get away. We still had Beth's money in my backpack, and I threw it at him. "Take the money. Run! Please." My voice broke. "Please run. Go! He won't really hurt me."

Mark took the knife from my side and put it to my throat, the metal biting the skin. I felt something wet. I was bleeding.

"Yes," he said, "I will."

Jamie's eyes locked with mine. I kept pleading with him to run, but it was useless. The boy who had always saved me wouldn't think twice about this sacrifice. He reached for my hand and squeezed. In his eyes were goodbyes.

"Jamie," I whispered.

"Shh," he said. "It's all right." He handed me my back-pack as Mark grabbed his elbow. Jamie traded places with me, and I was free.

"Let's go turn you in," Mark said.

They started walking away from me, and I watched them as they went, the space between us growing by the second. It was amazing how fast everything had fallen apart. But then Jamie elbowed Mark in the side, hard, sending him off balance. I watched in disbelief as Jamie broke away and ran back to me, dragging me with him as we took off again. For a second I felt relief that we were safe from Mark, but then he was on us again, spinning Jamie around by his shoulder. Jamie pushed him, knocking him back, but Mark lunged, grabbing for Jamie's arm. I threw myself at Mark's back, pulling his hair and punching—anything to get him to release Jamie. I yanked his hair as hard as I could, and he howled.

"You stupid bitch!"

He turned and shoved me, hard. Jamie and Mark resumed their struggle, and then suddenly Mark had his knife against Jamie's side.

"No!" I screamed.

Mark's breathing was heavy, his eyes full of rage. I'd never seen such rage. "You know what?" he said. "I've had enough of this. The odds of Louis sharing with me aren't good. I'll just take what's in the bag."

He shoved Jamie away and grabbed my backpack from the ground. He turned away from us, but then wheeled back.

"This is for my trouble."

He came at me, thrusting the knife, but Jamie was too fast for him. Jamie pushed me out of the way. I saw the knife as it went into him, and I felt it, like I was the one who'd been stabbed, my hand going to my own stomach. I screamed as Mark jerked the knife up, as the knife moved through Jamie, as Mark pulled the knife out and smiled. He smiled.

I heard more yelling and looked up to see a policeman running down the alley toward us, his boots beating on the cobblestone, his hand on his gun.

"Drop the weapon! Do it now!"

Instead of doing what he was told, Mark grabbed Jamie's shoulders, and the two of them began swaying back and forth, like they were dancing. The look in Mark's eyes said he couldn't believe he'd been caught.

"I said drop the weapon!" He said it like if he was just firm enough, Mark would straighten right up and obey. He didn't know it was too late.

The cop was on us all at once, cutting in between Mark and Jamie for his own dance. Jamie and I went one way, the two of them the other. There was shouting and chaos, and I couldn't make out who was yelling what, but when Jamie turned around to face me, his hands grabbing mine, everything slowed down. Swaying back and forth, now chest to chest, we slipped in between the spaces time could measure, our movements almost waltzlike. I felt wetness and warmth at my middle—Jamie's blood—and it made me press harder into him, hoping my body could heal him, seal him shut. We somehow made it out to the sidewalk, and Jamie leaned me back, or maybe he was falling. Either way, it was one last dip leading down to the street, and our dance was done.

Jamie slid to the side of me and lay out flat on the side-walk, his face to the sky. I heard my own breathing as I leaned over him. My hands went to his stomach, trying to keep the blood inside his body where it was leaking out, slow and warm. The look of it spreading on the sidewalk reminded me of his dad's blood on their kitchen floor, and I shook my head frantically, not ready for Jamie's debt to be collected.

"No, Jamie. No," I said. When I looked at his face, it was sad, and I knew the sorrow wasn't for himself but for me.

"I'm sorry," he said.

"I'm sorry, too," I whispered.

I wanted to say more, but my voice left, leaving me with an open mouth and no words. Jamie nodded, like he understood that, too. I kept my hands firmly in their spot, hoping the pressure could slow the bleeding, or that the hole wouldn't be there as long as it was covered.

The policeman's voice startled me. He was speaking not to me but into a handheld radio. I didn't hear exactly what he was saying, but I figured it out. Moments later I heard sirens in the distance, loud and alarming. Vicky's drug dealer was crumpled next to a bench across the street. He'd been handcuffed.

Above the sound of the sirens and my own loud breathing, I heard Maggie, her voice traveling to where I was, singing to me that she was coming. I looked up and saw her with Max. They were standing at the end of the street. At the sight of them, my vision blurred. It was safe to cry. Maggie ran toward us, and Max followed.

The policeman saw the two of them running and yelled at them to stop. Max listened, but Maggie didn't. She never does, just bulldozes ahead.

"Stop!" the cop screamed again, loudly. Then, seeming frustrated, he spit his command at her a third time. "Stop now!"

I looked at the policeman and saw that his gun was trained on her, like he was determined to have someone listen to him today. I looked back at her. *Stop now!* I willed her, but she didn't. The policeman looked at me, deflated, and brought the gun down, as if realizing one kid bleeding in the street was enough.

Then Maggie was next to me, not asking questions but simply putting her hands on top of mine. Jamie slid his eyes to her and apologized again, making Maggie cry, something she was getting better at.

"It's okay, Jamie. You're gonna be fine," she said. "You're gonna be just fine."

A few moments later Max stood over us, making me look up at him. I looked in the direction he was staring and saw the other policemen running at us. Maggie saw them, too, and stood up. She had Jamie's blood on her fingers, and she wiped them on her jeans.

The policemen yelled, telling us to step away from each other, hollering at us to step away from "the boy," but I didn't move. Maggie did, though. She stood and positioned herself so she was standing next to Max, making a wall.

I looked back at Jamie. In all the commotion his eyes had closed, and I'd missed it. Closing my eyes, too, I took my hands off his stomach and dropped my face down to his, my forehead pressing against his, our noses touching. His breathing was soft, and he was warm. *It's just me and this boy.* The other policemen were on us, breaking down the wall, pulling Max and Maggie in separate directions. Maggie's screams were feral.

A cop began to pull me from Jamie. I reached my head toward him one more time, my hair just touching his face, before being yanked away. The policeman wrenched my arms behind me, and even though I was sure they didn't naturally bend that way, nothing hurt. My eyes stayed with Jamie, my friend, my brother, sleeping on the sidewalk.

Other people were coming toward us then, paramedics. I was grateful. One stopped to look me over, and I choked out, "It's not my blood." They crowded around Jamie, blocking my view. I made deals with God. The policeman pushed at me from the back, his grip on my arms still tight. I had no idea what he was pushing me toward. I just knew it was in the opposite direction to Jamie, and the pain in my stomach exploded, the string between us pulling too tight, making me see white and bringing my knees in to my chest, forcing the man to half drag, half carry me.

Once we were down the street, he put me down next to a police car. He spoke to me, asking me questions, his face angry, his voice forceful, and even though I heard him I didn't process what he was saying. I didn't understand anything anymore. This immediately frustrated him. He shrugged his shoulders and grabbed my wrists, pulling them in front of me and forcing them together. There was pain from metal, cold and pinching. He pushed at my head, down and into the car, and I couldn't breathe. The sound of the door being slammed made me flinch.

Sitting in the back of the police car, I looked for Max and Maggie but didn't see them. Where were they? My mind went back to Jamie, to the sight of his blood spreading out on the sidewalk. My head hurt, matching the pain in my stomach, and I longed for a distraction. I heard a barge's horn coming from the river, blaring over and over again, warning everyone to get out of its way.

I understood then why my mother had walked into the river. I closed my eyes, and for the first time in my life, I saw her clearly, as if she was right in front of me. I had found her in the back of a New Orleans police cruiser.

The pain in my stomach was so great that even though I knew it was impossible, I wished for the river to reach out and take me like it did her, to make the pain stop. But I was too far from the river now. So I imagined that I had the power to pull the river into the police car. I felt for the water with my hands, and I watched as it began dripping from my fingers, slowly at first, then faster. It looked and felt so real, and even though part of me knew that it was a fantasy, and how dangerous it was to play with those, I welcomed it.

The water had a calming effect, taking my mind off what was happening to Jamie. Soon river water was pouring from my hands and washing across the floorboard, making me bring my feet onto the seat. But the water kept coming; it reached the seat, and I watched as it flowed over my lap, moving up my body. It was filling the car faster now, lapping against my neck, bringing chill bumps to my skin. I took one deep breath and closed my eyes as it washed over my face.

Once I was completely submerged, I sat in the darkness and relaxed into the water. When I opened my eyes again, I saw Max and Maggie through the window. They were making their way to me, each escorted by a cop, their hands pulled at uncomfortable angles behind them. They looked fuzzy in my underwater view, but as they moved closer I saw their faces. Max kept his eyes down, but Maggie didn't. She held her face forward. The look in it told me things had gotten worse.

My lungs burned, protesting the lack of oxygen, but I didn't give in. Any minute they would surrender to the lack of air and my stomach would give in to the pulling and I'd die. *Please.* The car door opened. The water rushed out, but the policemen didn't notice it. They didn't notice that I was wet and gasping for air; they just shoved Max and Maggie onto the backseat with me and slammed the door. My body immediately fell across Max like a deflated balloon, my head just touching Maggie's lap, and then kept falling deeper and deeper into them. Like the house of fallen cards we'd become, Maggie dropped her body down to cover mine, leaving Max as the only one of the four of us still sitting up.

The next thing I felt was the car lurching us forward, and then I heard more sirens. Max told us to keep silent. He said his dad was coming for us. That didn't comfort me, though—nothing could. The police car sped through the cobbled, bumpy downtown streets. I'm not sure how far we'd gone when we finally stopped. I closed my eyes tight at the sound of the back door opening, and Maggie's body pressed closer to me. They pulled her off me easily, making me sit up, my face close to Max's.

He leaned into me, his breath so close when he said, "I'm here. You're not alone. I'm here." He kept repeating it, like he knew it would be hard for me to understand.

My door opened, and then more hands were on me,

pulling me up and away from him. *He's here.* They led us into the side of a building; I guess it was the police station. Inside, I saw a long hall ahead of us. The man pulling me along handed me to a woman. She said she was taking me someplace special, as I was not yet eighteen.

This made me think back to Steven's words the night I saw him and his band snorting cocaine in the back room of the house on Oak Street. *This one's a baby.* Turning my head to Max and Maggie, I watched as they moved down the hall, away from me.

The woman led me to a room and took off my handcuffs. There was another woman in the room, and it looked like she'd been waiting for me.

"Take off your clothes," she said.

I just stared back at her. She told me again and motioned to my body. My middle and my hands were coated in Jamie's blood. She pointed to a shower in the corner and then to a pile of clothes on a table next to me, like I'd know what to do. She didn't realize I didn't know anything anymore. To her credit, she tried to explain again, but I still didn't move.

The woman who had walked me into the room came to stand behind me, and the other woman came to meet her. They must have been tired of giving me instructions, because now their hands were on me, stripping me of my clothes. My head yanked back, caught in my shirt. Soon I was bare, and I heard water running. They pushed me into it; it was cold at first and then too hot, the water beating down on my body, reminding me of the drowning dream and the rain. One of the women put a washcloth in my hand, but I didn't close my hand around it, so it dropped to the floor. She stepped into the shower with me, bent down to grab the washcloth, and took his blood from me by force.

❧

In a small room with one window, looking out onto an even smaller courtyard, lay a dead boy on a bed with white sheets. They told me he was Jamie, but I didn't believe them. They told me to step closer and I'd see, but I kept my feet where they were.

I was standing at the door of the hospital room with Max's dad on one side and a policeman on the other. There was no point in stepping into the room, because even at this distance I could tell he only barely resembled yesterday's boy in the street. He seemed smaller, somehow less, and I couldn't feel a pull to him; nothing in my body said this was the right boy. My Jamie must be in one of the other rooms. I looked back at the other two policemen in the hall, where I was told they'd been stationed since Jamie was brought to the hospital. Why were they necessary? Where was this dead boy going?

Mr. Barrow had rescued me from the police station a few hours after I arrived, a few hours after I turned off the switch inside me allowing me to hear or feel. He sat next to me for several minutes in the room they'd placed me in, but I didn't understand anything he was saying. He didn't get frustrated with me, though, just turned his frustration toward the other people at the jail, giving them harsh looks and gesturing with his hands. Whenever he turned his face to mine, it softened. He and Max looked so much alike that his presence comforted me. Eventually my hearing returned, and to prove his further connection to Max, Mr. Barrow leaned in to me and whispered, "I'm here. I'm here now."

He seemed reassured that I understood him then. He told me which hospital Jamie was in, and he promised to get me there. He said it was a condition put forth by Max, who wouldn't cooperate in any way until I was with Jamie. It would take a while, though, he said. There were my charges to consider, statements to give, papers to be processed.

"Max told me everything," he said. He registered the shock on my face. "Don't be mad at him. He just wants to make sure I understand what's going on. So I can help you." He looked at me knowingly. "I've prepared a statement that says you were an invited guest on the night in question. You were helping Louise Benton cook dinner when Tom Benton came home early from work. He and Jamie got into an argument that escalated. They began to fight. You witnessed Jamie hit his father in the head with a skillet, and then you saw Jamie stab him."

His words made me feel sick.

"Do you understand?" he asked.

Let me be the one who finally stopped him.

"I understand," I said, my voice hoarse. "But Mrs. Benton—"

"She won't contradict your statement."

He told me it would go quicker if I said what he told me

to say and signed where he told me to sign. He didn't have to persuade me too much, because the only thing I wanted was to get to Jamie.

"You won't be officially released until we get back to St. Francisville," he said. "I've spoken to your father. Apparently he was in New Orleans as recently as yesterday, looking for you. He's back home now. Once we get to St. Francisville, we'll file the paperwork. When the deal is finalized, you'll be released to your dad, and you can go home." He'd had a hopeful look on his face as he said this, like I'd take it as good news. He didn't know about the rival feelings inside me: the longing for home fighting the fear of looking into the faces of the people in it, my dad's especially, with his sadness and his worry. He didn't know I'd much rather be locked away somewhere small and alone.

And now here I was, in this room, with this boy.

Mr. Barrow touched my elbow. "It's him, baby. I'm sorry we didn't get here in time."

It was the *baby* that did it. Even though I knew it was just a Southern man's way of speaking, I couldn't stand his sweetness. I didn't deserve kindness or gentle voices. He was only doing it because he felt sorry for me, because he thought this boy was Jamie. I decided to prove him wrong, so he'd be angry with me, which was his right.

There were nine steps from the door to the bed, and I took each one slowly before climbing into the bed with the too-still boy. I could tell from the shifting of feet coming from the men behind me that they hadn't expected me to do this, but they didn't stop me.

My hand slid his hair back, and I saw fine, white-blond hair like the boy from my childhood once had. My other hand, knowing what to do now, began tracing, over his eyes, his nose, his mouth, the light from the tiny window highlighting his face and my fingers like a spotlight. I closed my eyes and did it a second time, slower now, just in case. Tears slid out from under my closed lids. They were right; this was Jamie.

My hands dropped from his face and went to my stomach, to the hollow feeling there, the absence of Jamie. The knife must have cut the string connecting us. I dropped down to Jamie and curved into him, my hand sliding up to rest over his heart with no beat. Just yesterday Jamie was breathing and he was warm. I thought about all the ways his face had changed over the years, and all the ways it wouldn't, like my mom's: forever eighteen.

Mr. Barrow and the policeman were at the bed, standing over me, crowding my periphery, but I didn't look in their direction. They didn't say anything, they just watched. Was this what it felt like to be the dead person at an open-casket funeral? I didn't think about them for too long, because my thoughts, like my body, were wrapped around Jamie and wanted to stay there. Memories of the two of us together collected behind my eyes. I heard the song coming from the river again, its lullaby sound snaking its way through the streets to find me, and I hummed its tune.

Chapter 14

It wasn't the river this time. This body of water was much smaller—so small. I felt my heartbeat in my ears. I was caught in a nightmare I couldn't stop, my head just below the water, drowning. I died over and over again, as if my body was practicing and the dream was a dress rehearsal of what was to come. *Once more,* my subconscious said, *with feeling.* The water was back in my lungs and burning in my chest, making me wonder how someone could be wet and on fire at the same time. I wanted to wake up, but I knew even when I did there'd be no relief. The new day would carry an underwater echo of this nightmare, and I still wouldn't be able to breathe. On top of that I'd have to move forward, one foot in front of the other, each step without him.

Road swept underneath me, trees flying past my face, a blur of brown and green. We were being transported back to St. Francisville courtesy of the Louisiana State Police, all three of us sitting side by side in the police van. Even though there was plenty of room, our bodies were touching, knees bumping, much the same way as they had on the front seat of Max's truck during another road trip. Only Jamie was being carried home a much different way. Mr. Barrow was following in the car behind us.

I blinked, my eyes cried-out from too many tears. Max sat closest to the window, and my face brushed his shoulder whenever I looked outside. The sun beat down through the glass, and I reached my hand across his body to touch it, to see if I could feel the sun's heat. It was no use. I couldn't feel anything. I kept my hand in its place and spread my fingers wide to see if that would make a difference. Max put his hand on the window right next to mine. We didn't say anything, just sat hand to glass and watched the out-side world speed by, the light moving through our fingers. When I relaxed my eyes, I caught glimpses of Jamie's face in the reflection, right beneath my fingertips, but when I focused them, he disappeared. Where did he go, and how did he get on the wrong side of the glass?

I entered a waking sleep. I saw Jamie everywhere, in the faces of the people in the cars passing us, the boy riding his bike on the side of the road. Jamie's voice came out of Max's mouth. But as soon as I looked closer or listened harder, he slipped away. So it didn't surprise me when I looked in the seat behind me, and it wasn't an empty seat that stared back at me.

Sitting straight up, like she'd been there the whole time, was my mom, the Mississippi River dripping off her skin. She wasn't solid; I didn't think I would've been able to touch her, but she sat there just the same, the sunlight slanting through her body. Now that I'd found her, she was following me everywhere. Her eyes met mine, and they looked sad. She looked back at me in a way that let me know she knew the line I'd crossed. We stared at each other for a while, and then she turned her head toward the window, her eyes taking in the road and the landscape around her.

"I've been down this road," she said, her voice young and sweet. Then she smiled at me, serenely, the sadness leaving her eyes for just a minute.

I turned back to face the front and slid down the seat, my shoulders slipping from their grip on the leather just like my sanity was slipping. I was sinking downward, where I'd puddle up on the floor of the van. But Max and Maggie pulled me back up, keeping me in my spot on the seat.

"Where are you going?" Max asked.

"You have to stay with us," Maggie said. "Stay with us."

Maggie looked at me and did a double take. I understood the gesture. Earlier we'd stopped for a bathroom break, and I'd risked a look in the mirror. In it was a lost girl. She was someone I hadn't seen before, or at least it had been a long, long time. One thing was for sure: I no longer looked like Lillian. The loss of Jamie had pulled my face in unrecognizable directions.

Maggie looped her arm in mine and dipped her head to my shoulder, making me look down at her. Her face was wet from her slow tears. She whispered, "I'm afraid they'll never stop."

I tried to wipe them away, but she was right. They were never going to stop. I gave up, and my hand went to my stomach, protectively covering the hole there, the one no one else saw, the place where Jamie had been cut from me.

"Do you think they'll still let me go to New York?" Maggie asked.

"My dad will make sure of it," Max said.

She leaned around me to look at him. "My dad and I can't pay him. We don't have money for lawyers."

"You don't need any," he said.

I thought about Maggie in New York. Maybe she would paint us on her walls so we could be together.

The van came to a stop at a red light in an unknown town, rural, with farmland butting right up to a convenience store, the only business in sight. On the side of the road sat an old man in a folding chair. He was holding up a wooden sign in one hand and held a megaphone in the other. The sign said we should all repent because the world was ending soon. He took advantage of his captured audience and stood up, bringing the megaphone to his lips.

"You are lost," he boomed at us.

You have no idea.

"You went astray a long time ago, and the time to repent

is now." He took a step toward the van and said, "Be careful, you're not on the right path. The road you are on is a lonely one."

I was sure he could see into my soul, and I waited for him to say something more, but he didn't; he only stared at the window of the van. I looked back to see if Lillian had heard it, too, but she was gone. I wasn't upset about it. I knew she'd pop up again. When I turned back to the window, the man was looking at me. His skin was worn, and his eyes looked tired. It was probably from warning people of their fates.

The light had long since turned green, but the van hadn't moved, the policemen in the front seat caught up in the man's side-street sermon. The old man's arm shook at the elbow, making me wonder how long he'd been holding up that sign. I wished I could roll down my window, so I could relieve him of his burdens, so I could tell him it was okay to rest. I wanted to tell him the world ended more than a day ago, and we were all living in this leftover space, a place with disjointed rhythm and no Jamie. He nodded at me as the van finally moved forward, like he got the message, but he didn't drop the sign.

As we drove on, I was aware of my own disconnect. The road home was purgatory, an in-between place where the pain and the present wouldn't be real until we entered St. Francisville. I knew the places purgatory was supposed to separate, and I knew life without Jamie could never resemble heaven, leaving me to wonder if we were on the road to hell.

I was suddenly cold, like my body was compensating for the heat it knew it would find in hell by cooling me from the inside. This scared me for two reasons: first, because it was the only thing I'd felt in more than a day; and second, because the feeling came from inside me. Maggie started rubbing my arm, like she was trying to warm me, or maybe she was trying to rub life back into me. "Quick, what's your favorite day of the week?" she asked.

I couldn't speak.

"Mine's Tuesday," Max answered.

"Why?"

"I was born on a Tuesday. What's yours?" he asked her.

"My favorite day is Sunday."

"Let me guess. Because Magnolia's and Bird Man's are closed on Sundays, and it's your only day of the week off work."

"My dad and I paint on Sundays. We spend all day on our sun porch painting in the natural light. It's our church."

"I like the sound of your church," Max said. "What's your favorite thing about St. Francisville?" he asked her.

"Olivia," Maggie said.

I looked at her.

"Olivia is my favorite thing about home."

"Mine, too," he said. "When did you start singing?"

"My dad said I sang before I talked."

She started singing softly, her voice making my eyes heavy, so I closed them.

Jamie's face appeared behind my closed lids, startling me and forcing them back open. I was sure this was a trick, too, and that if I closed my eyes again he'd be gone. But every time I blinked, he was there, making me smile, and making my blinks last longer and longer. I decided to keep my eyes closed altogether. His smiling eyes, a gift to me. *Stay with me.*

It was easier for Max and Maggie if I kept my eyes closed; they both sighed in gentle relief, and their bodies relaxed around me, like they were tired parents who'd finally gotten a sick child to sleep. Maggie's singing continued, and I lost track of time as I slid into dreamland. Jamie met me there.

It was late in the night when we crossed into St. Francisville. I didn't have to open my eyes to know we were home, because I recognized the feel of the van's tires on the familiar road. I knew each dip and bump by heart. When I did peek, I saw we were the only people on the road. Every other car or truck had long since been parked at home. At the first sight of the landscape, my eyes burned with tears. I couldn't believe how fast it happened, my protective shield melting away almost immediately. Max and Maggie scooted even closer to me, the feel of them the only thing that comforted me.

"I'm here," Max said.

"We're here," Maggie corrected him.

We pulled into St. Francisville's police station, and the sight of my dad's truck in the parking lot made my heart slide down to hide in my stomach. Reality was here, right in front of us now. The van's tires crunched on the gravel of the parking lot before coming to a stop. There was this moment of stillness, right after the engine died and right before the doors opened, when I begged God to please let the world stop spinning. But He didn't, and the van's doors opened with a creak.

"Let's go," one of the cops said.

Maggie, who sat closest to the door, exited like she was told. Then she glanced back at me warily. The policeman stared at me with the same look, stepping closer to the van, like he was unsure if I was able to walk. Maybe he'd been warned about my bouts of immobility and was getting ready to pull me from the van. His hands reached for me. Maggie stepped between the two of us. There was no sign of her tears. Her fierceness was no longer muted, and she was the old Maggie, ready to cross more lines for me. But I moved quickly, to defuse the situation and to show them my newest trick.

I had discovered during the course of the day that it was possible to move without thinking. It was possible to move and breathe and blink and nod, all without thinking. This was my life now, a series of thoughtless movements.

The wind blew, moving in and out of the leaves on the trees, making them rustle in that quiet way leaves do, whispering their welcome-home to me. Everything was so hushed outside. I'd missed the quiet of a small town after dark. The policemen herded us toward the front door of the station, Max's dad pulling up the rear. Max and Maggie came to stand on either side of me again. We went inside shoulder to shoulder.

Officer Tom met us at the door. We all knew him. He

exhaled loudly, like the feel of us in one room together squeezed the air out of him. I got the feeling he'd been dreading this, too. I was hesitant to meet his eyes, but when I did, they held a look I remembered.

Once, when I was eight years old, I wrecked my bike a couple of blocks from my grandmother's house. I had skinned my knee pretty bad—or at least that's how I remembered it. Officer Tom was on foot, for some reason, and he picked me up and carried me all the way home, telling me not to worry about my bike, that he'd bring it to me later. I remembered when he sat me down on my grandmother's front porch, he looked sad, like he wished there was more he could do for me. Looking back on it now, I realize it probably had more to do with who I was than with my bleeding knee. He was looking at me in that same way now, sad and wishing there was more he could do.

Only the light in the front room was on. Everything else was shut down for the night. Maggie's dad and mine were sitting across from each other on benches. At the sight of my dad sitting on a bench with his head in his hands, I felt my knees go wobbly, and I thought I wouldn't be able to stand. I had an impulse to run to him, so he could help hold me up, but we'd never had that type of relationship.

Maggie broke away from me and Max, running to her dad, throwing herself at him. He caught her. For a long time we all watched their embrace, like we were silently taking notes on what reunions should look like.

I felt my dad's gaze on me, but I didn't look at him right away. I looked to the floor and counted the number of tiles between my feet and his. There was only a little space between us, eight three-by-five tiles, but the distance felt much greater. He stood slowly, and my eyes lifted to meet his gaze. He was wearing a look of disbelief, like even though he'd been sitting there waiting for me, he was never really convinced I'd show up. With the only light in the room coming from the main office, the hall was dark and shadowed, hiding the lines in his face, making him look like the boy in the pictures, the one always standing next to Lillian. He stepped into the light, and he was my dad again. I wasn't expecting his tears, but then again I had come home, and the first girl he loved hadn't.

He looked at my face for a long time. I imagine he saw the miles there; he saw how far I'd gone. Then he stepped closer to me, and his hand reached for mine. There was no dramatic embrace like the one Maggie and her dad were still in. He just held on to my hand really tight, giving it a squeeze.

The policemen pulled us away and said there was business to attend to. They led us into a different room, our parents following. There were papers piled up and spread across a table in the center of the room. Our pictures were lying on top of them. Max's dad took over, telling us where to sit, what to read, and where to sign. He explained the details over and over again, the trouble we would still be in if we didn't listen to him. We just nodded.

"Go home and stay out of trouble," he said. "If you don't, I won't be able to help you." He looked at Max long and hard, and there was a pained look on his face that said, "I won't even be able to help *you.*"

We nodded again.

Everyone stood, and as the others moved to the door, Max and Maggie and I moved toward each other, coming to stand so close our heads bowed and our bodies touched. There were no tears, just a quiet moment of being connected and still, like we knew that after that moment we'd forever be moving farther apart, and our bodies wanted to remember the closeness. I felt the others watching us; I felt their held breaths.

"I love you," Max said.

"I love you, too," Maggie and I said.

Maggie's dad cleared his throat, and one by one we peeled apart. Soon the people I'd grown so close to were walking in separate directions.

Sitting in the passenger seat of my dad's truck, I looked straight ahead, too scared to look anywhere else. For a while we rode in silence, and that was fine with me, but then my dad spoke.

"Your grandmother doesn't really know what happened."

I looked at him as he continued.

"Well, she knows about Tom Benton, but she never connected that back to you. At first I worried town talk would upset her, but then I remembered . . . she only hears what she wants to."

I guessed that meant she'd believed the note I'd left her and was expecting Lillian to come home before her birthday. I wondered if that was good news. We rode the rest of the way in silence.

As we drove down Fidelity Street, I kept my head turned to the right, not wanting to see a single piece of Jamie's house. Soon we were pulling up in front of my grandmother's house, and it looked just like it did the night I left it. We sat in the truck for a little while, neither one of us looking at the other, but instead looking toward the trees that hid the view of the river. It was my dad who broke the silence.

"Look, I don't . . ." He stopped and took a deep breath, then blew it out slowly. "When you l-left . . . The—the night you left . . ." His words came out in a stammer, and he paused for a really long time. "I thought I might not ever see you again."

I thought about telling him how close I'd gotten to never coming home. I decided to stay quiet.

He turned to look at me and said, "I'm sorry about Jamie. I know what he meant to you."

I swallowed hard at his use of the past tense. Should I tell him about some of the things I had learned, about the things worse than death? I didn't, because his hand reached across the seat of his truck and took mine. Again, there was that squeeze.

"I saw you. In New Orleans," I said. "At first I thought I was seeing things. It means a lot that you came for me."

"I couldn't not come for you." After a minute he said, "I'm glad you're home."

"Me too." There was so much more we both needed to say, but for the night we needed to leave it at this.

He used my key to open the front door. I walked into the dark house before turning back to face him. I watched him, his feet planted firmly on the porch, not taking one step inside. This was as close as he ever got to coming into my grandmother's house. There was only a tiny space separating us, but it highlighted the line he wouldn't cross for me. I was suddenly angry, and I wanted things of him he wasn't ready to give me. I wanted him to step over the threshold of my grandmother's door and say, "You don't live here."

But of course he didn't move. I stepped toward him, but only to close the door. For a while we continued to stare at each other through the glass, but eventually he turned around, and I watched his back as he went down the porch steps to his truck. I made a mental note to tell Lillian, the next time I saw her, what she had done to him.

I turned my back on the front door and faced the dark living room. My mom's room was directly to my right, but I wasn't ready to face it yet, so I kept my eyes trained on the hallway in front of me. I walked down it, past Lillian's framed school pictures, and stopped outside my grandmother's bedroom door. She had left it open, and I watched the lump in her bed, her chest moving slowly up and down. Part of me wanted to go to her and wake her up, to get this over with, but another part said it could wait until morning.

I walked back down the hall to my mom's room, the wood floor creaking underneath my feet. I slid my shoes off right outside the door, but I didn't step into the room, just reached my hand in and flicked on the light switch. The light shone brightly on the shrine to my mom: the curtains hanging from the window, the quilt on her bed, even the lampshade; everything made with Lillian in mind, a collection of soft yellow and white, her favorite colors. My eyes stopped on my crib standing in the corner of the room. I wondered if my grandmother ever thought about the baby that had slept there.

At the sight of my mom's bed, I was instantly tired, deep-into-my-bones tired. With a deep breath I stepped into the room and felt myself stepping back into her skin. It wrapped around me, enveloping me, but it felt uncomfortable. It was as if in the days I'd been gone, I'd outgrown her. It was choking me, making me step back into the hall. I knew the days of playing dress-up in my mom's clothes were over. I turned the light off. I'd sleep on the couch instead.

I went to the front window and looked across the front yard to my tree. It stood solid and perfect in front of me, and for a second I wanted to open the front door and run to its waiting branches. The promise I had made Jamie that night not so long ago stopped me.

If you come down, I won't let anything bad happen to you. . . . I'll take care of you.

I knew I'd be held to that promise, the promise I made on Fidelity Street. I looked away from the tree, back to the couch. I slumped down along the length of it before turning on my side and forcing sleep. Jamie didn't meet me in my dreams, even though I looked and looked for him.

Sunlight streaming through the window and the sound

of my grandmother shifting in the seat next to me woke me up. I turned my face and lifted my eyes to her. There was this blissful moment, this tiny moment, when I'd forgotten why I was sad, and the only thing I felt was happiness at seeing her. I almost flung myself at her. It was the worry and confusion in her face that stopped me. And then there were her tears. These were old tears, ones that had been cried a long time ago but were back again now. I knew she knew who I was. This wasn't going to be a happy reunion. Because if my grandmother saw me instead of Lillian, it meant that Lillian was gone.

My grandmother leaned closer to me, and there was a smell like baby powder mixed with her perfume that made me homesick even though I was already home. I sat up slowly so as not to startle her. She looked so confused, and it was my face that was causing her distress. For a second I worried it had been too long since she had seen me as Olivia, that she might label me an intruder and send me from her home. She touched my knee, and her skinny fingers curled around it, shaking. I wanted only to make her happy, to rearrange my features so that she saw Lillian once again.

She got up and walked to my mom's room. I followed, but stopped in the doorway. My grandmother sat on the bed, on top of the quilt she had once made for my mom, her back to me. She rubbed her hand across the pillow sham, back and forth, and then she traced the stitching, so slowly, like her fingers were remembering the needlework.

Chapter 15

"**W**hat do you want to be when you grow up?"

It was a question I'd ask Jamie every so often, wanting to stay up to date on any life-changing decisions he might've made.

"I want to be a tree." That was the first answer he gave me, back when we were five and didn't realize our options were limited to the human realm.

"I want to be a kite flier." That was what he told me when he was a little older and had become slightly more realistic.

Because I thought it was my job to make sure he thought everything out, I asked, "What if there's no wind?"

"Then I want to be a wind maker," was his response.

I liked the idea of Jamie the wind maker. We ran around my grandmother's yard, Jamie blowing his wind and chasing me.

By the time we were teenagers, he no longer thought he could make the wind.

"I want to be the ferryboat captain." That was what he said on his sixteenth birthday, when we were camping under the stars in my grandmother's backyard. I knew he was deflecting to avoid telling me what he really wanted to say.

"No, that's *my* fallback plan," I said. "You can't have that one."

He smiled, but later, when we were almost asleep, he whispered the truth to me.

"I want to be a writer. When I write in my journals, I can be anybody and do anything."

In his stories he could be a wind maker again. I smiled, because I still liked the idea. We were quiet for a long while, both looking at the stars blinking at us through the leaves on the trees.

"You can be anybody and do anything," I said. "One day you'll leave this town, and me in it. But that's a good thing."

"You can come with me," he said.

"I don't know how to leave."

He sat up and turned to me. I could just about make out his face in the dark, and he said, "One day you'll know how to leave. Besides, maybe one day we won't need each other so much. One day I don't think you'll need me at all."

"That's not true. I'll always need you."

"When you're an old lady you won't need me."

"That's a really long time to wait, and what if I don't live that long?"

"You will live to be an old lady, and then you'll die," he said, like it was an order. He laughed then.

"You're the only one who thinks so," I said.

He got quiet again before saying, "You only need one person to believe it for it to be true."

"Fine. I'll live to be an old lady. And *then* I'll die."

He lay back down.

"Where will you be?" I asked.

His eyes met mine. "I'll be waiting for you."

Under the faint glow of the stars above us, I didn't question why he thought he was going to die before me; I just smiled, because I liked the idea of dying an old lady and Jamie waiting for me on the other side.

❧

The shovel was heavy, heavy and hard, the wood of the handle rough against my hand. I felt the blisters already forming, but I didn't care. I kept pushing the blade of the shovel into the grass, over and over again. No one stopped me. I thought someone might. I'd thought about it earlier while walking down the steps of my grandmother's porch. And as I walked to the shed in the backyard looking for the shovel, I was sure someone would stop me before I was able to finish what I wanted to do.

It had been a few days since we'd come home, and there was this thing I woke up knowing I had to do. With my backpack on and the shovel in my hand, I walked down the middle of the street with my eyes closed. I counted the steps, because I knew exactly how many there were between my grandmother's house and Jamie's, and when it would be safe to open them.

My arm was tired by the time I made it to the graveyard. I looked around, catching the eyes of a couple standing a few feet away. They didn't stop me, just watched. I dropped my backpack next to Lillian's grave and looked at her name in the stone for a really long time. Then I started digging.

After a time I had dug deep enough, and I dropped the shovel, sweat stinging my eyes. I sat down and brought my bag into my lap before opening it. I pulled out Beth Hunter's letters. I closed my eyes and imagined her face, the one in the photos on the wall in my mom's room and the one that belonged to the woman she grew up to be. She had wanted to use the letters to communicate with my mom.

I placed the letters in the hole I'd just dug. It was maybe two feet deep—just deep enough to be considered buried, but shallow enough so the rain could still get to them. It wouldn't be long before they decomposed. The rain would help. The letters would decay, word by word, and in this way they'd finally find their way down to Lillian. I found peace in that.

My bag had been confiscated in New Orleans. I'd since gotten it back, and everything in it, except for the money. Because we wouldn't tell them where it came from, they kept it. I'd already mailed Beth a letter and promised her I'd pay her back somehow. Paying her back was something I had to do.

I stood and picked up the shovel. The couple watching

me didn't move. The woman was Mrs. Copeland, my fourth-grade teacher. Every time I saw her, I thought about the look on her face when she finished reading our class *Old Yeller,* like she thought she'd made a mistake in reading us something so sad. I didn't know the man standing with her. I filled the hole back up, the sound of the dirt hitting the letters loud in my ears. I dropped to my knees and began smoothing the dirt with my hands.

It wasn't just me and the couple in the cemetery now. There were workers clearing a spot not too far from me, about fifteen rows behind my mom's grave. I sat on top of Lillian's tombstone and watched them digging, the two of them taking turns stabbing their shovels into the ground. It had taken me a long time to dig a tiny hole, but these men were expert gravediggers. They'd be finished in no time.

I knew it was Jamie's grave they were working on, and I watched their shovels do their work, deeper and deeper. It was his mom's family's plot. I'd already walked over there to see if Jamie's dad was buried there, and to my relief he wasn't. That made me feel better—the idea that Jamie wouldn't have to lie near his dad.

I felt heavy, and I turned my back to them before sliding down the front of the tombstone. I hadn't gone to Jamie's visitation the night before, and I wasn't going to his funeral today.

My body was so heavy that I imagined I sank into the ground a little—just enough to make my legs disappear. Someone would have to dig me up if I was ever going to move again. It was a good thing I was comfortable.

It was late in the afternoon when the cars began to line the streets. I heard the opening and closing of their doors, one after another. I heard feet moving in the grass as they came closer to that spot in the graveyard, the one that had just been cleared. I kept my eyes on my lap. They walked in from all corners of the cemetery, but I didn't look at them, not even the ones who walked past me. I didn't even look up when it was Max's hand reaching down to touch my face.

"I'm here," he reminded me.

He squatted down and cupped my chin in his hand. Eyes still on the grass, I leaned into his hand. He would hold me up forever if I let him.

Since we'd gotten home, he'd been sleeping on the swing on my grandmother's front porch. She wouldn't let him in, but he wouldn't leave me. The couple of times I'd been strong enough to get off my grandmother's couch, I'd gone outside to join him. He'd held me in the swing and whispered, "You'll be okay," over and over.

"When?"

"One day."

"Soon?" I'd ask him.

"Not soon, but one day."

He was so careful with me, touching me lightly and speaking to me in hushed tones. At one point he'd used his body to block the wind, like he was afraid the slightest thing might break me into a thousand pieces.

I'd wanted to protest and deny that I was this fragile thing, but I was so light, and I had this floating feeling. Without Jamie, there was no one to be my anchor, to keep me on the ground. I'd been grateful for Max holding me to him on the swing. I was scared that without him I'd drift away, up into the clouds, to a place where no one could reach me.

He looked at me warily now.

"Are you scared of me?" I asked.

"No, just for you."

As Jamie's graveside service began, he walked to the crowd. I kept my back to it, the top of my head the only thing visible above my mom's tombstone. The day was windy, and every so often the wind carried the sounds to me. I hummed that song from the river and stared straight ahead at an oak tree a few feet in front of me. I watched as the younger versions of Jamie and me ran around it, ghost children running and tripping over the roots, laughing and chasing one another. My ears filled with the sounds of their play, drowning out the town's crying behind me.

I was so content watching them that I smiled. Until they ran right by someone watching me, someone real. The playing children faded away, my dad's face making their laughter disappear. He was on the edge of the graveyard, leaning against the front of his truck, his hands in his pockets. We each stared at the other, neither one of us moving. He pushed off the truck and walked toward the tree between us, the one on the edge of the graveyard. I wanted him to come into the graveyard for the first time in eighteen years and dig me up. But he didn't, he just turned around and walked back to his truck. He drove away. I watched his truck getting smaller and smaller, and because I didn't want to look at its taillights any longer, I turned my head far to the other side and accidentally caught a glimpse of the service.

I only saw a corner of the casket, but that wasn't what made me puff out the breath I'd been holding. It was the person looking back at me: Mrs. Benton, Jamie's mom. At the sight of her, my stomach clenched and my hand grabbed at the hole there. I wanted to look away from her, but her eyes trapped me and held me still. She'd aged twenty years since that night in her kitchen.

I'd gone to see her on our second night back in town. I couldn't go into the house, so she'd come outside to talk to me. I was there to tell her that, according to Max's dad, Mark had confessed to killing Jamie and was being sentenced soon. There'd be no trial. Instead, I gave my own confession.

"I'm so sorry," I'd said. "Everything went to hell. I thought I could keep Jamie safe. I was wrong."

She didn't say anything for a long while. Finally she said, "I don't want you to feel responsible. I set this in motion. Jamie should never have been in the position of having to stop his dad. I should never have put him there. I should've left a long time ago. If I had, they'd both be alive." She'd started crying. "But I couldn't leave. I didn't know how."

I needed to acknowledge my part in this mess. "I hurt him, too."

She shook her head, much like Jamie had when I'd tried to take responsibility.

"No, this isn't on you. Jamie would never want you to take any blame. He'd want you protected from that. That's the last thing I can do for him. Protect you. So that's what I'm gonna do."

I'd cried then, and she'd held me.

At the sight of me, Mrs. Benton—her face still carrying its faint yellow bruises where Mr. Benton had hit her—brought her hand to her stomach, covering a hole I knew was there.

Max and Maggie were standing together, watching the exchange between Jamie's mom and me. They both looked like they wanted to join me, but I turned my head back around and hoped they'd get the message that I wanted to be alone. I could still see Mrs. Benton's face, though, even when I closed my eyes. I was surprised the bruises were still there, and I sank even deeper into the ground, because she had lost her whole family before her face had even had time to heal.

Much later, after the people had gone, I listened for the gravediggers again, for their shovels and the sound of the dirt filling up the hole. I only looked once, as they rolled out the grass they had cut away that morning, laying it across the grave like a blanket.

After they left, my legs began to itch, and just like that I was no longer comfortable where I was. I broke free from the ground holding me and stood up. I hoped Max or Maggie had hung around, but I didn't see them. They would've been a good excuse to put off what I had to do next. My dad was there, though, and I wondered how he'd snuck back without me noticing. He was standing in the same spot as earlier, still watching me. I walked to Jamie's grave, and my dad moved parallel to me, staying on the sidewalk.

There was a slight lump in the ground. How long would it take to flatten over him? My stomach felt like it was holding rocks, and gravity took over, pulling me down. I heard my name. It was only a whisper, but it carried on the wind, making me look over at my dad again. He watched me, his lips still parted. His hand went out to touch a car parked next to the graveyard, like he needed it for balance. His knees buckled a little, like the image of me on my knees was pulling him to his. I thought about invisible strings, like the one that had connected me to Jamie.

I knew how hard it was for my dad to be even this close to the graveyard; the strength it had taken to come here showed on his face. With a sigh I realized that the places where I was most comfortable, he'd never go. I lay down next to the grassy lump, ignoring the death and dirt, and turned on my side to sleep.

It was a deep, dead sleep, the kind it's hard to open your eyes from. Much later I did, just for a time, and they slid open to the moonlight. The ground below me had grown cool, but I didn't care. I turned my head to the side to see my dad still there, sitting on the sidewalk now, leaning against the back tire of the parked car. His eyes were closed, and like Max he looked younger when he was sleeping. The sky was a dark blue, the color it turns right after the sun sets and right before it slips into blackness. This time of night only lasts a few minutes, and I watched my dad through the blades of grass until the sky turned black around him.

The stars were just beginning to show. They were winking at me through the branches. The heaviness was back in my body, and this time it pulled at my eyes, pulling my lids back down. I heard Jamie's voice whispering in my ear.

"What do you want to be when you grow up?"

He was asking me the question this time.

"A gravedigger," I told him.

⍦

It was that special part of night when it's so dark outside that even the animals know to be still. The night had been going on for so long that I worried I'd slipped into a black hole and was now somewhere the sun would never rise. My dad was still out there on the sidewalk. I couldn't see him anymore, but I felt him.

I'd been awake for some time now, but I hadn't sat up, was just holding still, taking in the slight dips and grooves of the ground around me, feeling them out with my fingers. I'd decided I'd be in this spot indefinitely.

I saw something moving in the distance: a light, small and round. It took me longer than it should have to figure out that it was a flashlight. I watched as it bounced around the graveyard independently, whoever was holding it completely invisible in the black night. Only when it came closer to me did I realize it was two people. Max and Maggie were walking toward me. Max was carrying his sleeping bag in one hand and a bottle of whiskey in the other. Neither one said anything as they came near me and I sat up.

No one questioned what I was doing in the graveyard. They set about their business. Max laid out the sleeping bag, like he'd done on the bank of Lake Maurepas and on Steven's living room floor. Maggie sat down in the center and dropped the flashlight next to her. Without any prompting, I moved to her. My plan was to sit next to her, but my body had other ideas. As I got close to her, my head dropped to her lap, and without missing a beat she started stroking my hair and humming to me. Her fingers were so light in my hair as they worked their way down from root to end.

Max sat next to us and cradled the bottle in his lap. He didn't drink from it. He was back to just holding it. He was leaving for LSU in a week or so. Fall classes were starting soon. His major was now undecided. Mr. Barrow had worked it out so that Max and Maggie could fulfill their community service hours in Baton Rouge and Manhattan, respectively. They'd been assigned caseworkers and counselors to check in on them. In addition to completing our community service hours, we each had to meet with a psychiatrist so our mental health could be monitored after such a tragic experience. At least that's how they worded it for us. None of us were too excited about that, especially me, because I was pretty sure I was the only one of the three of us who was crazy, and I was also pretty sure any professional would recognize it immediately.

There was no college waiting for me, so I'd be fulfilling my community service in St. Francisville. I wasn't upset about that. I felt better knowing my debt would be collected right here. The judge reminded me that once my time was up, I could go anywhere I wanted. I wanted to believe him.

I felt guilty for not spending enough time with Max or Maggie these last few days. But they were here now, and at least I had a few more days with them. They could come visit me here in the graveyard.

Maggie stopped her humming and her fingers stilled in my hair. "I'm leaving tomorrow," she said.

I turned my head in her lap to look at her.

She tilted her face down to me. "My dad wants to do some sightseeing in New York before I move into the dorms."

Maggie's dad was pretty eager to get her out of here, to put distance between her and this town and the reminders of everything that had happened. I couldn't blame him. But still, it hurt, and I could tell from the stillness of Max's body that it was news to him, too. I sat up. We both stared at her.

"You'll come visit me, won't you?" She looked at me, and then her eyes flicked to Max. "Both of you?"

We nodded. The nods were slow but sure, and then there was this long pause. I reached out to touch her knee, like my body wanted to keep contact with hers for as long as possible. The magnitude of the physical space that would soon separate us made my heart hurt. A feeling like homesickness hit me. I nodded again; I'd come visit her.

My hands went to the tips of her hair as I saw in the dim glow from the flashlight that they were dyed hot pink, like she'd dipped them in something.

She smiled and said, "Just getting into character."

"I like it," I said. "It suits you."

"I made you a present. I gave it to your dad." Her hand

went to my face, and she tucked my hair behind my ear. "He said he knew where to put it, so if you want to see it, you'll have to ask him."

I knew that was Maggie's subtle way of getting me out of the graveyard and into a room with my dad. I didn't want to argue about the unlikelihood of either happening, so I just said, "Okay."

Soon we were all lying next to one another, Max and Maggie on either side of me. We fit together so well, our bodies molding to each other like there'd been no time apart. Muscle memory: our bodies immediately remembered how to fit. One last night together.

Because there were only three of us on the sleeping bag, my mind slipped to that dark place, traveling down to where Jamie lay. My body tried to split itself in two. Max and Maggie must have felt the tearing, because they held on to me tightly, like they were trying to hold the pieces of me together.

We stayed like that for a long time underneath the black blanket of the sky, and then with his lips on my ear, Max whispered, "Happy birthday."

Maggie squeezed my arm. Maybe the present she'd made had many purposes, one being my birthday gift. Since it was way past midnight by now, I guess it technically was my birthday.

"Thank you," I said.

We were quiet again. I was turning eighteen in the cemetery. Lillian was lying not too far from me. When I was little, I liked to imagine it wasn't her choice. That on the night of her eighteenth birthday, a switch flipped inside her, one she couldn't control. Her body moved to the water without her permission, sort of like she was a zombie or robot. Now I know that isn't what happened. When we were in New Orleans, I'd longed for the river to take me like it did her. The longing was less now, but I was grateful to have Max's and Maggie's arms around me, keeping me in my spot, just in case I couldn't stop myself from being like her.

As if she'd been reading my mind this whole time, Maggie whispered, "What if, no matter what, we grow up to be the people we came from?"

I knew she wasn't thinking about Lillian, that it was her own mom creeping into Maggie's mind, worrying her.

Her mom had disappeared that day in New Orleans. She never went to Louis's apartment.

"You won't be like her," I said to her, and to myself.

"You really believe that?"

"I do, and you only need one person to believe it for it to be true."

From behind me, Max said, "And you've got two."

At first light I woke to the soft whisper-kiss of Maggie's lips on my cheek and opened my eyes to see her sad smile. She didn't say goodbye, just stood and walked out of the graveyard, walking her Maggie walk right out of my life. I watched her for a time, observing her stride and steps, to see how you walk when you're leaving. She gave my dad a small wave—he was still sitting in that same spot, but he was awake now—and then turned right at the sidewalk.

My eyes stayed on my dad. He looked tired in the new light. How long would he wait before giving up and going home? I opened my mouth to say something to him, but not knowing what that would be, I rolled back over and scooted closer to Max. Max smelled like home still, and even though we were back and home was all around me, I pressed my face into his neck.

Sometime later, we woke up. I moved off his sleeping bag and watched as he took his time rolling it up before tucking the bottle down into the middle of it. Every move he made was slow and deliberate. He was dragging this time out. He kept his head down as he worked, avoiding my face. When he was done and there was nowhere else to look but at me, he finally brought his eyes to mine.

He looked tired, too. "Please," he said.

It was the quiet way he said it that affected me most, and even though I didn't know what he was pleading for, I wanted to give it to him.

"Please let me take you home. I don't want to leave you here."

I didn't know how to explain to him that it was okay to leave me, that I was already home. I thought about showing him the spot next to Jamie's grave. I wanted to show him where the grass had already laid down for me. But that would have upset him, so I shook my head.

"Will you at least keep the sleeping bag?" he asked.

"I don't want it."

"All right, Olivia." He bent down and touched his lips to mine, then, deflated, walked away from me, promising to come back soon.

I watched him go as I had Maggie. He stopped and

looked back at me once, like he was giving me time to change my mind. I knew he wanted me to make a different choice. He wanted me to leave Jamie and pick him. Part of me wanted that, too, but another part, the bigger part, knew I was right where I needed to be.

"I love you, Olivia," he said, the wind carrying his voice to me.

"I love you, too," I said. It didn't change anything, because Jamie was still dead and I still couldn't leave him. I could tell this made Max sad, but we both knew this wasn't the end of our love story.

After a time, he turned and walked to his truck. It was the same one we'd left in New Orleans, which had somehow remained untouched when it was abandoned, and found its way back home like we had. With nowhere else to look, I turned my face to my dad again. His eyes were closed. He looked stiff and uncomfortable, and I wanted to yell out, to wake him and tell him to go home, because I'd found my comfortable spot. I even tried opening my mouth, but I'd grown too weak, my strength leaking out and soaking into the ground around me. There was nothing left to do but sink back down. It wasn't long before I went back to sleep, something I was getting very good at.

"You don't live here," my dad said as he carried me out of the graveyard.

I opened my eyes and saw I was being carried farther

and farther from my comfortable spot. I fought him. I begged him. "Please take me back. Leave me here. Please!" I fought until there was no more fight in me. He squeezed me tighter to him until I was boneless and limp in his arms. He opened the truck's passenger door and slid me onto the seat, pouring me in like I was liquid.

We rode down familiar streets, connecting in the way they always did. My dad was sweating, and occasionally he took his hand off the wheel to wipe his face, his body over-exerted from crossed lines. I turned my head toward the passenger-side window and saw that we weren't headed to Fidelity Street, which made me look back at him.

"Where are we going?"

He didn't answer me, just kept right on driving in the same direction, past Bird Man's and the bed-and-breakfast. I guessed he was taking me to his apartment—a space that was only his. Being in it always reminded me that he didn't have room for me. But we passed the garage and his apartment, too. We crossed to the other side of town, far from the cemetery and the river.

"Where are we going?" I asked again.

"You'll see." His voice was soft, and I leaned closer to him, hoping he'd repeat himself, because I didn't understand what he was saying.

"I don't understand."

"You will."

We were going farther and farther into the woods on a road that had never been named. It was the kind of road cars had to take turns using, because it was too narrow in parts for two lanes of traffic. It was strange that there was a road in St. Francisville I'd never been down, but here it was just the same.

We stopped at what looked like the road's end and faced a house. It was worn and in need of paint, with a tiny front porch barely big enough to hold the swing on it. He turned to look at me, but I kept facing forward.

"We're here," he said.

"Where's here?"

"Come on. I'll show you."

He stepped out of the truck and walked around and opened my door. "Do you want to see inside?"

"You live here?"

He nodded. "I rented it a couple of days ago."

"What's wrong with your apartment?"

He didn't answer, just said, "Come on. Come inside with me."

He turned and walked to the front of the house. I watched his back as he moved to the door, and then he disappeared inside.

The living room was small, and boxes of his things were stacked here and there. He stepped out of the kitchen when he heard me come in the front door.

"Hey," he said, and I thought I saw a look of faint surprise on his face, like he'd never really expected me to follow him inside.

"It's not much, but it's got two bedrooms." He paused, then added, "I thought you might want one of them."

I stared at his face, at the little lines around his eyes. He walked down the hall. I followed. He stopped in front of a door before opening it.

"This could be your room," he said.

I stepped into the room. It was a perfect square, and it was perfectly empty.

"I bought a bed," he said. "Just in case you said yes. They're delivering it later today. I bought pillows and a comforter, too, but I didn't know what color you'd like for the covers. I didn't know what to buy."

He looked at me in a kind of hopeful way, like maybe I could help him out with that, but I didn't know what color I liked, either. That made me frown, because I was pretty sure that a favorite color was something an eighteen-year-old girl should know about herself.

After a minute or so, he dropped his head and stepped into the hall. "I'll be in the living room."

I walked farther into the room. This place was altogether unexpected. If I had to guess, I'd say it was about ten feet long and ten feet wide, making it one hundred square feet of space for me in my dad's life that had never existed before. It was the only space anyone had ever said was mine. There was a lone window opposite some built-in bookshelves. I went to it and opened it a crack, just enough to let in the breeze. I turned back to face the room and tried not to feel small as I stared at its bare walls and empty shelves. A room with no shadows.

Chapter 16

It was a perfect blue-sky day, and we were barely thirteen—the last time we'd both fit comfortably in the seat of my tree. Jamie and I sat and watched the people of Fidelity Street going about their day. My grandmother was digging in her petunia bed, humming a song she must have sung to Lillian, and Jamie's mom was swinging slowly on her front porch swing. They were flesh and blood but caught in between living and not, and we sat still and watched them, our hands holding tight to the branches. It was my favorite place in the whole world, my bird's-eye view of the tiny street with its green slopes leading down to the river and its people who wore their love like badges and made promises that lasted forever. We sat and watched, the smell of flowers mixing in with their devotion.

Jamie's face was sad. He was staring at his mom, which made me do the same. She looked straight ahead, flinching at slammed doors inside her house. I saw how tired Jamie looked—too tired for someone so young. I wanted him to be able to see the beauty around him, to see the tree holding him, the one that had stood in its spot for the last hundred years, but he couldn't. His mom was taking up all the space in his head, and it was only her face he could see. I wished I could take him somewhere new, someplace he'd never been, a place without sad mothers. So I said, "Let's go somewhere new today."

"Where?" he asked.

I shrugged and said, "I don't know, just someplace we've never been."

Our options were limited, because we were too young to drive. I perked up and said, "Close your eyes," and he did. He smiled when I leaned in to him, like even though he didn't know what was coming next, he thought it might be fun.

"Imagine you're somewhere new, someplace you've never been before," I told him.

He got very still and then leaned back against the tree. After a time he nodded his head, like he was there.

"Now imagine me with you," I said.

❧

We were having record rainfall for September, rain pouring down day after day, the noise it made loud on the metal roof of our front porch. It soaked into the mostly dirt front yard, leaving a muddy pond in its place. Day after day it fell, as if the sky was mourning him, too. There were days when I didn't think I could handle both our grief, but today was different.

The sun was rising with no clouds to hide behind, its light coming into my room through the window, spreading across the floor, fanning out, and sliding underneath the furniture. I sat up in my bed and watched it while I waited for it to reach me. It wrapped me in its velvet light. Today was the beginning of something new, even if that was just a day with no rain.

I'd been living in my room for a month now, but it didn't really look like it. Partly because I was adding the pieces of me slowly, and partly because I was still learning what those pieces were. My bookshelves stood empty except for the two photos Beth Hunter had given me, the one of my mom and me in the hospital and the one of her and my grandmother sitting on a bench in their backyard. They didn't have frames yet; they just lay on their backs and stared up at me when I went near them. I added some books but then took them back down, because I didn't know if I'd put them there because I liked them or because Lillian did. She and I were still tangled together, a muddled mess of mother and daughter, and it would take some time to separate the pieces of us out.

The walls were still mostly bare, with the exception of Maggie's present to me, a painting. I watched the sun bounce off it and change its colors like magic. I smiled at the painting, something I always did when I looked at it. I loved it, mostly because it came from Maggie, her hands, her art, but also because it was something only a few people in the whole world would be able to look at and recognize.

The painting carried its own sunrise, except this was a view of the sunrise over Oak Street from Steven's front porch. It shone through the cracked wood of the banister, the one we'd leaned our troubles against. It shone over Steven's front steps and the street we'd danced in—the place where we became something new. It burned its light through the alley next to the buildings, Maggie catching all the colors there, even the ones I didn't have names for, even the ones layering the sleeping homeless man on the street. Off to the side stood four silhouettes, dark shadows of the four of us watching the sun rise to its spot in the sky, like it knew it was rising over something special. There were days when it was the only thing I looked at.

Staring at the painting, I decided I wanted to do something I hadn't done in weeks. I wanted to go outside. My body moved slowly, my legs stretching out one at a time, testing to make sure the muscles hadn't atrophied from lack of use. I stepped down from the bed, and my feet landed on a piece of paper. It was crumpled, and I bent down to pick it up. When I unfolded it, I saw it had Max's handwriting on it. It looked like his attempt at taking notes. It must've fallen out of his backpack. I smiled at it, at the evidence of a secret I kept.

Sometimes, in the night, Max snuck back home to me, even though I was a sinking stone and it might not be safe to be near me. He didn't seem to worry about me pulling him down and would climb into my room through the window without warning and then slide in between the covers, always saying the same thing.

"I'm here."

I'd sink into him at those words, his touch reviving me. I knew it was wrong to use him as a life raft, but each time he came I wrapped my arms around him, holding on tight to the memories of our shared time, like echoes of a favorite song stuck in my head. He always slipped out sometime before dawn, but never before saying, "Tell me again."

"I love you," I'd say.

He usually left something behind, like the piece of paper. I kept each thing. It was my proof he was real and not some imagined comfort. Today he'd left more than one thing. I saw a smaller piece of paper a couple of feet from my bed, maybe trash from his pocket, and not too far from that another one. It was like he was leaving a trail for me to follow, one that led me to him. Maybe that was what the lost girl in the mirror needed.

I picked up each piece and smoothed it out before stacking them on my dresser, next to the college brochures littered there. I'd given myself a deadline for picking one. The brochures from LSU always found their way to the top of the pile after a visit from Max.

I pulled on clothes and walked down the hall. Mr. Barrow was sitting on the couch like he was supposed to be there. He smiled at me, a small smile.

"How are you doing?" he asked.

I was surprised to see him. He hadn't missed his son

by that much. "Better," I said, because that's what people wanted to hear.

"I'm sorry it's so early. I was headed out of town on business, and I wanted to talk to you about something. Your dad let me in on his way out. I hope that's okay."

"Yeah."

He stood. "I've managed to work out another deal. Y'all are so young, and I don't want the bad decisions you've made to affect the rest of your lives. If you all hold up your ends of the deal without incident, and stay out of trouble for the next five years, your records could be expunged. They'd be wiped clean. It would be like it never happened."

He smiled broadly, like he'd delivered good news. I thought about Maggie's painting as he talked about blank slates. I imagined the colors melting off the canvas, sliding down and dripping onto the floor like colored tears, leaving an empty white space behind. It would never be like it had never happened. It hurt to breathe, and I shook my head.

He frowned and said, "You need to think about this, Olivia. Don't give away a second chance."

I wanted to tell him that I didn't think we'd made bad decisions. I wanted to tell him about the things I'd learned, about sacrifice and perfect love, and how I wanted a record of that. I knew he wouldn't understand, so I said, "Thank you," so he'd go, and he did.

Once I was sure I'd given him enough time to leave, I stepped toward the front door. I paused in the doorway of my dad's bedroom. His bed was unmade. We were still figuring out how to navigate the same space, sometimes only circling one another, but each day we got a little more comfortable.

Stepping out onto the front porch, I felt like an animal coming out of hibernation, and my hand went to my eyes to shield them from the sun. I stayed like that for a while, giving my body time to readjust, before lowering my hand and staring with blinking eyes at the muddy mess that was our front yard. I turned my attention to my dad's gift to me: a car made two decades before I was born. I hadn't driven it yet. It might be a good day to do so.

I knew where I was going before I left the porch and carefully walked around all the puddles, then slumped down into the car's seat and used both hands to close its heavy door. It took three tries before it started. I drove down the quiet road and into town, my car the only moving thing in the still-sleeping streets, the morning dew shining brightly on the front yards I passed.

Turning onto Fidelity Street, I slowed the car to a crawl and kept my eyes straight ahead, coming to a stop right next to my tree. I turned to face my grandmother's house. Being there was like going back in time, and I wondered whether I'd always feel like a little girl when I stood in front of this house.

I climbed the front steps of the porch, and my hands shook a little.

"Lillian?" My grandmother's voice coming from inside stopped me in my tracks. I stood just outside the front door, my hand stopped in midair as I reached for the handle.

"What are we doing today?" she asked.

I moved to the window and looked inside. She wasn't speaking to me. She was standing in the kitchen, looking in the direction of my mom's bedroom, like she was waiting for Lillian's reply. She threw her head back and laughed, like my mom had said something funny. The laugh was a full-belly one, and her hand reached to her stomach to stop its shaking. My grandmother didn't need my face to see Lillian. I sat down on a little stool beneath the window and watched.

"Lillian, you are my prize," she said. My grandmother's head turned, like she was following the apparition of my mom as it moved from her room into the kitchen. I strained my eyes, trying to see Lillian, too, but she was invisible to me. My grandmother hummed and moved about her kitchen, and then she twirled, like they were dancing. She used to twirl me in just that way, and I closed my eyes, recalling the feel of it, my small hands in hers. I knew what it felt like to be her prize, and tears stung my eyes.

When I opened them, she was looking at me, stopped in mid-twirl, shocked out of her fantasy long enough to see the real me. Our eyes locked, and we each stared at the other. Her face looked like it did in the days after I came home and before Jamie's funeral: timid and somewhat remorseful. In those days she'd tiptoed around me as I slept on her couch, bringing me food and going to the window to see Max sitting on her porch. She did her best to ignore him and dusted around me, occasionally touching my face to make sure I was real.

The moment between us only lasted a few seconds, and then she looked from side to side, her eyes searching. She frowned, like she'd been unable to find what she wanted, making me wonder if Lillian had become invisible to her, too. Maybe she couldn't see both of us in the same place at the same time. Maybe I canceled Lillian out.

She turned back to me, and instead of looking sad she just shrugged her shoulders as if to say, "Where's that girl of mine gone now?" Then she smiled at me, a little unsure but smiling just the same. After a second, the smile widened, like even though Lillian was gone from the room, she was glad to see me in her window. I smiled back. Maybe Lillian and I could share her. That thought made me happier than I'd been in a long time.

She went to the edge of the kitchen counter and picked up her gardening gloves and spade. She gave me a little wave with her fingers, and I waved back. She smiled again and went out the back door. I got up from the stool and turned my back on the window.

Feeling something like hope, I spotted my tree again and moved toward it, then stepped onto the big branch that lay on the ground. My arms went out to my sides for balance as I walked up to my favorite spot in the whole world. Once settled, I looked over at Jamie's house, my breath blowing out at the sight of it. I'd half expected to see his mom sitting out front, but she wasn't. There was no one there, no car in the driveway, no noise coming from inside, just wood and glass and an empty front porch swing.

I couldn't look at it any longer. I turned my head to the

Mississippi River. The water had risen from all the rain. I closed my eyes and listened. Although the sound was fainter, I still heard the river's song, its sleepy lullaby rolling along the current, calling to me. My hands tightened on the branches as I felt the river pull at me. I became acutely aware of the tree around me, felt its solid trunk, and it felt like the tree was tightening around me, too, holding me in its seat. I knew I was safe, because my tree had stood in its spot for over a hundred years, and its roots were strong. It wouldn't let the river take me away.

My breathing slowed, my hands loosened their grip, and the sound of another song took my attention from the water. It was my grandmother, humming as she stooped over a flower bed in her side yard, checking the petals and smoothing them. It was the same song she'd sung to Lillian and me as babies, and the sound of it drowned out the river's song completely.

I listened to it as I looked at the landscape around me, and I thought about possibilities. I thought about where I'd gone and where I was headed, about tiny towns and big cities and all the roads in between. I thought about best friends and the word *forever,* about held hands and late-night promises made under stars. With the sound of my grandmother's humming in my ears, I thought about sacrifice. I remembered the words *I love you, I love you,* whispered by the boy I loved back. I leaned against the branch of the tree and closed my eyes. I imagined myself somewhere new, someplace I'd never been.

Chapter 17

We were headline news all over the state. The media said horrible things about Jamie. They said I made bad choices. They tried to explain the unexplainable, but they didn't know the whole story. Now you do. You know how I felt, what I dreamed. You know my part in it and yours, too.

We can stop pretending we don't know each other.

Your name is cold in the marble of your tombstone, no matter how hot the day gets. I'm obsessed with names on tombstones, another trait I got from you.

I finally went back in your old room the other day. I can still feel you there. I didn't stay long. I put your box of mementos back under your bed. I hope you don't mind, but I took your life list down from your wall and put it in the box. Some might say you didn't think your life was important. I put it there anyway.

I wrote my own list. There are 127 things on my list.

It's hanging in my room next to my painting from Maggie. Max helped me write it.

Dr. Green says I don't have to stick to it as long as I keep making plans. She says I'm getting better. Some days I don't believe her. Sometimes it's hard to reconcile all of my feelings. She says that's normal, that hope and despair aren't mutually exclusive. I hope she's right.

Some people might say that spending so much time in a graveyard isn't a sign of improvement, but I don't care what anyone thinks anymore. Dr. Green says that attitude alone is a sign of my improvement. And she told me not to be scared of the parts of me that are like you, that it's okay to embrace the Lillian in me. I like that. Those are some of my favorite parts.

Dr. Green was the one who suggested I talk to you, said it might help me to tell you everything. I started talking to your tombstone when I came to visit. Now you know all of it, even the part you played. I imagine much of it was hard for you to hear, and I'm sorry.

I finally picked a school. It's this tiny liberal arts school in Arkansas that nobody's heard of. It's in the mountains, no rivers in sight. I always wanted to live in the mountains. I never told anyone that, not even Jamie. Max was disappointed that I didn't choose LSU, but it's no more than a day's drive away, and he's promised to make the trip often. I have no idea what my major will be. Dad's excited for me and a little sad that I'm leaving. Classes start soon. He promised that I'd always have a room to come home to. I can count on his promises, because he doesn't make them lightly. He proved that by keeping his promise to you, that he'd love you for the rest of his life. Even if at the time he made it, he didn't know you were sick.

I'm sorry no one knew how to help you. If it's any consolation, you're their biggest regret.

I've outlived you by ninety-two days. It's weird being older than your mom ever was. I guess I'll get used to it. Maybe one day I'll stop counting the days. I don't know how many I'll get, but I hope Jamie was right and that I'll live to be an old lady. Maybe I'll live to be eighty-three and die in a bed with my love lying next to me, whispering memories of a good life in my ear.

The sun is setting, and I need to go. I don't stay in the graveyard after dark anymore. We both know I'm going to sit with Jamie for a little while. I'll only stay long enough to tell him I still miss him. Then I'll walk out of here on my own.

Before I go, there's something else I need to say. Dr. Green says it's important to say it out loud.

I love you, Lillian. And I think you loved me, too.

Acknowledgments

Having a book out in the world is a lifelong dream come true and would not have been possible without the help of some key people. The most surprising thing I've learned through this whole process is the number of people that it takes to make a book. I am floored by the amount of love and work that was poured into every page of this book by people who aren't me. I feel like we should all share a by-line.

First, I must thank my agent, Kate McKean, fellow Southerner and all-around best person, who offered me representation even though this novel needed so much work in the beginning. I am amazed by her dedication, and I am so proud to be a part of her team.

I want to thank the entire team at Knopf Books for Young Readers. I am incredibly honored to be a part of this legacy. A special thank-you goes to Melanie Nolan, my lovely editor, whose vision matched my own and who knew just what to say to help me get the characters to do what I needed them to do. I think she loves them as much as I do, and working with her was an amazing experience, for which I will be forever grateful. Also, a special thank-you goes to Karen Greenberg, editorial assistant and early cheerleader of my book, and copy editors Ellie Robins and Janet Renard, who made me sound a lot smarter than I really am.

I owe a huge debt of gratitude to fellow writer John Corey

Whaley, the kindest and most generous person I know, and one of the first people to read the book. He offered me support and advice at every turn, and I know, without a doubt, that this book would not exist if not for his encouragement.

Thank you to Lanette Kennedy Watson, one of my early readers and my best friend since high school. She is my Jamie, and like Olivia, I'd do anything for her.

To my brother Shadly, for being the best uncle my children could have and for being such a good and supportive brother.

Thank you to my mother, Sherlyn, who handed down her love of words and books to me. My fondest memories from my childhood are of her reading to me. Sometimes she read other people's stories, and sometimes she read her own. She is, and always will be, my favorite writer. To my father, Sheldon, who showed me what it looks like to work hard. His work ethic is unparalleled. And to both of them for always making me believe I could be anybody and do anything.

Thank you to my children, Eliza and Jake, for being amazing and giving my life true purpose, and for not getting too upset with me when I had to work late.

I must thank my husband, Erik, for his unfailing support of every crazy idea I have, and for building me up and always being ready to gift me with four amazing words: "You can do this." And also because he doesn't mind sharing me with my laptop. Most days. I love you.

And lastly, to the town of St. Francisville, Louisiana, and the people in it—thank you for inspiring me with your history, beauty, and kindness. You are a treasure.